DELIBERATE CRUELTY

BY MARGARET GRETEN

D1565466

PublishAmerica
Baltimore

At the specific preference of the author, PublishAmerica allowed this work to remain exactly as the author intended, verbatim, without editorial input.

First printing

ISBN: 1-4137-8657-X
PUBLISHED BY PUBLISHAMERICA, LLLP
www.publishamerica.com
Baltimore

Printed in the United States of America

For Michael—
my husband,
best friend,
and true partner in life.

Acknowledgements:

—To Nicole and Colin, I am proud to be your mother
—To my mother, Betty, my siblings, in-laws, nieces and nephews—thanks for your love and support
—To George Gillard, and Marlene Greten—you are both loved and missed.

—Special thanks to:
—Nancy Silberstein, my friend and a fantastic editor.
—Wojtek Mysliwiec for his help in cover design.
—fellow author, Linda Cookingham, for inspiring me not to give up
—Martino Studios Photography, Kenilworth, NJ, for the author's photo.

CHAPTER 1

When Julian McPhee opened his eyes, he saw the tip of his necktie hanging in a pool of vomit. His head was dangling off the side of a bench, and the cramp in his neck suggested he'd been in this position for some time. He sat up slowly, his head bobbing as passersby regarded him with disgust. He slid down the bench, pawing at his tie. The stain had seeped to the center of the tie and could not be wiped away. He began to doze in this upright position, his head falling forward, but was startled awake by the sound of an approaching subway train.

"Fuck," he breathed through the ache in his temples.

He looked around at the humid stone walls sprayed with graffiti. The pain in his head pulsed forward, approaching him, moving closer, like the subway train. *How did I get here? Where is my car?* The thoughts echoed between his ears as the train sped by, but the pain did not pass. He closed his eyes to try to retrace his steps: *Smokey's...I drove to Smokey's.* He recalled ordering a Martini and "accidentally" bumping into Cathy. She worked with him at Comptech, and they'd slept together a few times over the past six months. She was not like the women Julian usually found himself with. Nameless, faceless women who barked out instructions, thanked him for a good time, and went away. Cathy was different, but she came with a price—Julian's father was her boss, he was everyone's boss—which made for an awkward situation at work. Yet he recalled how Cathy had let her arm brush against him last night, making the hair on his neck bristle.

Yes, he had wanted to be with Cathy last night, awkward or not, he knew that. The memory of that feeling was the only clear thing in his mind. *But had he been with Cathy last night?* He thought about calling her, but what would he say? *Hi Cathy, It's Julian, did we happen to fuck last night?* He snickered at the idea of such a conversation, but then a sound rang through his head. A dull, cracking sound that he did not recognize, yet somehow remembered.

He raked his fingers through his thick, almost black hair and looked around at the feet rushing by him. Heels, briefcases, newspapers tucked under suited arms. *What day was it?* He stood up carefully and wobbled up to the street, almost stepping on a homeless man who was crouched next to a newspaper stand, elbows jutting out like baby bird wings. Julian stepped into the first coffee shop he saw, and his stomach lurched from the smell of eggs and bacon. He ordered a black coffee, then quickly went to the men's room before it was poured and vomited into the rust-stained toilet.

The thoughts floating through his brain began hissing out softly as he leaned against the cool, dirty, bathroom tile: *Asshole...You fucked up again. Why didn't you go home? You were supposed to go home early!* He braced himself against the sink and tossed some water on his face, shocked by his own reflection. A bright abrasion on his left cheek and a blood-crusted slit in his lower lip confused him. *A fight? Were you in a fight?* He closed his eyes and pressed his forehead against the mirror. He dozed again, the surface of the mirror drawing a red line across his temples. A small part of his mind was aware of his reflection even as he slept. It was like looking into a pool of water, and the feeling made him unsteady. Then his reflection became distorted into a new face, the face of a woman—beautiful—but a stranger. Her face came closer, so that it seemed to be rising from the imagined pool of water, closing in on him. He reeled backward, suddenly fully awake, afraid of the stranger in the mirror, afraid of the proximity of her eyes, afraid of the smothering sensation that suddenly blanketed his own face. Acid burned the back of his tongue, and he fought the desire to curl up in a fetal ball underneath the sink

His breath came easier when he stepped outside, but the bright sun stung his eyes. He stumbled into a cab, his head flopping against the sticky leather seat as he mumbled his address to the driver.

"It's in New Jersey. Forest Grove, do you know how to go?"

Julian lived in an affluent New Jersey town that was one of three towns that formed a triangle around one of the state's largest lakes, Marion Lake. The town of Forrest Grove sat majestically at the top of the triangle, above middle-class Orchard Park to the left, and the impoverished Little City. In the center of the triangle was Marion Lake Park, which boasted beautiful picnic grounds and a jogging trail along with its lake. The cab crossed from New York and into Little City, full of two to four family homes, strewn with long forgotten Christmas lights, small, anonymous, taverns and a large bus depot, and headed north toward the sprawling lawns and swimming pools of Forrest Grove. The main bus stop in Forrest Grove was bustling with the arrivals and departures of nannies, cleaning ladies, and pool maintenance workers.

As the cab approached his long winding street, Julian's mind began to focus more sharply on the inevitable scene that would take place when he arrived home. Actually, the scene would be one of the three that his screw-ups inevitably provoked. Scene A: he would walk in the door and his father would grab him by his wet tie and fling him into the nearest wall. He would feel the angry spray of his father's words, "screw-up, ungrateful bastard, I have given you everything I never had; what would your mother say if she were alive..." and every other cliché that applied to a spoiled screw-up twenty-three-year-old son of a self-made man. Scene B was the concerned father routine: "you have a problem...no one else can help you if you don't want to help yourself..." followed by attempts to bribe him into rehab or AA. Scene B usually took place after a marathon of sound sleep. The coffeepot would sit steaming between them in the stark kitchen, and Julian would swear he would be more responsible. Did his father think he actually enjoyed waking up in his own puke? Yet, there was a part of him that knew he had lost control, but he lacked the will to do anything about it. Lately a new scene—Scene C—had been introduced. This involved Julian slinking to his room while his father glared in hostile silence. His father had given up on him, justly so; his drinking had been the cause of several problems over the past few years. He'd been arrested for DWI twice. The first time his father's lawyer had managed to get the charges dismissed, but the second time the only deal they could get was a plea bargain to reckless driving. That had cost him his license for six months, during which he had to be carted around anytime he had to leave the house. A disorderly conduct arrest followed a nasty fight in a small tavern in Little City, and at work he'd been the subject of particularly vicious office gossip after dozing off during one meeting and missing a few others. Then there were countless other incidents that only Julian knew about: urinating on himself, waking up next to a woman who was old enough to be his mother, being picked up off a sidewalk by a stranger, wallet and watch missing. Julian didn't really blame his father for giving up; he'd pretty much given up on himself. Scene C had been the most common recently and he would have predicted it again except for the car. This time he'd left the car, somewhere...

He opened his eyes and told the driver to make a right onto his street, bracing himself for what his father would say when he told he had lost his college graduation gift: a navy blue Honda Prelude which was still less than a year old. It was the last time he could remember his father being proud of him. Before that it had been at his mother's funeral. *I'm proud of you, Julian, proud of the way you handled yourself.* The words still bewildered him, so many years later. He could still hear his dad saying them; he could feel the hand on his shoulder...

Julian dozed again, unable to keep his eyes open. He had the sensation of falling as he slept. He could feel air rushing past him, blowing his hair off his forehead. Deep in his mind, he braced himself for impact, felt his face smacking against something, crushing his nose and teeth.

Then he heard that sound again—a dull thud, a crack...

He must have cried out slightly, as he could see the driver's eyes looking at him in the rear-view mirror. He had bolted himself upright, spine rigid. Gradually, he relaxed and sank back against the seat, rummaging through his pockets for money to pay the driver. He sat up again, abruptly, when he saw two police cars in front of his house.

CHAPTER 2

Randy "the Face" Jenkins put a second sugar in his coffee at his usual time—5:30 a.m. He typically finished two or three cups before the commuter crowd hit the convenience store for buttered rolls, bagels, coffee or whatever else could be devoured neatly on a train. This morning—the sunny Thursday before Memorial Day weekend—was even quieter than expected. The commuter crowd was probably already sitting on the hot parkway en route to opening their shore houses. Two construction workers strolled in for two black coffees, a bagel, and a newspaper. Their skin was already tan from being outdoors every day. After they left, Face lit his third cigarette of the morning and grabbed a newspaper from the rack. He sat on the hard stool behind the counter, sipping and smoking, his legs crossed and a rubber flip-flop dangling from his big toe. He read the sports page first, then checked the Yankee's box score, even though he had watched the game the night before. The opinion page was his second stop. He enjoyed reading all the letters to the editor from every asshole in New York and New Jersey. He often wrote letters, too, on various topics of irritation, and a few had even been published. Occasionally during his reading one of his hands would creep up to stroke the thick salt and pepper mustache that hid a wishbone shaped scar on his lip, or tug at the small wavy ponytail that sat low on his neck, behind the receding hairline on the top of his head. Sometimes his hand would absent-mindedly trace the row of thick scars that mapped the area from his wrist to the inside of his elbow.

Face's reading was interrupted when just before seven two young girls in short cutoffs, chunky sandals and identical baby blue t-shirts came in to load up on paraphernalia for a trip to the beach. They looked like they should be in school, but that wasn't his business. He kept an eye on them as they raided the chip aisle and grabbed sodas and bottled water. He was still young enough to notice the way the t-shirt fabric pulled slightly in between one of the girl's breasts, but he was not young enough to *really* care. He noticed the strings of each of their bathing suits poking out the backs of their shirts, and he imagined pulling one of the strings, but only for a second. He was too weary for anything more than decadent fantasies about the nameless girls who breezed in and out of the store, using him for his beef jerky and bottles of Pepsi, then cruelly tossing him aside.

These particular bimbettes approached the counter with their chips, soda, water, and a tube of Chap Stick. He wondered if they were planning to share the Chap Stick. They each had their hair piled on top of their head and clipped with little butterflies of various colors.

"You ladies headed for the beach?"

"Oh, yeah," the bustier one smiled coyly. "And can I have a pack of Newports?"

"Well," Face teased, "I don't know if you ladies look old enough to buy cigarettes."

"We're eighteen," the flat one declared.

"Do you have I.D.?"

"Oh, it's in the car...do I *really* have to go get it?" She leaned in slightly; turning her heavily lined eyes upward, looking Face in the eye.

Face was taken aback by her flirtatiousness. He wondered for a moment how badly she wanted the cigarettes and what she would be willing to do to avoid being carded. Not that he could do much anyway, but it was a thought.

"Smoking is a disgusting habit, you know."

They both looked toward the cigarette burning in the ashtray behind the counter.

"I'm speaking from experience," he laughed in an equally flirtatious manner. "All right girls, but just this once, next time no smokes without ID."

"Thank you!" They squealed together. What could he say? He was a sucker for flirtatious adolescents with big breasts. Anyway he figured he owed them for his lewd thoughts. He went back to his paper as the bimbettes bolted with their purchase, and something on page twenty-three caught his eye. It was a photograph of a woman, and a wisp of recognition blinked behind his forehead. The eyes were familiar, as was the very straight hair and glossy smile. Veronica? He quickly skimmed the article, jumping over chunks of it, trying to figure out why her picture was in the paper. Veronica Lawson. She was dead. *Oh My God. Is it really her?* The article was small, just a corner of the page, with a tiny photo. He went back and read the article again, this time fully; killed in a hit and run accident. Tuesday night. Veronica was the wife of Collins University professor James Lawson.

James Lawson. Jimmy. Jimmy "The Cat" who always landed on his feet. Not this time, Jimmy old friend. Face put the newspaper down and stroked his moustache harder. Jimmy, *Jimmy*. The wake was Friday, funeral on Saturday. *Shit, she was dead? Should he send flowers? Should he go?* He imagined the scene: Jimmy, racked by grief, would throw his arms around his old friend, cry into his chest, and say it was time to forget the past and make amends. *I've changed, Jimmy. I forgive you, Face.* Or it could go the other way: *You have nerve showing up here, Face. Get the hell out…*

He recalled Jimmy and Veronica's wedding; a small but somewhat lavish affair full of academics and business people. Face had gotten plastered and tried to seduce someone's cousin in the coatroom, but she'd been scared off by his aggressiveness and shoved him away so hard that he fell on his ass. The brief chuckle that accompanied this memory was truncated by his shock. It was almost a year after the wedding that he was invited for dinner, in the middle of what he liked to call his *dark period*.

"So how did you get the name Face?" He'd noticed how her lips seem to glide over her teeth when she smiled.

The three of them sat in the couple's apartment, devouring veal Florentine and two bottles of expensive Chardonnay. Veronica found Face to be quite engaging, as he was always at his most charming when he was high. Jimmy had just gotten the job as a professor of American Literature at Collins University. All the years of struggling to get good grades had paid off for Jimmy. Face always felt that Jimmy was smart, but Jimmy's parents, both high school dropouts, never valued education. If Jimmy was reading a book, his father would tell him to go out and play ball, something useful. Face could recall the many times Jimmy would sit in the bleachers at the baseball field, reading. But now it had paid off for Jimmy. Face was impressed, but stung by jealousy. Two kids from Little City; grew up across the street from each other, lost their virginity at fourteen to sisters on the same night. They played high school baseball together, Jimmy still carrying books to read on the bus. They compared gifts on Christmas mornings, sometimes showing off a new bike or skates while still in a robe and slippers, and they got drunk the first time together on homemade wine stolen from Jimmy's grandmother. Their mothers used to drink coffee and smoke Paul Malls together in the middle of the afternoon, while the kids were outside riding their bikes or walking to the store for cans of soda or bread for dinner. Now the two kids from Little City were all grown up: one a professor of literature with a lovely young wife, the other a junkie loser.

Face's resentment of his childhood friend grew that night as his buzz wore off. He'd snorted the last of his coke—that was before heroin—his dark*er* period as he called it. He watched Veronica and liked the angle at which her hair was cut—so straight across the bottom. Why did Jimmy have all this? Just because he liked to read books? Why did his life have to suck so much? Why had he lost three jobs in two years? He watched Jimmy follow Veronica into the kitchen and slide his arm around her waist as she put the dishes into the sink. He excused himself and went to the bathroom. As he passed their bedroom, he glanced at the four poster bed and had a vision of Jimmy and Veronica making love, which angered him further.

"Hey," Jimmy had come up behind him and slapped his shoulder, interrupting an impressive fantasy.

"She's great, a lovely girl." Face had been sincere.

"Are you okay?"

"Yeah. Whadda ya talkin' about?"

"You don't look well," Jimmy had moved passed him and flopped onto the bed.

"What? I'm the *Face*—the Face always looks good."

Jimmy laughed, but it was slight—the kind of laugh that hovers over something serious. He fluffed a pillow and leaned backward "you look...strung out."

"C'mon Jimmy; don't give me shit."

"This is not shit, this is concern."

"Bullshit, Jimmy!" Face stopped leaning on the door and took a few steps toward the bed. "Worry about yourself. You've been toasted a few times, my friend."

"Not anymore," Jimmy stood up; shaking his head more times than Face could count.

"Oh, come off it, Jimmy, I've seen you snort coke till your nose was bleeding."

"I don't do drugs anymore, Face. That's a fact." Jimmy practically spat the words.

"Oh, yeah, I forgot…you're a *professor* now."

"It's not just that. I'm not a kid anymore, Face, and neither are you. I decided to grow up and build a life. Veronica and I want to have kids someday, I want to be an example…"

"Hah!"

"Why is that funny?" Jimmy sat up on the bed.

"You're not father material…or husband material for that matter."

"That's a horrible thing to say."

"Tell me, how many blowjobs does it take to get an A, professor?

"I'm not like that anymore." Jimmy stood and lowered his voice. "I love Veronica."

Face snorted. "Yeah, I know alotta girls you've loved, till the next one comes along."

"Fuck you! Don't turn this around on me. I'm trying to help. I'm just looking out—" Jimmy's words fell on Face's back as he spun and stormed out of the apartment, not even acknowledging the open-mouthed Veronica in the hallway outside the bedroom. She stood holding a coffee cup in her hand, her head following Face to the door.

"What the hell is happening, Jim?" Face heard Veronica's voice, full of concern as he left the apartment.

Face's memory was interrupted by an elderly woman asking him where the Tylenol was. He pointed without speaking and lit a fresh cigarette, sighing heavily as he exhaled. It seemed puzzling when he thought about it now. He had always been vaguely aware of jealousy toward Jimmy, yet he never acknowledged it to himself or anyone else. Even with girls Jimmy had always been more successful. Face knew he was better looking, but Jimmy's confidence made women want him, even though his brown hair and eyes were ordinary and his complexion did not have the glass-like texture that Face was blessed with. Face even found his own addiction a reason to be jealous of his friend. He knew, even then, that although Jim had dabbled in cocaine briefly, he himself was the one with the problem. But at that time he was aware of the problem on only a superficial level. He knew it in his mind, but his mind was not communicating with the rest of his body. Why could Jimmy snort blow for fun, then just stop? Why didn't Jimmy want more? Why didn't Jimmy think about cocaine all day? Why didn't he dream about it? Why didn't he long for that taste dripping down the back of his throat? Why didn't he do anything he had to do to get it?

The next time he saw Jimmy after that was the next year, at the height of his dark*est* period. He'd bankrupted himself from cocaine to crack and heroin and spent most of his time trying to get either drugs or the money to buy drugs. It was something like being a wild animal—all he thought about was the next kill, he was constantly on the hunt. One day he'd gone into a small tavern in Little City, looking to borrow twenty bucks from anyone in the place who knew him from around the neighborhood, and the owner had tossed him out into the street. So he sat on the sidewalk, shivering and sweating at the same time, running through a mental list of possible ways to get money, including selling his dick to the first offer that came along. Veronica Lawson, returning from a visit to her Aunt June, stopped her car when she saw him sitting on the sidewalk.

"Get in," she'd ordered in a way that prevented any discussion.

"Hey beautiful, ya left Jimmy for me?"

"Not quite."

The next thing he knew Veronica was pulling him out of the car in the parking garage of their apartment building, and struggling to drag him to the elevator.

"What the...?" Jimmy had bounded off the sofa when he saw them.

"He needs help...he was just sitting on the sidewalk."

Face spent the next two days in their spare bedroom in a sweaty fog of withdrawal. He had vague sensations of Veronica swabbing his forehead with a washcloth, and of Jimmy bringing him coffee and talking about what they should do.

14

"I don't want you to die in the gutter like some piece of crap," Jimmy had said without any show of emotion. "I'm going to look for a place..."

Rehab. Face knew he needed it, knew it would save him, but at the time he could not bear the thought. The only thought that would stay in his mind was getting high. He wanted it so bad that a few of the tracks in his arms screamed like babies wanting to be fed. So after Jimmy left for class late that morning, Face got out of bed, put the contents of Veronica's jewelry box in his pockets, and walked out.

The jewelry cost him a broken nose, and a childhood friend. Jimmy never even said anything. He just walked up to Face two days later, in front of his mother's house, as Face was leaving and punched him squarely and solidly in the nose. Face's eyes saw nothing but white as he reeled backward and hit the driveway. Then Jimmy kicked him hard, under the ribs, causing more blood to spurt from his nostrils as he struggled for breath. He looked into Jimmy's eyes, a look he would never forget. The dark brown eyes that usually looked warm and soft now looked like the eyes of a shark who'd just eaten your leg— nothing there. At this point, Jimmy's fist was re-balled and ready to descend, but they were interrupted by Face's mother who came running down the porch steps in her housecoat and fuzzy slippers, carrying a wet mop and a can of Raid. She ran toward Jimmy waving the mop and threatening to spray the Raid into his eyes, but stopped short when she recognized him.

"Jimmy? Whadda doin?" she screeched. Jimmy hesitated for a moment and Face was unsure if he would strike the old woman. He looked at Face, wiped his wrist across his upper lip and left. He walked away slowly, not afraid of a wet mop to the back of the neck, or Face jumping up to retaliate. Face knew he got what he deserved, and Jimmy knew he knew it. Face's mother had trotted after Jimmy, calling his name in bewilderment, wondering what her son had done to incur Jimmy's famous wrath.

Face and Jimmy had never fought as kids, although the skinny, docile young man that Jimmy was then was capable of exploding when provoked. His ability to fight and escape harm had earned him the nickname "The Cat." Even after the bloodiest brawl he would be on his feet, or the cops would show up ten seconds after he'd left a fight. That day in his mother's driveway had been the only time he'd

15

felt the cat-rage first hand. They had not spoken since, but Face thought about Jimmy often, especially when he looked in the mirror—which he did only when absolutely necessary—and saw a nose that was no longer in the center of his face, but on a diagonal. He never bothered to get it fixed. He had too many other things he needed to fix. He glanced around the store, which was clear of customers, and dialed information only to find that J. Lawson in Orchard Park was unlisted.

CHAPTER 3

James Lawson stared at the flatness of his dead wife's face. She didn't look real. He didn't feel real. Valium. Her hair was slightly teased on the top, and there was a spot where the lipstick was feathering slightly onto her powdered skin. James did not speak as the funeral director stood to the side, waiting for a nod of approval that never came. Veronica's Aunt June—next of kin after James— spoke up.

"She looks lovely, thank you." The man nodded and stepped away silently. James felt Aunt June, and his mother who'd flown in from Ohio, patting his back and lightly squeezing his hand, but was unable to acknowledge it. He didn't think she looked lovely at all. She looked flat and had on more make-up than she ever would have worn. She had looked the best after she'd just washed her face. He loved how she smelled right before she went to bed, with her hair pushed back with a white headband and her face freshly scrubbed and soft. That was Veronica. Sitting on the floor with her legs crossed eating pizza crust side first—that was Veronica

The next few hours were blurry for James. His face was patterned with lipstick marks, which were wiped away, then put on again by another friend of Veronica's…colleague…cousin. Even some of his students showed up. The scene was eerily reminiscent of his wedding—standing in the receiving line, shaking hands and being kissed. But Veronica had been standing with him, not placed in position like a doll, and there had probably been fewer guests at their wedding. As a woman he had never met gently pecked his cheek, he wondered what that said about them. It was Friday, Memorial Day weekend. They would have been at the shore by now, at Bonnie and Ed's. They had a huge house overlooking the bay with their own dock and deck and a Jacuzzi built in. Bonnie was Veronica's high school chum—Bon and Ron—partners in crime. Jimmy liked them well enough but still considered them her friends. He did enjoy the weekends at the shore, though. Once he and Veronica had made love in the Jacuzzi after Bonnie and Ed had gone to bed, then slept in a lounge chair on the deck. Just after dawn, Ed came down to get the boat ready for fishing. He walked right behind their naked, intertwined forms on the lounge chair and jumped onto the boat. Ed whistled as he disappeared into the boat's cabin, which allowed Jimmy and Veronica to run into the house where they burst into laughter. Jimmy smiled for a moment, then he looked at Bonnie and Ed sitting in the third row of chairs, Ed's arm draped around Bonnie's shoulder. It occurred to Jimmy that he's never seen Ed in a tie before. Bonnie looked different, too, in her navy linen suit and cream-colored blouse.

The room was hot and crowded, and after a while he needed some air. He excused himself from Aunt June and his mother and walked out to the front steps of the building. Several circles of mourners were milling about, smoking. His sudden appearance caused a hush, and the groups dispersed awkwardly, but he didn't seem to notice. His eyes were drawn to a man sitting in his car at the side of the parking lot, smoking and listening to the Yankee game on the radio, a little too loudly. Jimmy's breath became quick. *Face.* He almost smiled to see someone so familiar, but he clenched his jaw when he recalled Veronica sobbing over her mother's engagement ring, lost forever.

He looked around at the people outside and realized he didn't really know any of them. They were polite, well-meaning strangers. This was a great irony in his life. He and Veronica rarely spent a weekend without an invitation to a dinner party, picnic, boat trip, Bar-mitzvah. You name it, they were there. But who *were* these people? Which of them knew that Veronica liked chocolate chip mint ice cream? Or that she was allergic to perfume? Who knew that he had a birthmark in his armpit and a deformed small toe? Who knew that he had been arrested when he was sixteen for putting a chair through a wall in a hotel down the shore? Face knew these things, about him, anyway. Face met his glance for a moment, but never left his car, and Jimmy never left his step until his mother tugged him inside by the elbow, murmuring about his appropriate place. Face drove out of the parking lot, passing another man in a car parked on the side of the street. The other man was Darren McPhee.

CHAPTER 4

Three men arrived home later that night, all three churning with grief over one single moment, which had lasted less than a minute. One man arrived at a neatly-groomed, three-bedroom colonial in Orchard Park, to find his porch strewn with fresh flower deliveries and his oak kitchen table covered with trays of baked ziti, chicken cacciatore, a baked ham and a coconut cake. More food than he and his wife would have eaten in a week. He tossed his keys on the counter and spent the next ten minutes sifting through the thirteen messages that blared from his answering machine, all expressing their sympathy, all sorry they couldn't get there tonight. A few would be at the funeral. One was from his wife's dermatologist confirming tomorrow's appointment. He undid his tie, poured some coffee from the pot that had spent the day thickening on the newly tiled kitchen counter, and walked into his office. The books on his shelves were arranged neatly, heavy volumes of literary criticism along the bottom shelf to weigh down the bookcase, and lighter editions—novels and plays on the top shelf. He sat in his cushioned, rolling chair in front of his computer and let the small warmth of his favorite room comfort him. The large tree in the corner needed water, something his wife usually did. He went to the kitchen and returned with the telephone and a pitcher of water. He dialed information as he watched the dirt soak up the water and darken.

"Little City. Jenkins, Randolph."

The second man sat in the driveway of his Forrest Grove home, weeping over the steering wheel of his BMW. The street was dark and wooded, and he'd forgotten to leave the front light on. He sat there for a while and then went inside, where it was still dark. He stood in the doorway looking at his favorite part of his home, the staircase. Intricate patterns were carved in the wood along the outside of each step, and he loved the way the wood banister curled into a tiny ball at the bottom and how the spindles along the banister were so perfectly smooth and seemed to melt into the rail. The staircase was what sold Mary on this house. For a moment he was glad that his wife was no longer with him; glad that she had died peacefully in her sleep of a heart condition no one knew she had, that she had not lived to see her son in jail. She had not seen the bleary eyed little boy who used to thud down these steps in footed pajamas with his treasured stuffed frog tucked under his arm, led out of the house in handcuffs.

The ring of the telephone startled him and seemed to intrude on his quiet darkness.

"Darren?" The voice was abrupt, and sounded before Darren had said hello.

"Yeah?"

"It's me, John. I spoke to the D.A."

"How's it look?"

"They don't have a case, really. No witness has come forward. All they have is the car."

"What does Julian say?" Darren sat at his kitchen table without turning on the light.

"He doesn't remember anything, says he was in a blackout."

"How is he?"

"He wants to come home, Darren."

"No way." He closed his eyes and shook his head, as if to emphasize his feelings to his attorney. A familiar feeling returned. A body full of goose bumps, a heart that beat too hard for his chest to bear. The feeling he always had whenever the time Julian was expected home passed. He saw the familiar images that floated through his head on the nights he waited: Julian beaten and robbed, bleeding in some alley, or frozen stiff on the side of the road where he'd passed out, or his bloody, sliced face poking through a shattered windshield. He sighed deeply. "He needs to sit in jail for a bit. Plus I don't want to see him."

"Darren, we don't even know what happened. He doesn't remember. He wasn't at the scene. Who knows? The car could have been stolen. Be reasonable, bail him out."

"I'll think about it."

"Fine. I'll call you in the morning."

Darren hung up the phone and thought about pieces of flesh and clothing the police had found in the front grille of his son's blue Honda Prelude. His graduation gift, now it was evidence. He had surprised Julian with it. He was so proud that he had graduated college. He hadn't been sure he would make it, but he had done it. Now the gift had been used to run over a woman who was walking to the train after seeing a show in the city with some friends. Mowed down like a piece of trash, no brakes, piece of garbage, a pile of leaves in the street. Julian couldn't remember, he was blacking out at twenty-three. Julian must have done it. Darren knew he had done it; maybe he was so drunk he never realized it. But what if John was right? What if the car had been stolen? Ah, that was crap. Lawyer shit. He went up his beloved staircase and into the immaculate master bedroom. He could tell the cleaning service had been there today by the vacuum lines in the carpet. He brushed his teeth and flossed above the brass fixtures and marble countertop in the master bathroom, then returned to the bedroom and sat on the edge of the bed for a long time. The bed was high and thick with a fluffy down comforter, and a carved pine headboard. Instead of slipping into bed, he stepped across the hall to Julian's room. His was the only room with a sleek modern decor. The rest of the house was full of antiques and carved wood, but Julian's room had a black lacquer dresser, armoire and waterbed, cream-colored carpeting and a scarlet bedspread and curtains. Across from his king sized bed was a small sitting area with a black leather loveseat, large stereo and television, and to the right of his bed was a silver, metal framed desk which held a computer and telephone. Darren was a software innovator who had come upon much success in the early eighties with the computer programs he had invented. Julian could have had it all. He would be ready to retire in four or five years and he'd hoped to groom Julian to take over the business, and the house. He wanted to buy a condo overlooking a golf course and only come here to visit grandchildren, spoil them with trinkets, and leave. He wanted the house to be filled with smiles and Christmas trees and friends and marshmallow roasts in the huge fireplace; like when Mary was alive and Julian was a child. He longed with every muscle to be able to turn back the clock, to do things differently. Maybe he hadn't been a good enough father. He had spoiled Julian. He sunk into the leather sofa, on top of a Tommy Hilfiger t-shirt that was strewn across it and wept again.

The third man came home to a small second floor apartment in Little City. The building was small but neatly kept by the downstairs landlady, a widow who planted flowers in the flower boxes and put a new wreath on the door each month to correspond with the nearest holiday. May's wreath was a group of dried grapevines with red, white and blue ribbon wrapped around and tied in a large bow at the bottom. A wooden American Flag sat across the middle of the circle. Mrs. Murphy had even put red ribbons and little flags on toothpicks in the flower boxes, in between the pink and white impatiens. The sidewalk was newly swept, and a large fern in a white plastic planter greeted him in the downstairs hallway along with a mat that had little chicks and the word *Welcome* stenciled across it. Face was just past the fern when he heard his phone ringing. He climbed the stairs quickly, but dropped his keys before he could slide them into the lock. His daily intake of caffeine from coffee and cigarettes was getting to be too much. He paused for a second to catch his breath. The phone stopped a few moments before he swung the door open, and his three cats sidled up to his leg and began rubbing. His girls, Donna, Susie, and Jane were named after the girls who gave him the best head. If he ever got another cat it would be named Rachel who was a close runner up.

"How're my girls?" He scratched Donna's ears and she purred loudly while Susie and Jane pushed and shoved to be next. He waited for the answering machine to click on, but the caller hung up without leaving a message. He didn't care, it was more than likely a telemarketer. No one else called him. He went to the kitchen and scooped up a cup of Purina cat chow from its Rubbermaid canister on the floor and poured it into the large bowl the cats shared. Donna, the largest, always ate first, then the other two did their usual shoving match, but all three girls were quite plump around the middle so Face never worried about them eating enough. He sat in his tattered recliner in his living room—living "area" was a more appropriate term, as it wasn't really its own room. The living room, kitchen, and "dining area" were one large room, separated only by the line where the carpet turned to gold linoleum in front of the appliances. He sat back in his recliner and Donna, who had finished her chow, curled into his lap with a triumphant glance at the other two, and began purring. Face thought about Jimmy. He looked so tall and majestic on the top step of the funeral home, like a king coming to greet his subjects. But Face had also seen the set jaw of his former friend. He was tall, but looked hollow. If you touched him too hard he would cave in, like the chocolate rabbits he used to get on Easter, which fell apart after the first bite. He knew Jimmy had seen him and wondered what he thought. He wondered how Jimmy would feel if he knew that the Face had sold Veronica's diamond ring along with two of her bracelets for a total of twenty bucks, or two vials of crack. He stroked Donna's tail and began to channel surf with his remote control.

The next morning three editions of *The Daily Ledger* were delivered to each of the three men. In Orchard Park, the paper sat untouched under a blooming azalea bush, but in Forrest Grove and Little City, the papers were opened by six. In Little City, Face sat with his paper, as was his habit every morning, whether he was working or not. Today he was off, so he sat casually with his third cup of coffee and fourth cigarette at the small dinette in his kitchen. All the papers from the week were stacked on the chair next to him, ready to be tied up for recycling. Donna was crouched atop the papers watching the smoke from his cigarette drift past her whiskers. Susie was in her favorite spot in the corner of the top of the refrigerator, surveying the room like a nervous lifeguard, and Jane was sleeping on the arm of the sofa.

In Forrest Grove Darren was reading at such an early hour because he could not sleep, in the sunroom, just off the kitchen, where he often went to relax. He liked the thick cushions on the white wicker furniture, and large plants that shaded the room nicely. He had carefully measured out some of the fresh hazelnut coffee beans that he loved, ground them up and put a fresh pot on to brew. He inhaled deeply; he loved the aroma. He had tied his robe and stepped out to the front to retrieve his paper, although he was not anxious to read it. He knew the word would be out by now. Finally he opened the paper in search of the article on page four, which Face already found unintentionally:

SON OF COMPTECH PRES CHARGED IN DEATH

Julian McPhee, 23, of Forrest Grove, has been charged with manslaughter in the hit and run death of Veronica Lawson, 37, of Orchard Park. McPhee is the only son of computer mogul Darren McPhee, president of Comptech Computer Software. McPhee remains in custody, as the $50,000 bail has not been posted. New York City police say that Lawson was crossing 34th street at approximately 11:30 p.m. on Tuesday evening when McPhee, allegedly intoxicated, struck her, fled the scene and abandoned his car several blocks away. McPhee was arrested on Thursday when he returned to his father's home in Forrest Grove. McPhee's attorney, John Singleton, has stated that his client will be cleared of all charges.

Darren read the article four times, hearing John saying that maybe the car had been stolen. Maybe. The coffeepot gurgled behind him, sending the rich aroma of hazelnuts floating around the kitchen, and the pictures returned to his mind. Julian drunk, babbling, drooling, stumbling around god knows where for over 36 hours. Pictures of Julian in prison, beaten, raped, bleeding, curled in a ball on a filthy bunk.

Face pounded his fist into the table so hard that Donna fled her paper-perch in terror, and his burning cigarette seesawed in the ashtray. "Little bastard," he snarled to his cats. He felt like he was in high school again, wanting to punch out some guy who'd messed with his friend.

The man in Orchard Park never opened the paper that sat under the bush. He never even took it into his house, at six, eight or even ten. He never saw the article. He was watching as six men that he knew hoisted his wife's coffin atop their shoulders and marched it into the waiting hearse.

CHAPTER 5

Julian McPhee wasn't sure what he wanted more—a hot shower or a hot meal. He'd gnawed his fingernails until they were raw, not out of habit but out of boredom. John Singleton had been to his cell three times, trying to pry details that would not come. He remembered being in Smokey's, Cathy...but nothing else. Why hadn't he spent the night with Cathy? That's where it had been heading—so he thought. He sat balled against the wall in a corner of his cell, scraping the film off his teeth with what was left of his pinky nail. He'd been here once before, on DWI charges that Singleton had managed to get dropped by calling in a favor or two, but not this time. Yet John did seem hopeful. But Dad was a different story.

"It's not the money, you know that, Julian," John had said without gentleness.

"What did he say?"

"He doesn't want to see you right now."

Julian sank his head against his knees, staying that way until John tapped him on his head with one finger

"He wants you to get help."

"I've heard it, John. All of it."

"What are you going to do about it?"

"I don't know."

"He loves you. He just wants what's best for you."

"This is what's best for me?" Julian's hands spread in opposite directions, indicating two corners of his cell and his voice cracked.

26

After that visit, he sat scraping his teeth and thinking about what John had said. His father loved him. Right. His father loved what he *should be*, not who he was. He wanted a smart, gleaming son who won awards, had a fresh-faced fiancée and played tennis and golf. He wanted a son like brainy Jeff from the office, or an upstanding do-gooder like his ex-partner's son, Steve. Not what he had. A son who drank too much, couldn't commit to a woman, barely graduated college and preferred watching, rather than playing, sports. His life sucked. His job sucked. He was an office manager for one of Dad's divisions, and people only paid any attention to him because of who he was. He knew they laughed behind his back. He noticed the scoffing when he came to work in the same clothes two days in a row because he'd been out all night. But he never missed work. Didn't that say something? What kind of alcoholic never misses work?

He thought about the woman, Veronica something. The cops had shoved her photo in his face when they met him at his house. He could tell she was pretty, even in the grotesque photo from the morgue, her lips and eyelids blue, some rubber thing supporting her neck. They had nerve showing him that stupid photo. He would have remembered running over someone! He figured he'd gone to get the car, couldn't find it and decided to take the train home but fell asleep waiting for it. Okay, maybe, he'd been to a few other bars first, he had been gone a while. That had to be it. John said it was a good defense. Nobody saw him.

He tossed himself down on his cot and balled the flat pillow under his forearms. The photo of the dead woman kept floating into his mind, even when he closed his eyes. For a moment it reminded him of his mother, the way that she had looked the morning he tried to wake her and could not. She was in her bed, in her usual position, curled up on her side with the pillow folded in half. It was her lips that startled him—just like the woman in the photo, purple lips. Even though he was only eleven he knew lips should only be purple after eating a grape Popsicle. He'd even wiped his mother's mouth to see if she'd eaten one before bed. Then he'd called his dad who was already at work.

Now at twenty-three, the memories of his mother were hazy. He remembered small things like way her hair smelled, and the way she would let a bowl of cereal soak in milk for ten minutes so it would be nice and soggy before she ate it, and how her toenails were always painted bright colors like red and deep pink. He liked her feet, thought they were pretty. She used to rub his back whenever he couldn't sleep and taught him to make meatballs with crackers instead of breadcrumbs. He still remembered the way they had stood in the kitchen with damp meat all over their hands, rolling little balls and tossing them into the pan.

"Darren, listen to me. You have to trust me on this one. If you let him sit in jail it looks like you—his father—doubt his innocence."

"I do doubt his innocence, I can't help it. Something like this was bound to happen."

"He could go to prison, Darren, *real* prison, for a long time. You don't want the papers to start saying that his father thinks he killed this woman. It's *very possible* that he didn't..."

Darren closed his eyes and thought about the husband of Veronica Lawson, her family. He'd watched the people from his car, across the street from the funeral home. He would not have dared to go in, he just watched from across the street as people stood in the parking lot, tissueing their faces and delaying walking up the front steps. It reminded him of when Mary had died, the people everywhere, unable to park on any of the streets surrounding the funeral home. He'd been so angry when Mary died, and that was nobody's fault, so he could imagine how Veronica Lawson's family felt. What if Mary had died in such a stupid, senseless, horrible way? His whole body cringed at the thought of what other people were now saying about his son.

"Darren? You there?"

"I heard you, John." Darren hung up the telephone and stared out his kitchen window. He glanced at the shopping list that his housekeeper, Maggie, had asked him to approve. He read the items over in his head without really comprehending words like *V-8 Juice, granny smith apples, Ritz crackers and Head and Shoulders*...Maggie had worked for him every weekday and some weekends for more than ten years and she still asked him to approve the shopping lists as if she didn't know what she should buy. Although she referred to herself as his housekeeper, Maggie didn't do housework. She was more of a manager. She arranged for the cleaning service, the landscaper, dropped off laundry and dry cleaning, made his doctor's appointments, did the shopping, watered the plants and left dinner on the stove before she left each evening. Basically, she did the things Mary used to do, the things he took for granted. Darren scribbled his initials on the list and stood to put his coffee cup in the sink as he heard the front door open. Maggie stepped into the kitchen holding dry cleaning in one hand and a small bag from the pharmacy in the other. Her red hair looked more fiery than usual as she stood in the direct square of sun that came through the skylight and made a spotlight around her.

"Oh, Darren," her voice was gravelly with a slight brogue. He knew by the way she said his name she had seen the papers before he'd had a chance to talk to her. "Why didn't you call me, I would have come over."

"There was nothing for you to do, but thanks."

"That's malarkey and y'know it. Company woulda done ya good."

Darren couldn't help but smile for a moment, as Maggie's freckles seemed to blaze on her milky skin. She was dressed in a pair of tan chinos and a light blue cotton sweater with short sleeves.

"Sit down with me, for a minute," she commanded as she grabbed the kettle and put it on the stove. "I gotcha some herbal tea, for nerves. Calm ya down a bit." She practically pushed him into one of the chairs and sat across from him. He knew better than to argue, even though he hated herbal tea.

"The paper said he doesn't remember, is that the truth?"

"That's what he says," he puffed the words out through full cheeks.

"You don't believe him?"

"I don't know what to believe."

"May I ask why ya haven't bailed him out?"

"I don't know," Darren pushed his breath from his nose and ran his hand across his forehead. "I think I feel safer. I know nothing else can happen to him if he's locked up."

"You know," her small hand patted the interlocking ball that his hands had made in the middle of the placemat. "Julie's a good boy," she lifted her hand and pressed it between her breasts, which were very round. "In here," she pushed her hand harder against her chest, for emphasis, "where it counts, where The Lord sees. If he did this,

Darren, it was an accident. Your son is not a demon—oh, he has them, we know, but he is a good boy." She rose from her seat abruptly and took out two teacups and saucers made of pale blue china. She placed a tea bag into each cup and then added the whistling water to each one. She balanced them over to the table and retook her seat. "I think we both need this," she declared.

"Thank you, Maggie," Darren now patted her hand. "I know Julian's not a monster, but I'm sure a lot of people are saying that he is. I just don't know what to do. You know all the things I've done to try to help him. None of it has done any good, and I don't know what else I can do."

"Darren, isn't it possible that he didn't do it—somebody coulda got the car, it's a nice car that people would wanna steal. Maybe he's innocent."

"Maybe he is," Darren sighed, "*this* time, but what about next time?"

"Only God knows that, Darren. Maybe this will be his wake-up call; a big kick in the arse that will straighten him out once and for all."

"I don't know, Maggie..."

"I'm finishin' my tea, then I'm gonna get the groceries." She took the checkbook from its drawer and ripped one off for him to sign for her shopping. "You take this," she handed him the rest of the checkbook. "Just in case you need it for anything." Darren put the checkbook in his pocket.

CHAPTER 6

Cathy Colfax called in sick the Tuesday after Memorial Day weekend. She'd called in sick to friends as well, canceling her weekend plans to go down the shore, after she'd seen Friday morning's paper. Julian had been arrested. This time it was bad. She figured he'd be home now; Dad would have everything taken care of as usual. But she was afraid, afraid and sick. She'd spent the weekend chain-smoking and watching a marathon of the life stories of former teen idols on *VH-1*. Her friends thought she had the flu. She felt like she did anyway. She didn't know if Julian would be at work today, but she just did not want to see him.

She stood in the window of the living room in her modest but neat apartment. She forgot that she was only wearing a tank top and matching bikini underpants. She watched the people in the courtyard going about their business. A mother, around her age, was carting two little kids off to daycare with their lunchboxes and backpacks. Mr. Gerry, the retired salesman, was sitting in his usual spot in the courtyard, on his folding chair. He was wearing a familiar outfit— shorts, knee socks, sneakers, and a plaid button down short-sleeved shirt with a pen in the pocket and a Yankee cap. She wondered why he always carried a pen, he was retired! He just sat there, like he always did. Sometimes he fed the birds or the squirrels, and sometimes he read the paper, but he mostly just sat. But she had done that too, at least for the last several days. She should have listened to Grace and Janine.

"He's a loser," Janine had scolded, stabbing her chicken Caesar salad emphatically, "get over him."

"Listen to us," Grace had joined in. "If it wasn't for his Daddy he'd be in a gutter somewhere. Did you see him last Tuesday—a mess! Same clothes, God only knows what kind of diseases he has. I hope you've been careful. Imagine what he's *been* with."

"Thanks a lot," Cathy said, chewing her cheeseburger, unable to swallow.

"We're just trying to look out for you."

"I know, but..." she dropped her cheeseburger in defeat. She could not make them understand something she did not understand herself. Julian was different when they were alone. She knew what people said about him, but she really *knew* him. She was aware that he often drank too much, but she liked to drink, too. And Julian was fun when he drank. They did fun things, things she would have never done alone. Once they drank two bottles of wine behind some bushes in the park, then went skinny-dipping in the dirty lake and ended up making love on top of a picnic table. She smiled at the thought. It was stupid and crazy and they both could have been arrested, but it was the best sex she'd ever had. Julian was her third lover, but the only one she really enjoyed. She found herself making noises that she never thought any human could make. It was exhilarating and addictive. But it wasn't just great orgasms that kept them coming back to each other. She loved the way he kept his eyes open and really looked at her as he climaxed. She often felt him tracing the length of her hair as she pretended to be asleep and more than once looked up at work to see him watching her. They laughed often, they talked and talked, they made French fries at two in the morning and ate them naked in her kitchen, and they hungrily flirted with each other whenever people from work went out, as if they were getting together for the first time.

She'd gone to Smokey's the previous Tuesday with the hope of a rendezvous with Julian at the end of the evening. That's the way it was with them. They endured evenings with groups from work, all with the plan to leave together at the end of the night. It was an odd relationship, if you could call it that. But Cathy was determined to turn it into something other than sexual encounters at various intervals; even though sometimes she felt she was being made a fool of. Like Tuesday night. Their flirting routine began as usual—after she'd had two Cosmopolitans—but Julian seemed distant. When she returned from the ladies room later in the evening to see Julian sidled up to some bleached bimbo with protruding nipples, she finished her drink, chatted lightly with a few guys from the office like nothing was wrong, then politely excused herself and went home. She'd seen the pitiful looks people were giving her. She wondered if Julian had gone home with the bimbo. She wondered if she could have stopped him.

But the paper—she read the paper Friday morning, when she became "ill"—the paper said the accident occurred around eleven thirty. She had left Smokey's around nine-thirty. Not much time for a fuck with the bimbo, unless they'd done it in the parking lot, which from the looks of *her* was always a possibility. She'd gone home that night before ten, ate a pint of Ben & Jerry's Cherry Garcia, gave herself a pedicure and went to sleep. Until the phone rang around one in the morning...

"Cathy? It's me, Julian."

She moved away from the window and lit another cigarette, waving the smoke from the front of her face, and the sound of the voice on the phone from her mind. When he didn't show up for work last Wednesday and Thursday she thought he was dead, until the news hit the paper. She threw up when she read it. There was a voice inside of her that told her to just write him off—consider it over, move on. The voice sounded much like Grace and Janine.

She reclined on the sofa, smoking and staring at the ceiling fan. She was almost lost in the large, floral print pillows of her sofa, a combination of mauve and yellow. The same fabric fell over the two living room windows in an elaborate swag. Her "dining room" was a round oak table that sat with two chairs in front of the large window, and the kitchen was simply a narrow array of appliances with a counter and two oak stools. The coffee table in front of the sofa was usually arranged with a neat display of flowers, books, and candles, but on this morning it was littered with a full ashtray, a dirty coffee cup and an unfolded newspaper. She'd worked hard to support such a nice apartment on her own, and it occurred to her that if she didn't get her act together she might lose the job that kept her here. But she felt...*sick.*

The ringing phone at three in the afternoon didn't surprise her. She figured it was Grace or Janine or someone else from work checking to see if she was alive, or calling to tell her what a great weekend she had missed. She let the machine get it. Tomorrow she'd go to work.

"*Cathy? It's me, Julian.*" The voice made her jump. "They said at the office that you were sick…I guess you heard…I'm okay. Things are going to be okay. I'm home now. Call me later if you can. If not, I guess I'll see you tomorrow…"

By the time she heard this she was sitting up, staring at the phone. She didn't think as she grabbed the receiver.

"I'm here."

"Are you okay?" He sounded tired.

"I should be asking you that."

"I'm fine. John Singleton is working on my case. He thinks that if it goes to trial, which is unlikely, I won't be convicted. There's no evidence."

"What do you mean?" Her heart began beating faster.

"No witnesses, they found my car, but I was asleep in the subway. Someone must have stolen the car and hit that woman. It wasn't me. What is wrong with you, anyway? You have the flu or something?"

"Julian…?"

"What?"

"You *really* don't remember *anything*?" She'd read that in the paper but thought it was bullshit. "I thought…"

"No," he said quietly. "I blacked out, I guess. But I couldn't have done it, Cathy."

She was quiet for a long time. She sensed that he wanted to say more, but what could he say?

"How do you know that if you can't remember anything?"

"Like I said, I was in the subway. I woke up there after I passed out. My car was missing. Besides, I think I would remember something like that, no matter how plastered I was."

Cathy's stomach tightened with nausea. She was desperate to get off the phone. "Maybe we can talk more tomorrow," she breathed. "Are you going to work?"

"Yeah. John's working on things, there's no trial date yet."

"Okay. I'll see you tomorrow then. Bye." She hung up. It was the first time that she recalled ever not really wanting to talk to him, the first time that he had made her so angry. She heard Grace and Janine's warnings again, and this time she listened to them more closely. His words echoed through her head. *No witnesses...it wasn't me.* She looked at the phone where it sat on the coffee table. She picked it up and held it between her palms, thinking about a call she knew she should make. But thoughts of what she might say were mixed with memories of Julian's smile, his touch, the night they sat naked, steaming in his Jacuzzi, talking until dawn while his father was out of town. But how could he be so callous about something like this? Part of her never wanted to speak to him again, but part of her was desperate to see him. She knew she'd be at work tomorrow, even if she felt sicker than ever.

CHAPTER 7

Face Jenkins closed the downstairs door to Mrs. Murphy's house and wondered why there were no real holidays in June. The door wreath was now adorned with yellow ribbon and a sailboat. Sure, June had Flag Day, but the flag was used for May, and would likely be repeated in July. There was Father's Day—but how do you put that on a wreath? So a sailboat it was. It was just after dawn, and the street was silent. His doctor's appointment wasn't until nine so he did what he often did with the empty hours of his life—went to the park. He sometimes felt like a cliché—sitting in the park feeding ducks at the crack of dawn—but he liked to watch the ducks swim across the lake in a group, a line of water making a triangle behind them as they glided to the shore at the first drop of a breadcrumb. He often just sat on the bench, thinking. He had arrived at the point in his life where he was his own best friend. He liked his own company and kept only a few superficial acquaintances. Although he was not yet forty, he felt like an old man, which was why he avoided mirrors. His nickname, "Face" had originally been the result of his smooth, clear complexion, large gray eyes, and his big, straight smile that once sent the girls giggling and blushing. Years of drugs, booze, cigarettes and insomnia had dulled and slightly leathered the once glowing skin, Jimmy's fist had skewed his once perfect nose and a fall down a flight of stairs had added the lip scar. Although the eyes were the same, they did not have the same sparkle without the smile that was now hooded with his moustache. To him, "Face" had taken on new meaning. The name now stood for what he once was, and what he would never be again.

He watched a young woman jog by. She was wearing black nylon shorts and a yellow windbreaker. He watched her buttocks as she passed him and was awed by the fact that they did not move, even as her feet pounded the pavement of the running track. His face would have once gotten her attention, but now he no longer existed. Not that it mattered, as the plethora of pills he swallowed daily had rendered him impotent for the past two years. That was one of the great ironies of his life: when he was heavily involved in drugs, sex was not that important to him, but his dick would get hard from a strong wind. Now that he was clean, and wanted sex, it was out of his reach. He was impotent, but not unaware of desire—that was the hardest part. Sex for him was only a memory—a great memory. As the woman jogged by for the second time, he looked at her face. Her dark hair was pulled through the back of a white baseball cap, and she wore her keys around her neck. The keys on a string bounced from one breast to the other and made a jiggling sound with each stride. She reminded him of a prostitute named Claire he knew in his darker period. Claire's hair was the same shiny dark color, but it always hung around her face, and she never bothered to brush it away, nor did she wash it on a regular basis. He and Claire used to shoot up together behind an abandoned warehouse. He never knew why but she would often share her stash of heroin with him. She'd fuck, get paid, get drugs, and often gave him some. He never did the same. When he had the cash to score, he shot into his own arm before Claire even knew about it. It never occurred to him at the time that she was being generous. She sometimes gave him a blowjob free of charge, too. Right after they'd gotten high, she'd just undo his pants and dive into his crotch. What a girl. He was sure she must be dead by now, strangled by a crazed john, or overdosed in some alley, or the bug. He figured she was the one who gave it to him. Back in the day he'd never thought twice about taking the needle from her. He never noticed the tiny pool of her blood still swimming in it...

The woman was coming around the track for the third time. Now a film of sweat covered her forehead. As she passed him she slowed to pull her windbreaker over her head. As she did so, her keys slipped under the zipper and fell against her red t-shirt. As she rounded the corner just past where he was sitting, she tied the windbreaker around her waist. Face loved how the yellow material seemed to melt over her hips. He would have liked to just sit there and watch her forever, but he knew he had an appointment—an appointment with the real love of his life.

"Good morning, Mr. Jenkins," greeted Jean, the redheaded receptionist. All the girls at the clinic knew him by name. They liked his quiet manner and pretty eyes. He never snarled, complained or treated them rudely—just some harmless flirting. Face sat in the waiting room thumbing through *Sports Illustrated* and craving a cigarette, even through he'd smoked four at the park. After a brief wait, the receptionist called him into room seven, where his true love, Princess, was waiting.

"Good Morning," she smiled warmly.

"It is now, my dear." He took her hand and kissed it, and she blushed as usual. Her name was really Samantha, but he called her Princess because her sparkling blue eyes and short ash-blonde hair reminded him of the late Princess Diana of Wales with whom he'd also been in love. But this Princess was very young—twenty or twenty-one—and naughtily, voluptuously plump around the hips and bust. Face liked a woman round rather than straight like a pencil. And Princess had the most adorable dimples and a few light freckles sprinkled across her nose. She was his definition of cute, and he was dying to fuck her.

"I wish all the patients here were so nice to me," she crooned as she waved her tiny hand toward the scale. He stepped out of his shoes, knowing the drill too well.

"One sixty-three..." she looked at his chart and he saw her lips push together in the cutest way. He knew she was not allowed to say anything, that was up to the doctor. But he knew he'd lost four pounds.

"Four pounds!" He whistled.

"Haven't you had an appetite?' she almost whispered, like she was afraid the doctor would think she was being too inquisitive. The truth was that food was an afterthought for Face. He ate when he realized he was hungry, never planning his meals in advance like most people. The problem was that now he needed to keep his weight up, which meant three nutritious meals and several snacks daily. He often didn't remember to eat that much. Coffee and cigarettes were sufficient breakfast usually until noon, sometimes longer. When he was at work he might eat a buttered roll or Danish, or if he was home he might have pop tarts or sometimes grab a corned beef sandwich at the deli down the street. At night he'd grab a slice of pizza, an egg roll or a steak sandwich if Mrs. Murphy didn't send up some of her "leftovers." She usually had leftovers because even though her husband was dead and all her children grown she still cooked meals for eight people. Sometimes she'd drop off half a pan of lasagna or half a roast beef, which would last him several days or sometimes a week. For most of his adult life—with the exception of the heroin days—he'd maintained a thin, but healthy weight of somewhere around 175 on his small-boned frame which was a few inches shy of six feet tall. But now he needed to stop losing weight.

"Do you think I'll get yelled at?" he asked Princess in a tone full of mock fear.

"This is not a joke, Mr. Jenkins," she scolded. "You need to keep your strength up."

"For our wedding, right?"

"I haven't said yes, yet," she giggled.

"You will, when you realize you're madly in love with me." They walked into the exam room where he hoisted himself onto the table. She pulled a blood pressure cuff off the rack in the wall and wrapped it around his arm—his favorite part, as she was so close he could see the individual hairs in her eyebrows. She squeezed the bulb and the cuff tightened.

"You're a little high, Mr. Jenkins…"

"I've told you to call me Randy…you should call your fiancée by his first name."

"You'd better behave yourself or I'll take an extra tube of blood."

"You're cute when you're being sadistic."

She gave him her warning glare, but the dimples were trying to pry her face into a smile. The door swung open, and a stout man with curly hair—it reminded Face of pubic hair—which encircled the sides and back of his head entered the room. Nothing on top, not one hair. He wore square glasses that often slid down his nose and a white coat over a plaid shirt, Dockers and loafers.

"How've you been feeling?" he asked as he reached up to Face's neck and began feeling around. Face pondered the question as if he'd never been asked it before.

CHAPTER 8

By late June, Jimmy Lawson had stopped getting pans of food from well-meaning neighbors, the fall term was a long summer away, and his phone sat silently on the counter. Sometimes he would sit in his office and try to read, or type up a new lesson or work on the book he'd started—a collection of research on contemporary American drama for college students. He had been excited by the book, planning to finish it this summer, but now the words seemed almost like a foreign language. He couldn't decipher anything that required thought. It wasn't that his mind was drifting, it was numb. He had a feeling that he hadn't yet been able to name. It wasn't grief, exactly, or sadness…but a desperate feeling that he wanted things to be different. His appearance had changed as well. His usually neatly cut brown hair had grown out around the edges, so now it curled up slightly at the bottom. His usually clean-shaven face was neglected until it grew sharp as a cactus, then he'd hastily shave with only soap and let it grow again. Even his body seemed slackened. His shoulders no longer hung in a straight line, but were slightly warped, and his firm abdomen had loosened from lack of activity.

He spent some of his time wandering around his house, not really doing anything. He didn't sleep at night; only in brief fits during the day. He knew he was getting lost, knew he had to do something, but didn't know what. One sunny morning he decided to do some work in the yard, to help him pass the time, the day. Although a neighborhood boy mowed the lawn each week, it was he and Veronica who pruned and cared for the bushes, flowers and shrubs in front of the house. He stepped out onto his porch and his eyes recoiled at the unfamiliar sunlight. He was dressed in denim shorts and a wrinkled gray t-shirt. With hands on hips, he surveyed the front landscaping. The azalea bush's bright blossoms were now wrinkled scraps on the ground, and weeds had begun to poke up through the bed of cedar mulch, which had lost its moisture. After completing his mental list of what needed to be done he went to the garage to retrieve the necessary tools. The garage was neat and well organized, with just enough room for Veronica's Toyota, which surprised him when he tossed the door upward. He'd forgotten it. Her car. He stood in his driveway staring at his dead wife's car, unable to comprehend how he'd completely forgotten its existence for over three weeks. What should he do with it? He touched it gingerly, trying to imagine selling the car—watching some stranger push the seat back, look under the hood, and try to negotiate a lower price. He opened the driver's side door and slid in. For a brief moment, he contemplated turning the ignition on and closing the door. He imagined his lungs burning with the toxic air, and falling asleep...

Maybe Aunt June would want the car. He didn't want it, but he didn't want to sell it, either. He opened the glove compartment and began sifting through its contents: insurance, registration, a torn map, an unopened pair of pantyhose, a small flashlight, a pen, and a parking ticket she'd never mentioned. He wondered if he had to pay it now as he ran his hand over the leather interior and the steering wheel. It felt exciting to him to be touching things she had touched, to be sitting where she'd sat so often. He'd once tried to teach Veronica to drive a five speed, but she was never very coordinated. They had spent three hours in the high school parking lot on a Sunday afternoon, clutching, braking and basically getting whiplash.

"You're hopeless," Jimmy had laughed, rubbing the back of his neck.

"Oh, so what! I like to relax when I drive anyway. I don't want to have to think about all that stuff. What's wrong with an automatic?"

"They're more expensive, for starters."

"Don't be so cheap!" She had swatted his arm, and then smiled at him. She was just as bad at tennis, often sending the ball flying outside the fenced in court where he tried to teach her. He taught her how to serve, and she developed a decent backhand, but as soon she lost her concentration the balls were over the fence again.

"You're impossible!" He laughed in frustration.

"What can I say, I can't help my own strength."

After his reverie in the car he set his mind on the yard work, determined to do something of value with this day. He grabbed his gloves, a small shovel and the Garden Weasel off their respective hooks on the wall of pegboard that hung to the right of the car and lugged them to the front yard. As he dug into the dirt with his gloved hands, and beads of sweat began to sting the back of his neck, he felt alive. He yanked weeds and threw them into piles, he dug up mulch, moistened it with the hose, and tossed it around like a salad. He clipped the overhang of grass that invaded the sidewalk and trimmed the rosebush on the side of the house. When be began feeling a tug in his lower back, he thought he should quit. He wiped his dirty, gloved hands across his buttocks, then placed his tools into their correct pegs in the garage, this time ignoring the car. He stood in front of the house for a moment before he went inside, admiring his work. The yard looked fresh and he felt good. He glanced at his watch and realized that it had been nearly three hours, and he had not yearned for Veronica. That was the word he had chosen to describe his mental condition: a yearning. It was not a sexual yearning, although he felt that void as well, but an almost uncontrollable desire to just be near her, to walk in the house and see her in one of her yoga stretches on her mat in the living room, or to hear the water spraying over her body when she showered, or to hear her giggling at something on television. He yearned for her *presence*.

Three non-yearning hours was a start, he supposed; definite progress from yearning constantly. He decided this was the key. He needed to do things, anything to keep the yearn away. He went inside and upstairs where he peeled off his sweaty clothes and took a shower. The lather was warm and comforting as it slid over his body, but he was reminded of the many showers they'd taken together. He recalled the time he and Veronica had lugged a very stoned Face into the shower of their old apartment. She'd picked him up on the street, like a stray dog. He'd been angry, at first that she'd brought him to their house in this condition, but this was Face, his friend.

"He's a junkie, can't you see that?"

"You can't just turn your back on him. I know you care about this man," she'd said, her social worker instincts taking over. "I know you'd never forgive yourself if he died on the street."

He'd known that she was right. He'd wanted to help his friend. Part of him felt guilty for getting out of the city—away from the life that had captured Face. But understanding the addiction was beyond him—just quit was his philosophy—you can if you really want to. The image of Face sitting in his car at Veronica's funeral came back to him. He wondered if he was still using. Probably not, or he'd likely be dead. He hadn't looked stoned in the car, but he was too far away to really tell. But why had he come to the funeral home? Guilt? Why hadn't he come in? Jimmy noticed that during these thoughts his hand had involuntarily balled itself into a fist. He could feel Face's bone crack against it...he'd felt the rib catch on his foot...he wondered for a moment what might have happened if Mrs. Jenkins hadn't come out of the house. Could he have killed Face? It was possible. That kind of betrayal was not acceptable between friends. Face had grown up under the same code. Look out for each other...

Jimmy heard the phone ring, and stepped out of the shower, wrapping a towel around his waist. The answering machine had picked up as he got to the bedroom.

"Mr. Lawson, this is Marilyn Jones from the D.A.'s office. I'm just calling to let you know that there's a hearing in the matter of your wife's death next Tuesday at 10 a.m. You're not required to attend, but I thought you would like to know. Please call me if you have any questions."

The yearn hit him again.

CHAPTER 9

In the weeks since he'd been released from jail and returned to work, Julian felt even more isolated than usual, especially at work. No one in this office saw Darren regularly, so Julian accepted the fact that he was considered a "spy" for the boss. He'd been used to occasionally having a room full of colleagues fall silent upon his arrival, but he'd always accepted that as a hazard of being the son of the CEO. Now it was different. They weren't talking about the fact that his job was one of sheer nepotism, they had just *stopped* talking. Nobody knew what to say to him, and it was lonely. On the morning before his preliminary hearing, he felt the rift widen. No one even looked in his direction, let alone looked him in the eye. But what should he expect? A party? A card signed by all the workers wishing him success in his manslaughter hearing? How could he blame people for ignoring him when a simple question like, "How are you?" was dangerous. He knew it was dumb to expect these people to be his friends, but their aloofness still hurt him.

He noticed Cathy's car in the lot, in the same spot where it always was. It was early, before eight. He'd been trying to catch Cathy alone on their way in, or to talk to her like they used to every morning. But she was avoiding him, clearly, arriving quite early and slipping out quietly at the end of the day. He missed the days when they'd linger in the tiny kitchen room where the large coffeepot sat on the white Formica counter. She'd fill her large blue and neon green soup-bowl-like mug with the steaming liquid, then press one hip against the counter as she pinched a sugar packet, shook it gingerly and deposited the contents into her cup. She always held her mug between both palms, the way you might place your hands if you wanted to keep water from leaking out before splashing it on your face. It was a stupid thing to think about, he told himself as he walked into the empty kitchen. He hadn't even realized until now that those small moments had been a real part of his routine. He knew Cathy was already at her desk, mug filled, suddenly much busier than usual. She'd been willing to exchange polite greetings and small talk, but she wouldn't return his phone calls, or be alone with him, so he was never able to *really* talk to her.

People were arriving sporadically as Julian poured his cup of coffee and searched for a stirrer. Suzanne, the executive secretary on the floor, stepped into the room carrying a large bakery box. She was in her fifties, slim and attractive with short auburn hair and half-glasses that she wore around her neck with a gold chain and placed on her nose only when necessary.

"Good morning, Suzanne," Julian smiled his warmest, most sincere smile.

"Good morning..." she seemed startled by his presence. She set the box on the counter and fished through a drawer for a knife. She slid a long red fingernail below the red and white string to lift it, and then sawed it apart with the knife.

"What's this?" Julian set his mug down and peered into the box.

"Oh, just some muffins. It's June birthday day." She removed a large platter from the cabinet and began to arrange the muffins without looking up. The staff on this floor had agreed to limit birthday celebrations to one day near the end of each month. Before the company had grown, they used to have a cake on each individual's birthday, but that had gotten disruptive—sometimes three in one week—and fattening. Suzanne was the one who always organized the birthdays, baby showers, get-well cards, like a well-meaning aunt. Julian wondered for a moment if she had considered planning a "hope you don't end up in prison" muffin party for him. No, the more likely party would be, "Junior's in jail! Let's celebrate!"

"They look delicious."

Suzanne looked up, but not fully at him. He regretted this comment because it did not require a response from Suzanne. He had to remember to ask more questions, get people talking. He felt exhausted already. Planning each word was exhausting.

He walked by Cathy's office. The door was open. She was sitting at her desk with the phone pressed between her shoulder and her ear, her brown hair was tucked neatly behind her ear and she was chewing on the corner of a pen. She scribbled something on a yellow legal pad, then in one motion swiveled her chair and pressed the enter button on her computer. Julian liked the smoothness of her motion, the way she moved without seeming to move. He listened to the softness of her voice as she spoke into the phone and let out a small laugh. He wondered what she might be laughing at.

"Chief, would you sign this for me please?" Julian was startled out of his thoughts by Jeffrey Madison, the computer business wonder boy who would probably get Julian's job if he went to prison. *Maybe dad will just move him into my room and pass him off as his real son.* According to Darren McPhee, Jeffrey was smart, dedicated and had a bright future. Julian had grown tired of hearing about Jeff's brilliant contribution to this meeting or that idea. He imagined Jeff taking over his job, Cathy falling in love with him; his father already was. These thoughts paralyzed Julian for a moment, so Jeff repeated his request in a louder, slightly bewildered tone, which caused Cathy to look up from her computer screen. Julian grabbed the document from Jeff, whose eyes were flitting between Julian and Cathy, and scribbled his name without looking at it. Cathy hung up her phone, and Julian purposefully stepped into her office and closed the door behind him. He hadn't planned to do that, and had caught himself by surprise.

"Hi," she said, fiddling with papers on her desk.

"We need to talk, Cathy."

"I'm really busy, Julian, I have to—"

He stepped around her desk and pulled her hands away from the papers she was fiddling with. He noticed the yellow pad contained an intricate pattern of geometric doodles. He pulled her hands up and led her to one of the two chairs that sat in front of her desk.

"Tomorrow is my first hearing." He pulled the second chair close to hers and sat in it, almost touching her knees with his own.

"I know, I heard," she whispered, her hands gripping the arms of her chair. Her head was bowed slightly, causing her hair to hang along the sides of her face. He noticed her gnawing on the corner of her bottom lip, and reached over and tentatively placed his fingers on one of her hands, which was gripping the arm of the chair. He felt her stiffen.

"Cathy, what is it? Why can't you even look at me?" He moved forward in the chair as if leaning in anticipation of her response.

Cathy could not lift her face up. The voice on the phone flew around in her mind.

"Cathy? It's me, Julian"

"What time is it?"

"I dunno, late..."

"Where are you?"

"I...I dunno."

She signed heavily and stood up, trying to block out the voice and the sound of the ringing phone that had been playing in her head almost constantly. She looked tired, and something in her eyes made Julian sit back.

"I don't want to see you anymore."

The words seemed to deflate her, and she leaned against her desk. Julian sat back further in his chair and pinched his bottom lip between his thumb and finger.

"Why? Give me a reason."

"I just can't," she shook her head.

"It wasn't me, Cathy, if that's what your problem is." His voice had lifted into something angry and desperate. "I know things don't look good at this moment, but *I am not* going to prison, Cathy." He stood and grabbed both of her hands, but she wrenched her wrists away and stood very close to his face.

"You don't know that! You don't even remember what happened!" Her words were almost whispered, but full of venom. She stepped away from him, back behind her desk.

"I know it in my heart, Cathy. I couldn't just run someone over. I would remember that. No matter how much I had to drink. I would not have left some woman dying in the street..."

"Julian. Listen to me. You need to stop drinking, now. You have to promise me."

"Cathy, believe me, I've learned my lesson." He looked her in the eye.

She stepped toward him, grabbing both sides of his face between her palms.

"Swear to me, Julian. *Swear to God* that you will never get behind the wheel of a car again if you've been drinking."

"Cathy, I just told you…"

"Swear it…" she said through her teeth.

"Okay, I swear!" He reached up and removed her hands from the sides of his face. "What has gotten into you?"

"No one should have to die the way that woman did."

"I know that."

"Do you?"

"Yes." He put his hands on her shoulders, but she shrugged them off.

"Just go away, Julian!" she plopped into her chair and rolled it forward. "Please."

He watched her for a few moments as she tried to ignore him, pretending to be engrossed in something on her desk and doodling on her pad. She didn't look up again, so he left her office.

When he walked out, she leaned back in her chair and stared at the door for a moment, waiting for him to return, expecting the door to move. Despite her efforts not to, she could not help recalling the first time he had kissed her. She had been leaving the Christmas party last year, walking out to the parking lot alone after an enjoyable night. She'd danced with Julian a few times, but had danced with some other guys as well. She was putting the key into the lock of her door when he came running up to her.

"Cathy?" He stopped short, breathing fast.

"What's up, Julian?" His cheeks were reddened with the cold air.

He hadn't said anything, but just stared at her for a moment, then he'd placed his hands squarely on her shoulders and given her a quick kiss on the lips. She was bewildered and just stared at him.

"I just felt like doing that," he'd smiled and shrugged slightly.

"Oh," was all Cathy could think of to say, berating herself as the words came out. She wished she could have said something really, really clever.

"See ya tomorrow," he'd stepped back and given a half wave.

Cathy grasped her keys again, but she was still confused. "You ran all the way out here, just for that?"

"Yeah," he shrugged. Then he took another step toward her and picked up both of her hands, her keys still in the right one, and kissed her again. This one was a little softer, a little longer. "It was worth it," he whispered. He turned and hurried back inside, holding his arms against the cold, turning to wave as he reached the door. She drove home that night thinking about his impish smile and the way his lips had tasted.

Cathy stared at the back of her office door, relieved that he had not come back in, but unable to focus on her work.

After some numb hours of signing, reading, and gazing out his office window, Julian left to go to lunch alone. None of the triads or quartets that were discussing where to eat today bothered to invite him along. Even the few workhorses who were having sandwiches delivered did not even bother to ask if he'd like something ordered. Cathy was included; he'd heard her order a turkey on rye. He drove out of the parking lot in his rented car, which smelled like Lysol, and drove to the closest place. The closest place just happened to be Smokey's.

"Cheeseburger, medium, and a coke."

The waitress at Smokey's smiled and wondered why this hot young guy in a nice suit was eating alone. Julian had brought a newspaper so he wouldn't feel so self-conscious, but he didn't feel like reading it. Instead, his gaze was drawn to a corner of the bar, a small table...for some reason that table held him there, as if trying to tell him something. He pictured himself sitting there...and there was a woman...it occurred to him suddenly that he was here on that night, at the bar. He wondered if somewhere in his subconscious he was trying to torture himself by coming back here. He'd been here with Cathy and others from work many times before. Everybody seemed to like Cathy. She had a way of making people smile without even doing anything. It was just the freshness of her presence...

The ringing of the ceramic platter against the table jolted him from his thoughts.

"Can I get you anything else, sir?" The waitress was a very young girl wearing khaki chinos, a white shirt and a black apron with the name Smokey's embroidered across the top. She had a tight plastic choker around her neck, the kind that looked like a tattoo. Julian wanted to touch it to see if it was really was a necklace, but he resisted the urge. He shook his head and she scampered off to her next table.

The choker...now he remembered! He glanced back at the table behind the bar and remembered sitting there with a girl who was wearing a similar choker. That was how he'd started talking to her, he'd asked her if her neck was tattooed all the way around, and when she said it was a necklace he didn't believe her so she invited him to feel it for himself. Could it have been her? Maybe she'd stolen the keys to his car out of his pocket...

He swallowed the last of his cheeseburger—with difficulty—and handed the waitress his credit card. Then he went over to the corner table and sat down. He ran his hand over the top, caressing it into revealing what it knew of that night. Meanwhile, the waitress was looking panicked when she returned and could not find him. His credit card was in her hand, and she picked up his plate and looked around. She sighed when she saw him sitting in the bar section and came to hand him the card, looking confused.

"Can I get you anything else, sir?"

"No, thank you." He added a sizeable tip to the amount and scribbled his name. She walked away looking confused but smiled when she looked at her tip. Julian sat glassy eyed and thought back to that night.

"Go ahead, see for yourself." The woman had taken his hand and guided it up to her neck where he ran a finger over the pattern and felt both the necklace and her skin. His hand had lingered for a moment at the woman's neck—he didn't even know her name—she was blonde with large braless breasts that bobbed beneath her shirt. He strained to recall what had happened next. Had he gone home with this woman? Had she fished his keys out of his pocket under the guise of some physical flirtation? But what about Cathy? *Shit.* That's why she'd left, at least now he understood that part. Cathy left because he'd been in, well, a compromising-looking position with a strange woman. No wonder she was so angry. *Why did he always pull shit that messed things up?* What had he done after Cathy had left? Although he'd messed things up with Cathy, at least if he'd gone home with her, he had an alibi for the accident. Maybe he had left his car here and gone home with her and someone had stolen his car from this parking lot. That had to be it! He closed his eyes and tried to remember her name.

"What can I getcha?"

Julian was startled by the young man who was hovering next to where he was sitting. He looked around the room, which was peppered with a few tables finishing lunch, but the bar area was empty except for himself and an older guy who was at the bar drinking a beer and watching the Mets game on the overhead television. Julian looked up at the new waiter, a young man in a black Smokey's polo shirt. It was like he was watching himself, he was unable to speak, to excuse himself and leave. He knew he should get up and get out, go back to the office, but it was as if he had no control over his body. He *knew* what he *must not do,* and he tried with all his might *not to do it.*

"Gin and tonic," he said.

CHAPTER 10

Cathy tried to finish all the crap that was strewn across her desk, but her mind would not allow it. She could not complete any task, no matter how small, without Julian popping into her head. She was proud of herself for standing her ground, but it had been difficult. When he was in her office, she'd had to resist throwing her arms around him and telling him everything was going to be all right. She was afraid for him; she knew he would never survive if he had to go to prison. He'd never really been on his own before, never had to fend for himself. He was weak in so many ways, and part of her was attracted to his weakness, his neediness. But he needed love and understanding, not prison. She looked at her watch, it was close enough to five to escape criticism, and she was anxious to relay her success story to Grace and Janine. She knew they disliked Julian and would be happy that her involvement with him was officially over. The three women met for drinks after work several times a week. Sometimes they had one round, chatted and left for other engagements, other times some of their friends showed up and they hung out until late. Occasionally, the three of them stayed for dinner, sharing a bottle of wine and intimate girl talk. It was Grace and Janine who'd given Cathy the courage to break it off with Julian once and for all with their advice and pep talks and their blatant disapproval of him. Even if it had taken her over a month to do it, she'd done it and knew they'd be proud.

After stopping at the cash machine and the drycleaner, she was a few minutes late, and Grace and Janine were already sitting at a table by the front window, waving at her. Each of them already had a glass of wine. Gracie had gorgeous tanned-looking skin and very short dark hair. She was one of those women who could wear short hair and only lipstick and still look feminine. She was very lean, an exercise buff who never missed a workout. Janine was lighter— brown hair, green eyes, and thin face—too thin, Cathy thought. Janine's thinness was a bony thin, which contrasted with Grace's healthy-looking physique. Being with both of them made Cathy feel like a blimp.

"Well, I have an announcement!" Cathy declared as she placed her purse on the empty fourth chair at the table.

"What?" They said in unison, both their tones thick with skepticism.

"Julian is history! We're totally over."

Grace and Janine looked at each other as Cathy fiddled with her napkin and unrolled her utensils. "And to celebrate, let's order a big, greasy appetizer." Grace and Janine were still silent and looked at each other again, and then started laughing. Cathy kept her face behind her menu as she admonished them.

"I do not *hear* that! Nachos or potato skins?"

"You are so full of shit!" Grace yanked the menu out of Cathy's hands.

"No, really. I told him today."

"You mean you actually spoke to him…words, you spoke words?" Janine sipped her wine while Grace continued giggling.

"Yes, I actually said the words!" Cathy mocked her friend's voice, then looked up into the face of a very young waitress who pulled her pad from the pocket of her black apron.

"I'll have a glass of Chardonnay, please, an order of nachos, *and* an order of potato skins!"

"Oh!" Gracie screeched and held up her glass to Janine who clicked it in a mock toast. "I guess you said the words! Here's to you, Cathy, took ya long enough!" The three friends giggled and joked good-naturedly for a few minutes, but by the time their snacks arrived, the tone had become more serious.

"Really, it's the best thing you could have done." Grace scooped a nacho into her mouth. Cathy admired the way that Grace seemed to handle men with ease. She was always "seeing" someone, but never seemed hurt when the relationships ended. She was always in total control. Her most recent flame was an aspiring actor who was currently working on a shampoo commercial.

"It was so hard, though," Cathy lamented, searching her friend's eyes for some flicker of compassion. There was none.

"C'mon, Cathy, can you picture yourself on visiting day in prison? Haven't you ever watched any prison movies? You know what kind of stuff goes on there. They even strip search the visitors you know…" Janine had a potato skin on her small plate and was picking the pieces of bacon off the top.

"They do not!" Grace interjected, "first of all, that's only in the movies, second of all they don't allow conjugal visits in this state…"

"Aren't we getting a little ahead of ourselves?" Cathy slid two fingers along the stem of her wineglass. "Julian hasn't been *convicted* of anything…he probably won't be. There is no proof he was driving the car. No witnesses," her voice broke slightly, and her friends grew silent.

"Come on, Cathy. The guy has a major problem. This has been coming for a while." Janine stared at her.

"Oh my god," Grace sighed and touched Cathy's hand. "You're really in love with him, aren't you?" Cathy just shrugged and blew her nose in her napkin.

"I'm afraid for him, I can't stop thinking about it. I just want to help him," she whispered, then sipped her wine. "Let's please just talk about something else, okay?"

They sat in silence, sipping their drinks.

"My boss touched my ass today," Janine interjected. Cathy and Grace stared at her for a moment, and then the three of them began to laugh again. Cathy listened politely to their banter, smiled and giggled when she knew they were expecting it, but she kept wondering what would happen tomorrow, wondering if she was in love with a man who would soon be in prison for as much as ten to fifteen years.

When the plates were practically licked clean and their second round of drinks finished, Grace stood to excuse herself.

"I'm off ladies; I've got to meet Mark on *the set.*"

"Oh, *the set,*" Janine mimicked, "you mean he's actually *in* something?"

"Yes, smart-ass!" Grace hoisted her purse off the empty chair. "He had to wash his hair seventeen times yesterday, for your information.

Do you guys wanna have dinner here tomorrow? I can tell you about Mark's commercial. He looks so hot with soap all over his head."

"I'm not busy," Janine said, handing her credit card to the young waitress.

"Cath?" Grace said.

"Yeah, tomorrow's okay...is it my turn to pay?"

"No, I got it already," Janine said. "You ready to go?"

"No, you guys go on, I have to visit the restroom."

"You want me to wait and walk out with you?"

"No, go ahead, I'm parked in front." Cathy kissed both her friends on the cheek. "Thanks, guys. You helped take my mind off things." Cathy watched her two friends saunter out to start the rest of their evenings and wondered what she would do. Part of her wanted to go home and curl up in bed and cry, but the other part of her wanted to stay here and find people she didn't know and have small meaningless conversations with guys who were flirting with her. That always made her feel better. She gathered her purse and headed back to the ladies room, which was behind the bar in the back of the restaurant. The bar was somewhat crowded, the after work crowd starting to linger into the weeknight singles crowd. As she stepped to the back end of the bar, her heart stopped. Julian was sitting there, alone. His shoulders were hunched downward, a tumbler enveloped between the palms of his hands. His tie was loosened, and his credit card sat on the bar in front of him. She stood staring at him. *What the hell was he doing?* She had a sudden impulse to run away — just turn and run away and not look back. She thought about calling the police, but she knew that would destroy his life. Having that power terrified her. But what about innocent lives that he might endanger? Where would this end? Part of her wanted to go back to hiding again. She had a budding career, a nice apartment, and nice friends...a nice life. She had a sudden paralyzing fear that getting involved in this mess could destroy her nice life. But instead of listening to this voice of reason, she went over to him and touched his shoulder. He looked up slowly, then broke into a wide grin.

"Hey, Cathy!" He reached up and touched her cheek.

"Julian, what the fuck are you doing here?"

He snickered sarcastically. "I could say the same about you. Whadda ya doin'? Looking for your next lay?"

"I was here with my friends..." she began before she realized the insanity of even answering his question, explaining her presence. She hoisted herself onto the stool next to him. "Why are you doing this? You promised me. You swore."

Julian looked perplexed as he surveyed his surroundings before he turned to look directly at Cathy. "I don't know," he sighed, rubbing his hand over his forehead. "I was here for lunch, and I felt like having a drink."

"You've been here since lunchtime?"

"Yeah. Like you care anyway. You told me to piss off, basically, remember?"

"That doesn't mean I don't care about you."

"Yeah, yeah, everybody cares about me; everybody has to save Julian because he's such a prollem."

"I can't believe you would do this a few hours after you promised me you wouldn't."

"I was going to call a cab."

Cathy summoned the bartender to square away the bill and then guided Julian up from the stool by his elbow, surprised at how heavy he was as he leaned against her.

"I'm taking you home," she declared.

CHAPTER 11

It was after seven by the time Maggie finished putting away dishes that could have waited until morning. She usually left at six or seven, but tonight she was purposely stalling, sensing from Darren's brooding that Julian should have been home for dinner. It made her feel good to help Darren in times of difficulty. Her husband had died of lung cancer when Maggie was in her early thirties. She'd never even dated since his death, let alone married again. She worked in a number of jobs—waitress, salesperson in a clothing store, until a friend who worked as a nanny in the wealthy part of town told her of a widower who was looking for someone to manage his household and help with his young son. Maggie arrived for her interview the next day, making a cup of tea for Darren as he spoke to her. She loved her job, it was pretty much all she had. She rented a small garden apartment across town, but spent the bulk of her time at the McPhee house. She'd even, in a small part of her mind, come to think of it as her home. She'd helped redecorate it a few years back, and Darren had deferred to her opinion on several colors and fabrics. She also felt a maternal inclination toward Julian. He'd been around ten or eleven when his mother died, so Maggie did not feel that she could take credit for "raising" him, but she knew that she'd seen him through his difficult adolescent and teenage years. She was the one who had taken him shopping for new clothes whenever he had a growth spurt. She would check the length of his pants and press her thumb into the front of a new shoe to see if his toes had enough room. She'd also nursed him through a bout with pneumonia in seventh grade that had kept him home and in bed for two weeks. She'd taken his temperature, doled out medication, and helped him keep up with his schoolwork so he wouldn't fall behind. She'd administered home herbal remedies for a sudden bout with acne when he as a freshman, and provided emotional support when he was cut from the football team.

As he grew, however, his problems became more serious. He was sixteen the first time he came home drunk. She'd had to clean up after he'd vomited and urinated in his bed, but both she and Darren dismissed the incident as that of a teenage boy's experimentation. Maggie was the one, however, who'd bailed him out two years later when he got his first DWI just after his eighteenth birthday. Darren had been out of town, so Maggie had taken the money from her own account, and Julian had paid her back without Darren knowing about it until after he'd spoken to his detective friend, Steve Curtis. Darren had felt betrayed by Maggie at first, but softened when he saw that she was trying to protect him in the same way Julian's mother would have. They had managed to get that case dismissed, and a second one reduced, and Maggie wondered now if that had been the right thing to do. As the evening grew later, Maggie was becoming just as nervous as a mother as she sprayed the marble counter with Fantastic and wiped it down for the third time. Maybe he had some errands to run after work, but what? She did most of that stuff for him. Maybe he was with friends, but if that was the case he was probably drinking.

"Maggie?" Darren's voice came from the sunroom, off the kitchen. She put the towel and Fantastic away and stepped into where Darren was sitting.

"I think the kitchen is clean enough, don't you?" He was sitting in his wicker rocking chair alongside a large potted tree that hung over him like a canopy. He was looking straight ahead, rocking slightly, an unread newspaper folded on the small table alongside him. Maggie stood defiantly in the doorway and put her hands on her hips.

"Whadda ya think you know about clean, mister? When did you ever clean in your life?"

The corner of Darren's mouth tugged a bit, as if he were trying not to smile. Maggie walked in and sat in the chair beside him, looking, as he was, out at the yard.

"He'll be home in a bit, I feel it." She tentatively patted his hand, which was gripping the arm of the chair.

58

"I'm not so sure," Darren sighed. He regretted that he didn't force Julian to stay in rehab two years ago. He'd felt so guilty when Julian had called to tell him how horrible the place was and how he wanted to come home and really apply himself. He'd been okay for a while…

"Maggie?" Darren's voice was soft. "What if he doesn't come home? He's supposed to be in court tomorrow."

Maggie rocked back and forth, keeping time with Darren even though her chair was not a rocker. "It's not that late. He'll get home…" she put her hand on Darren's again and this time left it there. "Maybe we should call Steve Curtis?"

"I don't want to bother him, Maggie. He was just here after the accident. I'd feel stupid calling him again. I can't tell him Julian's gone. Besides, I don't want to bother him; his wife just had a baby."

Steve Curtis had known the McPhees for many years. Darren was well aware that Steve had never had much respect for Julian, but he knew the young man would help in any way he could. Steve's father had worked with Darren, holding a prestigious position at Comptech for several years. Then he left Steve and his mother for Darren's twenty-three-year-old receptionist, moved with her to California, married her and had three little kids. Steve never heard from his father again, nor did Darren.

Although Steve had known Darren McPhee through his father, they didn't really become friends until the year before Steve had been promoted to detective, the youngest in the department. He had been doing some security work on his off days, and was hired to do a security evaluation of the executive offices at Comptech, where a recently burglary attempt had made Darren nervous. Steve made his recommendations, talked with Darren about the computer industry, major league baseball, college prospects for Julian, Curtis' recent engagement, and his hopes for his future in law enforcement. Darren saw in Steve a maturity, a sense of purpose he wished for in Julian, and Steve enjoyed having an older male to talk to. They had lunch one day, and Darren talked about Steve's father, expressing his disappointment in his friend for abandoning his family. The two had become close enough that Darren had come to rely on him for assistance with Julian's various troubles over the years. The accident had been no exception and Darren knew Steve would be in court tomorrow if he could.

"Maybe I should go look for him," Darren said to Maggie.

"He's a man now, Darren." Maggie's fear was turning to anger at Julian for causing his father to look so defeated.

"I realize that…" his shoulders seemed to shrink from their usual height.

"Well, I'm thinkin' it's time *he* realized it."

"Did I baby him too much? Is that what I did?" Darren's voice cracked, and he stopped staring at the yard and looked at Maggie, who leaned toward him.

"You did nothing wrong! He's sick. Drinkin's a disease, no different from the cancer that killed my Joseph. Julian can't stop it until he's ready. Maybe he won't be ready until he's lost everything. My father was a drinker, Darren. I never tole ya that, but I'm tellin' ya now so ya know I know what I'm sayin'. My father'd come home and holler and slap us all an' fall asleep in his supper. He was a good man, sweet as a lamb when he was sober. He had a good life, till the drink just took him over, like the devil, he lost everything he had…"

"This is not making me feel any better…"

"Lemme ask ya, then. If Julian tole ya he had cancer, like my Joseph," she crossed herself, "wouldya be sittin' here blamin' yourself?"

"I suppose not…" Darren took his hand from the arm of the chair and grasped Maggie's hand. "I just want it to stop."

The sound of a car in the driveway made them both stand up.

CHAPTER 12

Just after dawn the next morning, Face was downing his army of large pills. He chased them with water from a gallon jug while he waited for his coffee to finish brewing. The girls were circling his feet, mewing for their breakfast. After he set down their food he went out to grab his newspaper from the front stoop. He needed his coffee in order to sit and read his paper, so he pulled the pot out from under the stream of hot liquid and placed his mug there until it was full. He started to read the paper, but this morning his mind was elsewhere. First, there were his T-cells. Face had read books and pamphlets about AIDS until he could not stand to read another sentence. His T-cell count was low, the doctor had told him, but he felt okay, just a little tired. He had been toying with the idea of telling Mrs. Murphy about his condition, just in case there was an emergency and he needed her to feed the girls. Donna was hissing at the other two, who had dared to approach the bowl before she had finished. Face wondered what would become of them when the inevitable happened. He knew it was a stupid thing to worry about, especially when at the clinic he saw people who were much younger and appeared much sicker than he was. There were women who came with young children, and all he had to be worried about were his cats. There were days when he thought of tossing his meds into the trash and letting the chips fall where they may, and other days when he thought he should swallow the contents of one of the bottles and be done with the whole thing. But thoughts of his girls always stopped him.

His other distraction this morning was the court appearance of the man who had killed Veronica Lawson. He was going to be there, for Jimmy. He'd made up his mind that he would *talk* to Jimmy that day. He figured he owed the man a show of support for his prior betrayal. There was a code in the old neighborhood—you took care of each other. Of course, stealing from Jimmy violated that code, but Face rationalized that as behavior controlled by drugs, not by his own personality. Not that this was meant to excuse his actions; he had totally gone against everything that had once been important to him, but drugs had that power. Now that he was clean, sober, and terminally ill, he was determined to make amends to the friend who had once been like a brother to him.

As was his routine, he sat in the park watching the joggers and walkers—especially the female ones—and feeding the ducks for a while. Today, however, he was dressed in the only suit he owned. It was a bit old, and he'd had to wipe some dust off it when he fished it from the back of his closet, but he had not wanted to look out of place in the courtroom. He'd surveyed his appearance in the mirror before leaving his apartment; he looked good, despite his T-cells. No, he wasn't the handsome youth who had once had to fight the girls off, but he wasn't bad, well, not *too* bad. He did have to pin the suit in several places where it had gotten baggy and he hoped he'd be able to sit in court without being stabbed by his own clothes.

The courtroom was fairly full, but not too crowded. He noticed that there were a few representatives from the press; mainly the local papers. He sat toward the back of the room on a hard wooden bench that reminded him of church. He could see the back of Jimmy's head in the front of the room. A young woman in a very short light blue suit was standing in front of him, talking. Face noticed how the jacket of her suit flowed smoothly over her thin but somehow round hips. He liked her knees, too, they were cute little ovals, not thick or square like some women. Then he saw the scumbag kid and his scumbag father. They had the same almost black hair and were both tall with very straight posture, which was probably helped by the expensive suits they were wearing. They didn't talk to each other; the kid was sitting at a table in front with his lawyer and the father was in the front row next to a lady with red hair, who Face figured was the mother of scum. A very blond young man with a crew cut came to join them. Face saw that he was carrying a gun as the man pushed aside his jacket to put his hand in his pocket, and figured that the kid's family must be in good with the cops. Face noticed the father leaning forward and glancing at Jimmy furtively. He felt like punching him and telling him he did not deserve to even look at a decent man like Jimmy Lawson because he had raised a scumbag killer as a son. Although it occurred to Face that only luck, the suspension of his license, and the repossession of his car had kept him from being in the seat where Julian McPhee was now sitting, he shook off those thoughts before they were fully formed.

The anger he felt seemed to temporarily revive Face. His pale, sallow skin had reddened with the fury he felt, and his adrenaline pumped ferociously. He felt young and ready to fight; he could almost feel his blood rejuvenating itself. This bastard was going to fry, and Face felt invigorated. He practiced in his mind what he would say to Jimmy after the hearing. He'd been rehearsing it for days. He would approach Jimmy, shake his hand, and express his sympathy. Jimmy, in Face's fantasy, would then grab him in an embrace of friendship and tell him how happy he was to see him. Face would apologize about the stealing, and tell Jimmy that he'd been clean for over three years. He would explain that he never would have betrayed him had it not been for the drugs, and Jimmy would apologize for breaking his nose. Then they would go for coffee and talk about all the old times and everyone they knew. Face would listen patiently as Jimmy described his loneliness and grief over Veronica and how he really needed a friend now.

Face stood with the rest of the room as the judge entered. She was a woman in her forties with short, cropped hair and square silver earrings. She was attractive, but in a domineering, scary, almost man-like way. The young blue suit stood first and spoke about Veronica Lawson. Face caught pieces of her sentences in his mind: "brutally run down and disregarded like a piece of trash in the street." Face was mesmerized by her long flowing hair that undulated against her shoulders as she spoke, and the thin, long-fingered hands that swayed to the words that flew from her coral-painted mouth "innocent victim...loving wife and friend...life cut short...callous disregard for human life...previous DWI arrest...reckless driving conviction...left the woman bleeding in the street...using his car as a murder weapon." An invisible crane on the back of Face's neck was pulling him up taller with each word. His excitement level was nearly equal to that of being at Yankee stadium when they won the World Series in 1996...okay, he was in the left field bleachers and could barely see but his blood was pumping then, before he knew about his illness, before his life had become what it now was. He watched the young scum's hands as they were in constant motion, twisting, rubbing, and lightly tapping. Face could tell he was shitting his pants and he was glad.

Jimmy sat looking straight ahead, trying to avoid looking at Julian McPhee, but his profile was still in Jimmy's range of view. The kid was pale, and seemed unable to sit still. Jimmy tried to listen to the voice of Marilyn Jones...but he'd heard it all before. Veronica was a piece of trash in the street, a dead leaf...these thoughts made Jimmy recall a poem by William Carlos Williams that he'd taught in American Poetry last semester. In the poem, a young woman is compared to a dead leaf in the road and a car runs over it. The students had been bored, but he loved the poem. He thought about the plans he and Veronica had made for the rest of the year. Christmas in a small cabin in Maine, just the two of them in front of a large blazing fire, a possible cruise to Hawaii in May, at the end of the spring term...and next year, a baby. The baby that would never be. The baby that Veronica wanted to name Lawrence, Lawrence Lawson...she'd joked. He took a tentative look at Julian McPhee's father. The man was sitting quite stoically, but the swollen puffs of skin below his eyes showed that he had not slept well in some time. Part of Jimmy felt pity; the other part felt hatred. He hadn't been sleeping well, either, through no fault of his own. That man had raised a son who'd shown "callous disregard" for his wife's life. As for the son himself, Jimmy could feel only rage, that old rage that he hadn't felt in years; the rage that Veronica had quelled. He'd had so many fights in his youth when he hadn't thought twice about pummeling someone who deserved it. Sometimes it had even felt good to slam his fist into soft flesh that would break and bleed. Fighting had always made him feel better, a catharsis. Although he once felt good about the time he broke Face's nose, he regretted it now, because Veronica had been furious about it.

64

She'd noticed his bruised knuckle and immediately figured out what had happened.

"What did you do to him?" She'd demanded, tossing his hand down after she'd held it up to inspect the damage.

"He got what he deserved."

"For God's sake Jimmy, what are you, some kind of thug?" Her voice had been pitched with anger as she followed him into the kitchen where he was retrieving ice for his hand.

"You don't understand this sort of thing." He said, calmly placing some ice cubes in a small Ziploc bag and placing it gently over his knuckles.

"What sort of *thing?* A *male* thing?" she said the word, *male,* with mocking in her voice.

"No, it's not a *male* thing," he mimicked. "It's just the way we grew up—you don't betray a friend like that. We were like brothers; he was from my neighborhood. That ring meant so much to you, and he didn't give a shit. We're supposed to *watch* each other's backs, not *stab* each other in the back."

"Well, excuse me for not understanding this bullshit code," she was walking around the room, rubbing her hands over her thighs. "I grew up in *civilization*, where we have *compassion* for those who are in trouble, and desperate, and we learn that violence is not a solution...he has a problem, Jimmy."

"Don't give me your psychobabble crap! This was something I had to do, now it's over, so just forget it."

"Jimmy, I hate violence, you know that. You need to promise me that all this stuff is behind you," she sat next to him on the couch, and gently touched his injured hand. "I want to have a baby with you someday...maybe two or three babies. I don't want my children being the bullies in the playground. I want to teach them to use their minds, not their fists...please tell me that's what you want, too."

Jimmy had paused before he answered. He knew he could be violent, yet his years of education had deflated its place in his life. Hitting Face was the first fight he'd had in years, and it had felt good, but he wanted Veronica's love and respect more. So he told her. He promised. That promise was what kept him from jumping out of his chair and pounding his fist into Julian McPhee's face as he listened to the defense attorney use phrases like "reasonable doubt...no witnesses...lack of evidence...car was stolen...defendant was not found at scene...irresponsible, not criminal behavior...no proof...his DWI had been dropped and could not be used against him...move to dismiss the charges, they would not hold up in a trial..."

The judge listened to both sides with folded hands and an intense stare. She asked a few questions of the lawyers and then called a recess for thirty minutes.

Jimmy sat outside on the steps of the courthouse, looking at Marilyn Jones, who stood on a step in front of him. Face watched them talking as he lit a cigarette. He couldn't hear what Jimmy was saying, but he could hear Marilyn Jones as she expressed her concern that the judge might dismiss the charges. Face watched as Jimmy put his face in his hands.

CHAPTER 13

Julian sat alone on a hard, shiny bench outside the courtroom. He was afraid to go outside because he'd seen James Lawson and the District Attorney head that way. He didn't want to stay in the courtroom, either, afraid to face his father after the fight they'd had last night. He wished Cathy had come inside the house with him, but she'd said no when he asked her to last night. She said she'd meant what she said about their relationship being over, she was just driving him home as a favor, and she no longer wanted to be involved in his life. She'd waited in her car until he was in the house, then left. Things did not go well from there. His father and Maggie both confronted him at the door. He was used to his father's varied reactions, but Maggie's face distressed him, and he and his father had said some terrible things to each other.

"I love you, Julian; I just want you to get well. You need help…"

"That is such bullshit!" Julian had spat, walking past both of them. "You don't love *me;* you love what you *think* I should be. Mr. perfect, computer whiz's son."

"That's not fair!" Darren yelled, following Julian into the very clean kitchen. Maggie was tentative, but followed a few paces behind. "I have always done everything I could for you."

"Oh yeah, you set me up good, Dad. You set me up in a job for which I am totally unqualified, where I am ridiculed by my co-workers on a daily basis."

"I just wanted you to be successful," Darren sat at the kitchen table while Maggie hovered in the doorway and Julian leaned against the counter.

"Yeah, and you knew I was such a screw up that I would never be able to do anything on my own, right? I could never be brilliant like friggin' Jeffrey Madison or driven like five-o Curtis."

"I didn't know that's how you felt…"

"Because you never bothered to ask me how I felt. You never have, not when Mom died, either…we never talked about that, did we Dad?" Julian took off his jacket and loosened his tie, as if it was choking him. Darren was stunned by the question at hand. Maggie took a few steps forward.

"Julian," she whispered. "You father loves you."

"What the hell do you know about it? You never even had kids; you just had me as a substitute."

Darren stood and grabbed Julian's arm. "Don't you ever talk to her that way!" he said through closed teeth. "This woman has been nothing but good to you *and me*, and don't you fucking forget it!"

Maggie's mouth fell open, as she'd never heard Darren speak in that tone, let alone use profanity. She was on the verge of crying, Julian's remarks had stung her, but she didn't want either of them to see that, so she turned around to leave. Darren called after her, but she wanted to be out of that house, away from the yelling that churned up memories of her own father.

Julian's anger could not be contained. "You want me to go to prison, don't you Dad? Then I'll be out of your hair for a good seven years or so. You won't have to worry about me drinking anymore, I won't have time, I'll be too busy getting fucked in the ass. But you won't have to worry, Dad. You can move Jeffrey right in to my room."

Darren grabbed both of Julian's arms, "I don't want you to go to prison…I want you to be well. You're going to die if you don't do something Julian. I don't want you to die…"

Julian had watched his father sobbing in front of him, but at the time the alcohol had numbed his sense of compassion. He'd pushed away from Darren and gone to bed.

This morning, however, along with a dry mouth and pounding head, came remorse. He could not face either of them so he'd left early, leaving a note and taken a cab alone to the courthouse. He wouldn't have blamed his father if he'd not come to the hearing, but deep down he knew Darren would be there. Maggie, however, surprised him. He'd been a total bastard to her and yet she came. He knew he'd miss both of them if he ended up going to prison. He thought briefly about the things that he'd have to do before his trial ended just in case he was found guilty. He'd already decided that he would tell Darren and Maggie not to visit him, he would never be able to face them through glass. He figured Cathy would not even consider visiting. But there was hope—a real hope for a dismissal, or so his lawyer said. What then? How did you go about starting life over at twenty-three?

Maggie and Darren sat inside the courtroom, quiet with concern. Each of them kept replaying last night's scene in their mind. Maggie had come in around eight in the morning as she usually did, as if it was any other day, as if Julian had not been so hurtful to her. Darren came downstairs to find her making coffee in the kitchen.

"Prince Charming left early," he said, opening the cupboard for a cup.

"It was the drink talkin'...ya know that," she sat down across from Darren and stirred some sugar into her coffee.

"You've been like a mother to him for more than ten years; there's no excuse..."

"Well, you've been his father all his life, and that didn't stop him from cuttin' you up, now did it? Anyway, if his mother was here, she'd a been the one gettin' the tongue lashin'...a drunk's gonna lash out at whoever's in the room."

"Maggie, you never cease to amaze me," Darren took a gulp of coffee.

"I suppose your goin' to court?" Darren nodded in response. "I'd...like to go with ya, if ya don't mind." Darren stared at her for a few moments, her face was soft.

"That would be great," he smiled.

Cathy Colfax was in her office when she heard the news about Julian's hearing. People around the office were buzzing like crazy, so she stuck her head out of her door

"What's going on?" She asked lightly. The office grew suddenly quiet at her question, as they all knew her history with the defendant.

"The case has been dismissed, the judge said there was not enough evidence to prove that he was driving, and there were no witnesses." Suzanne said without emotion, not knowing what Cathy was hoping for. Others were not so discreet:

"What a lucky son-of-a-bitch!"

"If you're rich, you can get away with anything."

"I can't believe he got out of this one."

These and other comments were being tossed around as Cathy closed her door and sunk into her chair. She was relieved for Julian, but the phone call still haunted her. She felt the sensation of being jarred from sleep by a screaming telephone all over again.

"Cathy? It's me, Julian"

"What time is it?"

"I dunno, late..."

"Where are you?"

"I...I dunno, Cathy. I...I'm scared...help me...I think...It's bad..."

"What?" She sat up in bed, her heart pounding. *"What happened?"*

"She's bleeding, Cathy, she's bleeding..."

"Who?"

"I dunno, I ran away. I just ran away...she's hurt...I didn't mean it..."

"Julian where are you? I'm coming to get you..."

"I'm so messed up...I saw her face...so much blood...I saw her face, she looked right at me."

"Please deposit fifty—five cents," the nasal operator's voice broke in.

"Okay, I got money," she could hear the phone banging against the phone booth as he searched his pockets. *"Julian,"* she yelled, *"give me the number, I'll call you back—"*

But the line had disconnected. She sat by the phone the rest of the night, waiting for him to call back, but he never did. She called his cell fourteen times, but it wasn't on.

Now Cathy sat at her desk, looking out her window wondering if she had done the right thing. No witnesses. She'd saved Julian from prison, but she wondered at what cost.

When the judge announced her decision, Julian stood and embraced his father without considering their previous argument. Face ran into the men's room where he kicked one of the stall doors so hard that it almost came off its hinge. Jimmy just walked out of the building without saying a word. Face sat on the toilet, breathing through his nose until he calmed down. He checked the mirror before he walked back out into the hallway, but Jimmy was already gone.

Chapter 14

That afternoon Julian sat in the sunroom of the McPhee home with Maggie and Darren. He rocked nervously in the rocking chair while Maggie sat where she had the previous evening and Darren sat on the small wicker stool where he usually rested his feet.

"I just wanted to thank you both for your support, and tell you how sorry I am for everything…especially last night. I didn't mean it."

Maggie reached over and patted his knee. "I know ya didn't." She stood up and went to the kitchen in response to the call of the kettle.

"I wouldn't have blamed you if you didn't show up in court today."

Darren opened his mouth as if to speak, but the only thing that came out was a small sigh.

"Dad, I know I screwed up, but it's over now. I know I have to stop doing this."

Darren straightened his legs across the floor. "Excuse my skepticism, but I've heard it before."

"I know you have, Dad, and I don't expect you to believe me until I prove myself. I'm just telling you…and this time I really mean it. This whole experience has been a nightmare. The thought of going to prison scared the shit out of me." Julian bent his head and rocked the chair harder. Maggie returned to the room with three cups of her herbal tea on a bamboo tray. She balanced skillfully as she took one off and handed it to Julian, then one to Darren.

"I hope you know I never wanted that, Julian."

"I know. I really didn't mean what I said...not about that anyway."

Darren's brow furrowed. "But you did mean some of it?"

"No. Not the way I said it. But the stuff about my job...you know it's true."

"No."

"Yes, you know it, Dad. You're kidding yourself if you think I am cut out—"

"I think if you really applied yourself—"

"No, Dad," Julian put his tea on the table and leaned toward his father, touching Darren's hands, which were laced together across his knees. "Your work is *your* work. It's not me, I suck at it and I hate it. I'm sorry if that hurts you, but I'm quitting Comptech. I need to do something on my own, something I can feel good about." Julian sat back, deflated but relieved.

"What are you going to do?"

"I'm not sure yet. I have to think about it. I just hope you understand."

Maggie sipped her tea, her eyes flitting between father and son.

Darren stood and looked at both of them, then held out his hand to Julian. "I hope you can do it, son." The two men shook hands, and Darren walked into the kitchen and put his cup in the sink, then headed upstairs.

Maggie leaned over to Julian and spoke in a hushed voice, "he'll come 'round, hon. Now drink your tea."

"Maggie, you know I hate this stuff."

"Oh, shut it. Ya know it calms ya." She swatted the side of his head.

She picked up her cup and carried it into the kitchen. Julian followed her and touched her elbow as she turned the faucet on.

"I hope you know how much I love you." She turned around and placed her palms on each side of his head, then kissed both his cheeks. He encircled her in his arms and hugged her tightly.

"I know," she said, "I know."

CHAPTER 15

By the end of September Jimmy Lawson had returned to his role of Professor of American Literature, but with less than his usual spark. Although he knew Veronica's death would change his life, he had not realized how the little every day things would be impacted. He had started making only half a pot of coffee in the morning, and it had taken time to adjust the measurement of coffee to scoop into the filter. He no longer bought eggs at the store, because he didn't like them. Veronica had been fond of egg salad, so eggs had been a regular item on the shopping list. On his first post-accident trip to the market he'd had eggs in the cart, but when he reached in to place them on the conveyer belt in front of the cashier, the thought struck him: why? He no longer ate pizza on Thursdays, as one pie was too much for one, and the dishwasher often sat idle for days at a time because it was never full.

Although his work provided a worthwhile distraction, the comments he scribbled in red pen in the margins of student papers had taken on an *edge*. He sometimes had to read the same paper three times before he was actually able to focus. He didn't notice this himself, but the discussions in his classes were less passionate this year. He fulfilled his duty as a professor—he questioned, agreed, disagreed, gave new information, analyzed, but gone were the times when his voice would go up a bit in response to a comment he disagreed with. Also gone was the way his heart once quickened when a student came up with an insightful comment, and gone was the smile that would crawl across his face when he read a truly excellent student paper.

In contrast to previous years, he now preferred to work in his school office, rather than at home. His school office now had a rumpled look, kind of like a couch that has been slept on. Books and papers were stacked in corners of the desk, hiding coffee-mug rings, and fast food wrappers often filled the garbage can. His computer was speckled with tiny post it notes which formed a frame around the moving star screen saver at which he often sat staring. In contrast, his home computer sat idle, a thin film of dust across the screen, a few cobwebs beginning in the corner of his bookshelf.

He finished a paper written by a student named Patricia Callahan, and wrote in some detail the justification for the grade—a B. She certainly had potential as a writer; her paper was well organized and well supported. He simply thought there were a few places where her focus veered away from her point, and she needed a bit more close analysis of the literature. He knew the grade would disgust her, as she was what a teacher might label a "shark" when it came to her GPA. An appearance of Ms. Callahan at his next open office hours on Wednesday would be unavoidable, but maybe deep inside him, that was what he wanted. Conversation.

He put away his papers, even though it was still early. The head of the Literature department, Lou Zaits, had asked Jimmy to make an appearance at a student poetry reading, which was taking place in the open courtyard behind the freshmen dorms. Lou often attended such functions himself, but this conflicted with his daughter's sixteenth birthday so he'd asked if Jimmy would mind stopping by for a bit, just to have a faculty member there. Jimmy, having nothing else to do, agreed. He didn't bother to pack his leather book bag these days, because he spent sufficient hours at school to complete all of his paperwork in the office. He considered this quite an accomplishment, not ready to acknowledge that he was just avoiding being alone in his own home.

The evening was warm, and the sun was still fairly bright when he arrived at the courtyard. There were groups of students seated around the few rows of folding chairs that were arranged in a horseshoe shape around a center podium. Seated in the chairs were mainly those who would be reading their poems, while the spectators sprawled on blankets on the outskirts of the folding chairs. Some were eating sandwiches and drinking wine, some smoking quietly under trees. Jimmy stood against a large tree, next to where two girls were sitting, eating peanuts and drinking out of small plastic cups. A skinny young man with a large Adam's apple was reading a rather bawdy limerick, which made Jimmy smile without meaning to. Veronica would have liked it—she would have laughed. As he watched the young man enjoying his moment in the spotlight he thought of Julian McPhee. He had not thought much about him since his acquittal, in fact, this was the first time he had ever thought of him by using his name. The name sounded foreign, like Jimmy had not heard it before—usually any image or thought of McPhee was acknowledged with names like murderer, monster, bastard, or the all encompassing—*him*. The full name as part of his thought process startled Jimmy, and he wondered briefly if there was any deep psychological significance that he should attach to it.

It wasn't that the boy at the podium even remotely resembled McPhee—this boy was awkward and gangly where McPhee appeared strong and confident. It was the sense of pleasure that exuded from the boy—the way he seemed in love with his own creation, that troubled Jimmy. He knew the pleasure of pride in his own work, but was reviled that Julian McPhee was now free to experience such pleasure. He might be home now, strumming a guitar, or designing a computer game or drawing a landscape—he could be just home, just doing these things. Things that Veronica could not do, and Jimmy could no longer enjoy. He shifted his thoughts from McPhee and tried to focus on the happy spirits around him as the boy finished his second dirty but humorous creation and sat down.

"Professor Lawson?"

Jimmy looked to his left, to find one of the girls who'd been on the blanket near him. She was a senior, a bright girl, but he could not recall her name.

"Hi. How are you?" He said, straining to find the name.

"Do you remember me? Ginny Fraez, junior seminar last fall?"

"Of course, Ginny," he shifted his feet with relief.

"Listen...I just wanted to tell you...I heard about, your wife. I'm very sorry."

"Thank you," was all he ever said to such remarks. Although she was not the first student to express her condolences, he felt that she was honestly sincere. "Are you reading something?" he asked in order to make it clear that the subject of his wife's death was not open for further discussion.

"No, my friend is, she's next...so I'm gonna go back and sit down."

"Good to see you, Ginny." She turned and waved a bit, then joined her friend on the blanket a few feet away. They both clapped loudly and yelled when a girl named Melinda was introduced.

Jimmy was surprised that Melinda seemed quite different from Ginny. Now that he recalled her name he remembered that Ginny had always seemed like a very preppy, serious type. Melinda was the opposite. She was wearing a yellow poncho and bell-bottom jeans— a flower child of the new millennium. Her hair was dark, wavy and very long and it swayed as she spoke.

"Hi, I'm Melinda," she said quietly. "I just want to explain a bit about the poem that I'm going to share with you. I used to be a heroin addict." A sudden hush grew over the crowd. "No, it's okay, I've been clean for nine months, three weeks, and four days." Clapping and cheers burst through the silence. "I found it really hard in the beginning, I missed being high...so I started writing about the feeling...kind of a poetic high, I guess...well, anyhow, here I go..."

Jimmy stepped forward, intrigued. He'd never heard someone spill their guts in front of a crowd and sound as if they were talking about the weather. Melinda's face lit up as she read her poem, her hair and poncho swirling around her in opposite directions. She seemed to dance as she read, her voice spilling out without hesitation.

"...I am flying, a bird, a flowered bird...so pretty,
everything pretty, everything flying, clouds are my pillows
as I nap in the flowered sky..."

Jimmy did not admire her literary skills but he did admire her courage, honesty and the way her face seemed to shine as she read. She sounded like heroin was something she really missed. Jimmy thought of his old friend, Face, and the way he had looked that day when Veronica had brought him to their house. He had not looked at all like someone who was enjoying being high.

When Melinda was done, she stood still as the crowd leapt to its feet and celebrated her victory. Jimmy found himself clapping with enthusiasm without planning to. When the clapping began to subside, Melinda bounded back to the blanket where Ginny and the other girls sat, and they embraced her simultaneously. Three mediocre poets later the reading was concluded and Jimmy walked across the courtyard to the faculty parking lot. But before he reached his car something seized him—it was early, a little after seven o'clock. His days lately were spent in his office until at least 10:30 or so. Now he faced what he had grown to fear most—an evening in his house—an evening alone. He stood by his car for a few moments. He did not even have any work with him, and in actuality, he had nothing left to do. He left his car and started walking toward the area of town that was designated "off campus" despite the fact that almost everyone who lived there was affiliated with the school. The "off campus" area consisted of several garden apartment complexes, several older homes that served as boarding houses, a few small restaurants and taverns, a large bookstore and a coffee house. Jimmy walked through the small town, his hands in his pockets, looking around at the people coming and going. He thought about the girl, Melinda, and what she'd said about how writing poetry had helped her overcome her addiction. Maybe he should start writing again. He had written a few short stories in college, but that was it.

He milled around in the bookstore for a while, scanning the course book lists for other professors, just to see what his colleagues were teaching, then he roamed around the fiction department, looking for recent collections of short stories. He found a few, along with a volume of American Poetry and sat on one of the leather chairs to skim them. He thumbed through the poetry, stopping to read the Williams poem that he could recite by heart. "…shy, uncorseted, tucking in stray ends of hair…" he smiled and ran his hand over the page, stopping at the last stanza: "…the noiseless wheels of my car rush with a cracking sound over dried leaves…" He shut the book and put it back on the shelf. He stopped as he passed the section of medical books and looked up every symptom he'd had in the last few months: headaches, insomnia, loss of appetite, lethargy. Then he looked at a book about addictions. He wondered what Face Jenkins would think of Melinda's poem. He wondered how far Face had actually fallen before he had gotten clean—if he *was* clean. Jimmy didn't know for sure. He glanced at a few books on grief and dealing with death, but he didn't go further than the table of contents.

After checking out the bookstore for over an hour, Jimmy entered the coffee shop. He spotted Ginny Fraez as she was getting up from her table, and he was relieved that she did not see him. Part of him just wanted to wander around as he had been—like he was invisible. When Ginny and her friend left, he saw that the poet Melinda was alone in the booth, sipping the froth off a cappuccino. He ordered a regular coffee, and before he realized it, he approached her.

"I enjoyed your poem," he said to her. She lifted her eyes, a film of froth still hanging on her upper lip.

"Thanks," she said, as she wiped the froth with her index finger. "Have a seat..." she pointed to the empty bench opposite her, as if he had not noticed it. "Are you a poet?"

"No," he laughed, "a professor."

"Oh, really? Here?" She furrowed her brow and pulled a cinnamon stick out of her cup.

"Yes," Jimmy put his cup down and extended his hand. "James Lawson."

"James Lawson...Professor Lawson, English department?"

"That's me."

"Oh," she sucked thoughtfully on the cinnamon stick, then as if a voice from beyond had told her to mind her manners, she shook his hand, "Melinda Devereaux. So, you're the famous Professor Lawson."

"No, I'm just the regular one, the famous one must be someone else."

"Oh, no you're the one. I have a few friends who've had you. You're quite a monster with your red pen, I hear."

"A monster?" Jimmy was genuinely surprised. He knew he had a reputation for being demanding, a tough grader, but monster was something he had not heard before. He felt defensive. "I am demanding, but not a monster."

"That's not what I hear from my friends."

"Well, don't believe it. I just have high expectations."

"Mmm," she sipped her coffee again, seeming not to really drink, but just dip her upper lip into the foamy top. "So, you liked my poem, really?"

Jimmy felt a sudden pang of guilt. The poem itself, was awful, it was the exuberant energy surrounding it that intrigued him. "I thought it was very...honest."

"What does that mean?"

Jimmy was startled by the question. *Honest* was a simple word, wasn't it? He groped his brain for how to answer. "You sounded... really happy."

"What about honest?" She'd taken to stirring her froth with the cinnamon stick.

"I mean you were honest about being happy...on heroin." Jimmy took a sip of his coffee. It was very hot, and he felt its heat travel down his throat. Melinda looked at the table for a moment, seeming embarrassed. "I'm sorry," Jimmy said, "if I embarrassed you."

"No, I'm not. I really was happy on heroin."

"Then how did you get clean?"

"Well, it's not the happy part of heroin that made me get clean, it was what happens after the happy is over that really scared me. It's like you are just in the greatest moment, the greatest feeling, then bam! You go from floating to slamming headfirst into concrete." She had punctuated her statement by slapping her palm against the table, causing the spoons to jump and a bit of coffee from each of their cups to spill over onto the table. She didn't stop talking as she wrapped a few napkins around the bottom of her cup, sopping up the spill. "That's the part that made me get clean...you can only slam into concrete so many times before you become road kill. I didn't want to be road kill."

"So why not write about the bad part, isn't that what you need to do to stay clean? Remember the bad?"

"Not me," this time she actually swallowed a mouthful of her coffee. "I like to relive the happy moments, because that's what I miss the most. I don't miss waking up and feeling like my head is in a vice and my arm is sore and stinging and I don't know where I am or what I did the night before. But I do miss the happy feeling...*the high.*"

Jimmy wrapped his hands around his mug, as if he wanted to hold his thoughts together. "Aren't you risking going back, if you keep thinking about the happy part?"

"I don't know, it's worked for me so far. I almost feel high when I write...it feels good, like heroin did. I need that feeling someplace in my life...and I can't go around having sex *all* the time."

They both laughed at her joke, but Jimmy felt that she was watching his reaction to her comment with a bit too much interest. He felt warm suddenly and tried to refocus the conversation. "I just enjoyed listening to you read. You had *joy* in your voice."

"Why don't you have joy in *your* voice, professor?" He looked at her for a long moment. Her eyebrows were arched in a genuine inquiry, and her face looked so clean, and fresh, like she had just washed it, and her hair was slipping over her shoulder a few strands at a time. She did not know his story, he realized, and a great feeling of relief washed over him. She'd heard of him, heard he was tough on students, but she knew nothing else about his life. He didn't have to explain, and that was comforting to him.

Chapter 16

The month of September found Face at a double low—his T-Cells had dropped, as had his weight. The princess had not even looked at him the last time he stepped on the scale. 155. Down eight. He now felt the sharpness of his anklebones when he crossed his feet, and his razor had difficulty traveling down the new valleys of his cheeks, and his pants sagged in the waist. Mrs. Murphy had been helpful in his campaign to eat more—clearly his emaciated form concerned her enough that she left pans of food by his door on almost a daily basis. Eggplant was his favorite, but a child-sized portion was more than enough to fill him. He even started to drink vile cans of milkshake like crap that was supposed to give extra nutrition, but he sometimes had difficulty keeping these down. Sometimes he would try to force himself to finish a can, tipping his head back, and tossing it down his throat like a shot of Jack Daniel's. This worked a few times, but on more than one occasion, half of the can ended up in the cat's dish. Donna would approach with caution, take a few sniffs and then lap the bowl clean without regard for her counterparts. Her small bumpy tongue would then stretch out to wipe any remnants from her nose and whiskers. Face thought he saw a question in her stare—like she could not understand why Face did not finish this stuff—it was so good.

As he sat one morning with his fourth cup of coffee and third cigarette—two things he always managed to have an appetite for despite a hacking wet cough that shook his frame—he watched the sky grow light with the new day and wondered how many days he had left. It was unfair to know that the time was coming, without knowing when. The slow brightness of the sky reminded him of what he considered his last night of *real* life: his senior prom. He'd sat on the beach at sunrise, interlocking fingers with those of his true love, Angela Pavone. He'd watched her freshly pedicured toes rake like a fork through the sand, the soft granules skittering off the shiny red nails and falling between the toes. It was the most beautiful thing he'd ever seen. He thought so then—and now. He'd kissed Angela that night, using his nose to gently guide her face from its downcast position and the tip of his tongue to widen the slight part in her lips. They had only kissed, even though most of his friends, Jimmy included, were screwing their prom dates at the Plumrose motel. Angela was different. Face thought her too good to be groped on a dirty mattress. He was perfectly happy to sit there for the rest of his life and watch her feet. She had written a few times after she left for a college in Connecticut the following fall, but by the time she finished her first year Face had forgotten her for a new love: cocaine.

Donna rubbed her growing belly against his ankles, purring in a demanding, "time for breakfast," tone. Susie and Jane joined in the chorus. Face pushed himself out of the chair and filled the bowl. Susie leapt into his lap when he sat down again, waiting for Donna to eat her share. Susie's marble green eyes reminded Face of her namesake, a twenty-year-old girl he'd fucked in the laundry room during one of three short stays in rehab. She was small, so he was able to sit her on top of the dryer and stand on a stool to reach her. When her back pressed into the controls and turned the dryer on, the heat and vibrations drove him wild. He signed himself out of that place the next day, and he never saw her again, he didn't even know her last name. Her memory lived only in the marble eyes that looked up at him with what Face for an instant thought was concern.

"Ah, Susie, those were the days." He breathed, scratching behind her soft ears. It occurred to him for a moment that he ought to stop taking his medication, then maybe the impotence would go away. How much time would he have to give up to fuck one more time before he died? He smiled for a moment as he ran through a list of candidates for his going away fuck, but the smiled dimmed when he realized that he would never find a woman willing to fuck a formerly handsome skeleton who might die mid-fuck. Where was Angela now? Probably married and fat with five kids. Maybe, just maybe, Princess would do it if he sincerely expressed it as his last wish, but he would not want to risk giving her the bug. So he downed his pill case full of morning medications, feeling it deflate his dick just a little more. He paused for a moment, wondering what would happen if he swallowed a whole bottle. Would it be painful? Would he thrash about in an uncontrollable seizure before the end came? Susie jumped onto the counter and rubbed against his arm. He gulped the last of his coffee, and headed to work.

CHAPTER 17

Julian had spent part of the summer in deep thought on a chair by the pool, staring at the ripples of water shooting out of the filter, occasionally grabbing the skimmer to fish out a bug or leaf, but never going in. Often in the mid afternoon he would tire of the pool, and head for the park where he spent time sitting on a bench and staring into the dirty lake. The lake where he and Cathy had once peeled off each other's clothes and splashed around without regard to the creatures sleeping beneath the mud. They'd emerged from the water, muddy and laughing as they fucked on a picnic table where unsuspecting families would eat their lunches the next day. Cathy came to his mind often. He sent her a few E-mails, but they were ignored. He'd called numerous times but never had the courage to talk to her machine. The park would also make him think of a dead woman named Veronica Lawson. A woman he'd never seen, the woman some people would always believe he'd killed. He'd received a few supportive notes from old friends, including a "hang in there" card from his college roommate, but no one from Comptech. He'd always had faith in the justice system, until now. The charges had been dismissed, yet there were still people who had convicted him in their minds. Some days it felt like people would always stop talking as he entered a room, or whispering about him as he passed. That was what he liked about his days outside by the pool and in the park. He felt invisible.

Without regard for ultra violet rays, his outdoor days had turned his skin a deep bronze color, which made his eyes leap off his face.

He'd quit his job at Comptech, despite Darren's assurance that people would forget about the incident and things would get back to normal. He did not want things to get back to normal. He'd worked for three weeks in August as a golf caddy in a nearby town, but gossip about him persisted. Many of the people he came into contact with either knew or *knew of* his father and the company. He was often bewildered at how his father was able to keep such a low profile, to be so grounded, despite his success. People did not gossip about Darren. In fact, people respected how the "poor man" had survived the tragic death of his wife and still maintained his successful company while raising his young son alone. He quickly had his fill of the country club crowd, so he began interviewing for various entry-level business jobs, but with no luck.

"Morning." Darren was tightening the sash of his bathrobe as he strode into the kitchen on a mid September morning. Julian nodded his greeting then returned to the folded newspaper in front of him. The columns were full of question marks, cross outs, and small notations such as "too far?" Darren passed behind his son to fill his cup with the fresh pot of coffee, and peered over his shoulder at the want ads.

"I'm proud of you," were difficult words for Darren, but he pushed them out anyway. He'd initially despaired at his son's poolside wallowing. He'd tried cajoling and threatening him back to work, but Maggie convinced him to let him search his soul on his own. Now, at least, some progress had been made. Julian was looking for a job. Even though Darren was a bit stung by Julian's rejection of what was rightfully his, it was progress.

"I haven't done anything," was Julian's response, his eyes still scanning the paper.

"You're trying." Darren brushed his fingers across Julian's shoulder and added a splash of milk to his coffee.

Julian was bewildered by his father's statement, he had not really done anything yet. One minute his father was begging him to keep a job where he was ostracized and ridiculed by his peers. The next minute he was proud that his son was circling low-paying entry-level jobs. But Julian did feel hopeful—he had an appointment later this morning with an insurance company that needed an office manager. The salary was laughable, but money was not the issue. After his interview, he had an appointment with a real estate agent to look at a condo, then with his therapist. He had not taken a drink in six weeks.

Chapter 18

Cathy Colfax also used the summer to change things—primarily herself. She decided that she no longer wanted to be the doormat that a person like Julian McPhee could control. Her teenage years had been spent in pursuit of acceptance, and she was determined to change that. College had been easier. She'd made some good friends, Grace included, and had a few serious relationships with guys she'd met in class or at clubs, but she had never felt totally confident with anyone—men or women. She always viewed other women as smarter, prettier, more sophisticated or funnier than she. With men, she often found herself the friend, the one they could talk to about the girls they wanted to date. Since graduating college and landing the job at Comptech, she'd been making progress at changing herself. She liked her job and performed it well and had a nice social life with friends and people from work. She had been basically content with her life until she met Julian. She'd only worked at Comptech a few months when Julian was moved into his position of manager of their department. The stories that had arrived before him were enough to make her wary: he was a boozing, womanizing party boy who wouldn't do anything he was supposed to do. But he had struck her differently. She tried to keep her distance at first, but she could not resist the greenish gold flecks in his eyes and the way his lips looked like they were being tugged into a smile against his will. She found him quite timid, not at all like the playboy she had expected. One night she asked him to come along when a group went out after work. A few others had given her a hard time for inviting Darren McPhee's son, but she'd felt sorry for him. Later, toward the end of the evening, he'd made a point to thank her.

"Cathy, thanks for including me," he'd said to her while she was in a corner gathering her purse and coat.

"No problem," she'd smiled. "We're glad you came. I hope you had fun."

"I did," he smiled. "You leaving?"

"Yeah," she glanced around. Everyone else was already gone or on their way out.

"Why don't you stay, let me buy you one more."

"Oh no," she waved her hand in protest, imagining every cliché about drinking with the boss. "It's late."

"Please, just keep me company." It was the first time she'd seen him smile to his fullest ability. They stayed for two more hours, two more drinks each. They talked about college, relationships, and work. Julian had confided his insecurities with surprising candor.

"I know what people think." He poked at the ice cubes in his drink. "For the most part they're right. There's no way I would have my job if not for my father. He thinks he's doing me a favor, but he's not."

"What do you mean?" This revelation had surprised Cathy.

"I don't know if I belong in this business."

"What else would you do?"

"I don't know. I mean, I've never had to think about that before. Everyone around me always assumed that I would just take over Comptech. Become Dad someday."

"Your mom, too?" It was an innocent question, but Cathy immediately saw the green eyes cloud over.

"She's dead."

"Oh. I'm sorry," she'd turned away.

"No. It's okay. She's been gone for a long time. Since I was a kid."

"Oh. That must have been bad."

"I think it's worse for Dad. I mean, I don't really remember her that much, but he does. I know he misses her."

"Do you remember anything about her?"

"Yeah, sure." He was thoughtful for a moment and Cathy studied his face. "I can remember little things, here and there, although I'm not sure how much of it is my actual memory and how much is stuff I've been told."

"That's sad." She made a mental note to call her parents.

"Mostly I just wonder about things."

"Like what?"

"Like how would things be different if she was still here. I think I would be different, a different person, but I'm not sure how."

After that night, Cathy could not stop thinking about those eyes, and the smile that he seemed only to show to her. She started being more careful when choosing her work clothes, worrying about her hair, becoming more conscious about how she sat and moved. She had reverted back to her high school self.

But now she really wanted to be different. She quit smoking with the patch, and had her chestnut brown hair professionally highlighted. She had her upper lip waxed and lost ten pounds on a high protein-frequent exercise diet. By September she was almost able to keep up with Grace in spinning class. The makeover, however, was not only physical. Her new sense of confidence and determination spilled into her work and social life as well. She'd had six fairly enjoyable dates with men that she met through various friends, the gym and one in the supermarket. They were all very nice, three had kissed her goodnight, but none of them really sparked her interest. Work was getting better, too. She'd been relieved when Julian resigned; their game of hide and seek had grown tiresome. Her desk was now routinely cleared, then brimming with fresh assignments, which she handled deftly. She was proud of the way she had been resisting Julian's relentless attempts to contact her, but every so often she needed reinforcements.

"So far I've successfully ignored six E-mails and thirty-seven phone calls," Cathy told Grace as they entered Cathy's apartment after a Thursday evening spinning class.

"Yeah, but who's counting, right?" Grace helped herself to a bottled water from the door of the fridge and handed one to Cathy. "Can I have a few of these strawberries?"

Cathy nodded and gulped from her water at the same time. "It's not that I'm counting. He only left a message the last time. Before that call I went through my caller ID to see if there was a pattern…"

"I killed my knee today," Grace reached behind her back to hold her foot up and stretch her leg. Cathy noticed how the white stripe along the outside of her workout pants remained without a bulge of fat as she did this. Grace put her palm against the refrigerator and stretched further.

"Are you listening to me?" Cathy walked into the living room and plopped onto the sofa.

"No, not really."

"C'mon Grace. Just listen to it, please...this one is different. He sounds different."

"Okay, I'll listen." Grace said, walking to the chair next to the couch. "But I *will* give you my *honest* opinion, no matter what it is."

"Fair enough." Cathy reached over and pressed the play button her answering machine.

"Hi, Cathy. It's Julian. I know you don't want to talk to me, but I wanted to tell you that I'm working on getting myself together. I had a really good interview today, and I have a second one...so I might have a new job, and I 'm working on getting my life together. I've used this whole mess to wake me up and make me change things...I...I haven't had a drink in six weeks...what I really wanted to say was...well, I've been thinking about you a lot...about—"

The words were severed by the loud beep of the answering machine. Grace stood from her chair, placed her hand on her hip and arched one eyebrow very high.

"What do you think?"

Grace stared at her in disbelief. "You know what I think!"

Cathy lowered her head, "but...didn't he sound..."

"Same old, same old!"

"But..." Grace held up her palm as a stop sign. She grabbed Cathy's elbow and dragged her like a disobedient child into the bedroom and closed the door. She put her hand on Cathy's chin and pulled her face up, so that Cathy was looking into the full length mirror on the back of the door.

"Look at you. Take a good look at yourself. I do not see the word *sucker* on your forehead." She pushed Cathy sideways in the mirror and slapped her left buttock. "You look fabulous, look at that new ass! You feel fabulous. You are doing so great! And why is that?" Grace's hand circled in an effort to cajole the correct response. Finding no success, she placed her hands on the sides of Cathy's lips and helped her form the words. "I look and feel great because the loser is out of my life! You can have any guy you want. Stay away from him, he's a mess."

Later they sat watching a sappy chick-flick and ate the rest of the strawberries with fat free whip cream. Cathy hugged Grace when she left.

"Thanks for almost beating the shit out of me," she laughed.

"I was trying to beat something *into* you—sense." Grace smiled.

When she left Cathy paced around her apartment for a while, fighting the strong urge for a cigarette despite the patch on her arm, then she listened to the answering machine message again.

"What were you going to say?" She yelled at the blinking light. "What was the rest of it?"

CHAPTER 19

"Jamie, time to get up," she murmured with a swat at the clock radio. *Jamie*—a small piece of himself recoiled at the name she'd given him. A voice deep within laughed a vicious, mocking, laugh whenever he heard it. *Jamie*. What a joke. But he knew, with her, he *had* to be someone else.

"You're not a James, or Jimmy. You're a Jamie..." she'd declared after the first time they had had sex. They were in her apartment on her living room floor. Jimmy was still reeling from the thought of touching a woman who was not Veronica. He was not exactly sure how he had ended up there. He knew when she had asked him over what was going to happen. She'd love to show him some more of her poetry, she'd crooned after two more coffees and two hours of conversation about the school, her writing, the book he was working on, what she wanted to do after college, and her childhood in Arizona. He had never mentioned his wife and Melinda never asked. The omission was quite deliberate on his part. In fact, several times Veronica almost flew into something he said. It was quite an effort to not mention her at all, but he liked being with someone who did not look at him as *that poor man.* He knew what would happen if he went home with her, and he did not want it to happen, but he did not want to go back to his empty, silent house, either.

They sat on her living room floor with her collection of poems spread out around them, and before he was conscious of it, she was kissing him. He closed his eyes, trying to imagine that she was

Veronica, but her smell and the taste of her tongue were different. He was different. With Melinda he was *not* Professor James Lawson. He was the skinny, insecure kid who grew up in Little City, fighting everyone and everything to be taken seriously. He never had "girlfriends" back then, he just had sex with whatever girl was willing, and many of them were. He was charming and confident with just enough aloofness to make him desirable. He was never good at talking to the girls he actually liked, so he never really got to know any of them. Eventually he had just gotten used to sleeping with the ones he did not care about. After he had graduated from high school, he fought hard *not* to be that kid, to rid himself of the rage that had caused him so many scuffles and bloody noses, to escape the insecurity that once left him speechless around girls he liked. Veronica had helped him move away from that kid, to become a proud, well-educated man. She showed it was okay to be smart, to use his education. The fresh-faced girl he'd met at a campus blood drive run by her sorority had saved him. He fed her a Twinkie when she became lightheaded, and she sat alongside his cot and talked him through his pint. He hadn't felt a thing as he watched her cute way of tucking her hair behind her ears then letting it fall alongside her face again. Now that seemed like a lifetime ago. He was a different man.

"Jamie?" It had been only five months since his wife's death and he knew what people would think about him. Another woman was waking him up, making sure he would get to class on time. Sleeping with another woman was bad enough, but she was a twenty-year-old student and a former drug addict. She would have been someone he would have slept with in high school, because he didn't really care about her. He had let her call him Jamie because it was someone he had become. Jamie could allow Melinda to hover above him at night in constant motion—swirling, twisting, moaning, laughing. He hid from his life in her tiny, cluttered, mouse-infested apartment where clothes were strewn across the floor, where they ate Chinese food right out of the carton and drank wine out of paper cups, where noise from above and below sandwiched them…where Veronica did not exist.

"C'mon, lazy. It's getting late," she tongued his left nipple, sending a ripple through him. "Or you could blow off your class and stay with me." She licked again, her brown eyes upturned toward his face, her hair trailing across his abdomen.

"I can't," he breathed. "I did that last week, twice, remember?" He slid himself away from her, and she propped against the headboard and lit a cigarette.

"I'm sure that class was totally devastated to have a free hour." She gnawed at her fingernail, then picked the chewed sliver off her tongue. "You coming over tonight?"

"I don't know," was always his answer.

"Okay, whatever." She jumped up and pecked him on the cheek before strolling into the bathroom. He listened to her urinate and then he heard the shower go on. He was tempted to go in and kiss her, hard, against the wet tile...to carry her back to bed and stay there for a week...but he resisted the urge. It was as if the old Jimmy was fighting him, trying to get out from the muck that has seeped into his life. Sometimes it felt so good to hold Melinda that he wanted to just tell her everything and cry and let her comfort him. He sometimes rubbed his face into her hair, smelling the mixture of shampoo and cigarettes. Melinda's hair was similar in color to Veronica's but had a slightly thicker, wavier texture. He would sometimes grab a few strands and pull it as straight as it could be without causing her pain.

"You freak," she would laugh. "What are you doing?"

"I'm trying to picture you with straight hair."

"I look like a dork with straight hair."

He showered and dressed and was ten minutes late to his class. The students grew quiet as he strolled in and plopped his briefcase onto the desk. He opened it and was surprised to find a stack of papers, which he'd promised to return to the class this morning, sitting, untouched, ungraded, and completely forgotten. He mumbled an excuse, which was met with a medley of groans which caused an involuntary clench in his fist. It suddenly occurred to him that he had not reviewed the material they were studying, he could not even remember what they had discussed last class. What were they reading? He felt suddenly naked and child-like as he surveyed their faces: a few were bright and eager, notebooks open, pens poised, some were drowsy and disinterested, hands branding their cheeks with a red imprint, a few cocky and defiant, arms crossed, books closed. He felt a brief sense of fear that no words would come out of his mouth. His breath began to get stuck in his throat and his heart beat fast. He felt their impatience in the air as they watched him on his imaginary stage; the comic in front of an audience that would not laugh. He cleared his tightening throat, trying to force air out of it.

"Let's get started," he mumbled and was met by a clear but faceless response:

"Yeah, let's."

He surveyed the faces again without being able to determine the identity of the heckler, and unsure what he would do if he could. He felt his face growing warm.

"Last week we spoke about the role of women in American drama. Today I'd like to get your thoughts on a poem by William Carlos Williams." He flipped open one of his books and pretended to read the poem which he had memorized. He read each word carefully, deliberately. He was aware of the student's questioning looks at each other, but he could not look up from the book. The room was very quiet, no one even seemed to be breathing.

"...tucking in stray ends of hair..." his voice had fallen to just above a whisper.

He imagined Veronica, and her habit of tucking her hair back behind her ears. She did it unconsciously, in one swift, fluid motion, sweeping the strand back over her head, hooking it behind her ear. Sometimes she would look up and catch him watching and smile. He read a few more lines, unaware of the words he spoke, until he came to the end of the poem.

"...I compare her to a fallen leaf. The noiseless wheels of my car rush with a crackling sound over dried leaves as I bow and pass smiling." Jimmy steadied himself against the corner of the large desk, his heart hammering, his throat tight, the sound of leaves cracking beneath wheels echoing in his head, morphing into the sound of a body thrown against a hood, flopping back onto the pavement. A dull thud, the cracking of bone. He felt a film of sweat across his forehead.

The students seemed to be assessing Jimmy in silence, minds miles away from the poem.

"Is the wife supposed to be dead at the end?" of the more eager students spoke. Several heads turned to the young woman in disbelief, looking like they would kick her under the table if they could.

"No," Jimmy said so quietly that the students seemed to lean toward him in unison. "The wife is not supposed to be dead."

A few others chimed in, purposely seeming to veer the discussion away from the last few lines. Jimmy stood in front of them, but did not provide direction. They had finished talking fifteen minutes before the scheduled end of class. They did not even wait for him to tell them that class was over, they sensed it. He stood quietly in front of the room while they stared at him for several moments, then one by one began getting up and walking out. He hoped the unexpected free time—an invaluable commodity to most college students—would squelch any complaints about the ungraded papers, but none of them seemed happy as they milled out. He was sick of trying to please these spoiled, reckless little punks; they were never happy. They complained about too much work, they complained about too little work. He ground his molars together and felt his fists tightening again. A feeling of apprehension toward this particular group was spreading across the pit of his stomach and he promised himself that he would be dazzlingly over prepared for their next meeting. *Shit.* He realized he had forgotten to give them their reading assignment. He knew he had to buckle down; he'd already dealt with four disgruntled students this week: one who insisted he'd scrawled a profanity in the margin of her paper, one who complained that he'd been in "another world" during a conference, and two who said his lectures had become impossible to understand.

"Prof Lawson?"

"Yes?" The young woman's voice found him despite the fact that his head was purposefully burrowed in his briefcase. *Tanya Hill.* It was no surprise to him that she was asking to speak to him after class, he knew she would be a pain in the ass about her paper. *Fucking Bitch,* he thought as he imagined slapping her, her head slamming into the chalkboard.

"I was wondering if you had had a chance to look at my paper *at all.*" He frowned at the accusatory tone of *at all.* " I had some concerns about…"

"Sorry, Tanya, I have an appointment. I can't talk to you now, I have to run. We'll talk next time, or stop by during my office hours." He feigned a glance at his watch, scooped his briefcase off the desk and trotted out of the room, leaving Tanya Hill standing there looking dumbfounded.

His jaw was tight with tension as he walked across campus, feeling the newly crisp air pinch his face. He walked fast, his buttocks contracting with each step, his breath heavier after a while. He watched the students milling about. A few were curled under trees, reading, or wiping highlighters across pages of words they tried to comprehend. Some were smoking outside the doors to the smoke-free buildings, leaving their discarded butts flattened against the sidewalk. A group of boys were in the center courtyard, red and sweaty, tossing around a football. He felt absolutely invisible. Like he could walk through any of them and they would not notice. He watched himself, too, the invisible professor, walking through the world of the living. He heard the voice deep within sneer again. *Look how pathetic you are.* He walked to the edge of the campus and sat beneath a large tree that was tossing its leaves around him. He thought of a day last fall when Veronica came waddling home with her arms wrapped around a twenty-five pound pumpkin, which she declared she would carve for Halloween. She sat on the back patio, her jeans pulled tightly along her rear end as she sat straddling the pumpkin with her arm elbow deep inside it, spooning heaps of its orange guts onto pieces of newspaper. He'd watched her from the back porch, then chased her around the backyard, threatening to weave some of the stringy goop into her hair. Later they roasted the pumpkinseeds in the oven, and sat eating them by the fireplace, talking about future Halloweens with their future children.

By late afternoon the rumbling in his stomach broke through his reverie and he realized he had not eaten all day. He looked at his watch and realized he'd been sitting there for several hours, but he couldn't recall exactly what time he'd sat down. He was close to town, so he stopped in a small coffee shop and ordered a tuna sandwich and a 7-Up. Self-conscious about sitting there alone, he opened his briefcase and pulled out his stack of papers, with Tanya Hill's on top. He stared at the cover page, with her name above his in the bottom right corner. *She was such a bitch!* She thought he had nothing else to do in his life but worry about her stupid paper! He doodled some small pictures in the margin of page one, an ugly face with a grotesque expression that in his mind mirrored Tanya's face. He read a few sentences, then found a map, which was stenciled on the paper placemat, more interesting. Later he returned to his campus office. When he opened the door he stepped on several notes that had been slipped under his door. Two students had been waiting to see him, and he'd missed his scheduled office hours. He crumbled the notes into balls and threw them basketball-style into the wastebasket and then sat at his desk and took out the papers again.

This time he thought about Melinda, doodling her triangular breasts on the paper in front of him. He did enjoy talking to her, her life was so interesting for someone so young.

"How did you get into drugs, so young I mean?" he'd asked her one night as they sat on the floor of her candlelit apartment eating from a bucket of greasy take-out chicken.

She shrugged and licked her fingers thoughtfully. "I was a pretty wild kid."

"What about your parents?"

"What about them?"

"Didn't they try to stop you from taking drugs?"

"Well it's not like I woke up one day and was a junkie. It was a very slow, very quiet process. They were pretty oblivious, and I was pretty good at hiding things from them. You would not believe the places on your body where you can hide needle marks, like between toes and stuff. They trusted me too much, I guess. They never thought they had to do the 'just say no' business with me."

"Didn't they know something was wrong?"

"Sure, after a while, they figured it out." she wiped the side of her mouth with the back of her hand. "But I think they took a while before they were really ready to face it. But eventually I stopped caring about having any marks and just shot up in my arm, where it was fast and easy. Maybe I wanted them to see, I don't know. They eventually sent me to therapy and rehab and the usual crap."

"Are you close to them now?"

She shrugged again, "define close."

"I had a friend who was hooked, a good friend." James put his drumstick down and moved his foot from where it rested beneath him.

"What happened to him?"

"He's still around. But we haven't spoken in years."

"How come?"

"He stole my..." he'd stopped just short of the words *my wife's jewelry*. Veronica was always on the verge of falling into their conversations. "He stole something from me when I was trying to help him."

97

"Were you angry with him?"

"I broke his nose," Jimmy could not believe he had told her this, even as he said it.

"Wow," she stared at him for a moment, as if assessing his strength.

"It was stupid, but I was just so hurt and angry. We had been like brothers since we were little kids."

"I used to steal money from my parents. You know, slip a ten or twenty out of their wallet and they never knew. Sometimes I would make up things about school. You know, we're going on a trip to see a play, it costs forty dollars, or I need a deposit for a yearbook, blah, blah, blah. They never checked."

"Did it hurt them when they found out?"

"Yeah, sure. But I wasn't doing it to hurt them. It had nothing to do with them. I just had to get high. No matter what I had to do. You can't take it personally."

"Yeah. I guess that's how my friend was."

"Do you still care about him?" she flipped her hair behind her shoulders.

"What do you mean?"

"If you had to do it again, would you help him if you could, even though he stole from you?"

Jimmy pondered the question, "I guess I would."

"That's kinda the way it is with my parents. I've caused them so much pain," she stopped for moment, as if making a list. "I've hurt them so much, but I know they'd never be gone from my life. They would always help if I needed it. I'm sure we would be closer if all this stuff hadn't happened. Sometimes we don't talk for a month or two, but they're never gone. They're never absent from my life."

"That's kind of how it is with me and Face."

"Face? What kinda name is *Face*?" she laughed.

He thought about her candor and decided that that was what kept him going back to her, even when he felt awful about it. She was so aware of things for someone so young, and she talked about anything from the color of her urine that day to the hairiness of his feet to how she felt about abortion. She was an open book, and he found that refreshing.

When he returned to his house that evening he did not notice the dehydrated, crumbling plants, the dirty coffee cup in the sink, or the unopened mail on the kitchen counter. The mail was in two piles—his and hers. What do you do with a dead woman's mail? Most of it was junk: catalogues, store flyers, credit card applications, a professional newsletter, but he could not bring himself to throw it away so it gradually grew into a heap on the counter.

He tapped the play button on his answering machine and listened to Aunt June's droning, his mother asking him to please call she hadn't heard blah, blah, blah, please contact Mr. Smith at American Express…he sat at the desk in his office and listened to them, while his hand gingerly wiped a film of dust from his computer screen. His book was behind that screen, somewhere, sitting untouched. He showered, changed his clothes, and plopped onto the sofa on top of the rumpled sheet and pillow. He listened to the hum of the refrigerator, the ticking of the clock, and the occasional car passing on the street. He hung on these sounds, waited for them, as the silence of the house felt suffocating. It sat on his chest and forced the air from his lungs. He turned the television on loud—too loud, but soon he could not hear it anymore. He tossed and turned for a while, afraid to close his eyes; afraid he'd see Veronica's face smashing against a car windshield, her nose shattering, teeth flying, or he'd see Julian McPhee laughing, dancing with Veronica. Or he'd hear the baby ghosts…souls cheated out of the bodies they were supposed to inhabit.

Eventually he stopping trying to be in the house and drove out of the driveway, fleeing from it. After driving around for a while, he ended up where he recently had been finding himself more and more frequently. A place that was noisy, a place full of movement. A place where the sounds and images that haunted his home were quiet. A place where he could watch her long dark hair swirl around…

"Hi, Jamie." She wrapped her arms around his neck and pulled him inside as something deep inside him recoiled again.

CHAPTER 20

Julian had decided that the key to solving his problem was a simple matter of discipline. His second interview with the insurance company had not gone as expected. The chubby, balding head of human resources had shaken his hand and said, "Mr. McPhee, Sorry, we've filled the position," in a curt tone that told Julian the real reason: they knew about his problems. The same ad was still in the paper, he had checked. He was fed up with whole system. A bunch of middle-aged, bitter underachievers who took out their life's frustrations on people like Julian who were trying to start out in the world. After that interview, he'd walked around Little City for a while, as he liked to do when he had things on his mind. He loved to watch people and wonder what they were doing at the moment he saw them. He saw an elderly woman, taking small deliberate steps as she approached the corner drugstore. Was he picking up a prescription? Arthritis maybe? A young mother pushed a baby carriage out of a small shoe store. Julian figured she was getting the baby's first pair of shoes, and he suddenly wondered if he and his mother had once done that. Had she pushed him around town in a stroller? Had she held his sticky, post-lollipop hand before crossing the street? Or walked with her shopping bags in one hand and her other arm draped around his shoulder? He watched an older man enter Nick's Tavern, a small out of the way place at the edge of Little City. He stood looking in the window for a while, watching the man talk to the bartender and point at something on the television. Was he retired, or did he know the owner? Or maybe he was just a die-hard baseball fan who went in to watch the game. He hadn't planned to, but his arm, acting on its own, pulled open the door like he was going to work or school. He went in like it was something he might do on any day, sat down and ordered a gin and tonic. He did not even think that this might not be a good idea. *One drink. Why couldn't he have one drink, just like anyone else?* Amazingly, he was able to sip that single drink for an hour, and he did not feel the slightest bit drunk, nor did he have a strong desire for another one. He felt good, relaxed. The drink tasted good. He'd missed the warm feeling in his feet that always came when he drank. This place was quiet, but friendly, and best of all no one seemed to care who he was or why he was there. He confidently paid the bill, left a generous tip and went home. It was just a matter of self-control. He would just have to be conscious of what he was doing, not let himself go. When he was on the wrestling team in high school he had been able to go without food sometimes for an entire day in order to make his weight. He had been able to do it because he had been focused, disciplined, and had a goal. He knew he could be that way again. *Self-control was the key.* His father had not even noticed anything unusual when he arrived home.

"Hey, Dad." Julian tried to sound casual as he told Darren about the lack of success he had encountered in his job search. He hung his jacket in the closet and took a seat in the chair that was the furthest away from Darren, afraid that he reeked of Nick's Tavern.

"Why don't you consider coming back to Comptech?" Darren was sitting on a high back leather chair in the living room; he folded the book he'd been reading across his knees as he spoke. "It just makes sense, I've built it for you. It's *all* for you. You can have it *all* someday."

"I don't want it." Julian sat down carefully, acutely conscious of each movement he made, worried that something in his actions might cause Darren to detect the drink. "I was never any good at my job," he watched his father's face, "I'm sure Jeff is much better than I was."

"You know I respect Jeff. But this is not a contest," he paused for a moment. "I 'm sorry if you felt I was comparing you to Jeff, or Steve Curtis, or anyone else. I didn't mean to make you feel…"

"Come on, Dad. You know I didn't mean that stuff I said." He thought about the drink he had just had. The taste was still on his tongue.

"Oh, you meant it. Maybe it wasn't supposed to come out the way it did but I know you meant it."

"They're great guys, Dad. Of course you would want me to be like them, anybody would." He was thoughtful for a moment. "I wouldn't want me as a son, either."

"Oh, Julian," Darren sighed and looked out the window. "I wish you could see what potential you have. You're just as smart as Jeff, and as hardworking as Steve. You've just had a rough time, that's all. Losing your mother at such a young age…"

"Don't make excuses for me. Steve's old man treated him like shit and he turned out okay. It's *me*. There's no excuse for *me*." Julian pressed his knuckles against his lips.

"I am certainly not excusing your behavior. I know it's a problem, Believe me, I know. But I think if you just found something you love to do, something where you couldn't wait to get to work each day, you would be okay. You need something like that in your life."

"No one is willing to give me a chance."

"You can't wait for someone to *give* you anything. You have to take it."

"I'm not sure I know how."

"What are you interested in doing?"

"I'm not sure, that's part of the problem. I don't have a direction."

"Well," Darren leaned forward, folding his hands beneath his chin. "I am posting a new position this week. If you want it, it's yours."

"Come on, Dad."

"No, this is different. It doesn't involve software, and you don't have to stay. I promise I won't push that. Use it as a starting point to begin a new career."

"What is it?"

"Community relations rep. I want the company to get into doing some community service, you know charity stuff. It's been a growing trend in a lot of companies and we have not stepped up, and we need to." Darren sat back and Julian stood up.

"Do you think that's funny?" Julian stepped closer to his father, but then turned away, remembering the drink. "Me? Charity work? You've got to be kidding. That's even funnier than me as manager."

"I realize you've dealt with some bad publicity, but this is your chance to make amends."

"What do you mean?"

"Do something good, feel good." Darren removed his book from his lap, slid the bookmark in and placed it on the table next to his chair. "I want you to have the chance to do something you'll be proud of...hospital donations, blood drives, programs for underprivileged kids, that sort of thing. You grew up with everything, now here is a chance for you to give something back. Plus you can make your mark in community relations, then eventually move on to a company with a larger PR department. I don't want you to stay with Comptech forever—I realize it's not what you want, but here is a chance for you to get a new career off the ground."

"People aren't going to take me seriously, they never have. I think you're taking a big chance here, Dad." Julian raked his fingers through his hair, pacing in front of his father's chair. Darren stood up and touched his shoulder.

"It's a chance I'm willing to give you. You just have to take it."

The next week Julian was still considering his father's proposal. Part of it seemed ridiculous, but maybe it was his chance to redeem himself for the hurt he'd caused his father. He pondered the question each night as he sipped his single drink in a dark corner of Nick's Tavern. He was happy to be socializing again. The happy hour snacks tasted better than anywhere before, and he was moved by the enjoyment of watching a ballgame with a handful of strangers—cheering and cursing like brothers. There was no substitute for the feeling of camaraderie found in a few beers a good ballgame. He'd missed his days of chatting with bartenders about politics and current events and flirting with women. In fact, he'd also decided that his new, disciplined self would not call Cathy again after she'd ignored his last heartfelt plea. He had given her a chance to forgive him, now it was time to accept her rejection. He would not permit himself to turn into a begging fool.

His new system worked quite well for several weeks. So well, in fact, that he was able to up his intake to two drinks per day without any sign of intoxication. He still sipped slowly, prolonging the desired social contact he deserved. He was young, and entitled to some fun and relaxation in his life. He'd decided to stop feeling bad about the whole mess—he was sorry that that woman had died, but even the judge saw that it wasn't his fault, so he was not going to walk around like a monk for the rest of his life, it was time to move on. He was even considering taking his father up on the job offer. He could do a good job in community relations—he was sociable, well informed, and he had some great ideas for an ad campaign about all of the "good for publicity" stunts that Comptech would be doing. He was feeling quite confident and hopeful about this as he sat with his new group of friends—the regulars at Nick's—watching a Yankee game on the large television that dangled from a bracket above the bar.

"I don't get that, why didn't he run?" said a tall woman named Janice. She had very curly black hair and a hoop ring through her eyebrow and she had apparently decided that she needed Julian to tutor her on the rules of Major League Baseball.

"The runner can't leave the base until the outfielder catches the ball," Julian felt confident as he shoveled some peanuts into his mouth and pointed to the television. He felt much different here than he had felt at work or going out to Smokey's. Most of the people who came to Nick's were a bit older, and he greatly enjoyed being the best-looking and most well dressed person in the room. This was not the young business crowd with their cell phones and designer shoes. That crowd had never let him in.

"But how does the runner know if the outfielder is gonna catch it?" Janice sipped her beer and arched her eyebrows as if she had just made a great point. Julian liked the way she tilted her head back slightly when she drank, like she was swallowing aspirin.

"He doesn't know for sure, so he has to—" He was suddenly aware of the closeness of her body as she leaned toward the peanuts. "—take his chances." He purposely let his hand brush against her arm and watched her face for a reaction. She looked him right in the eye.

"So, Julian, what do you do?"

"Uh, public relations," he said quickly.

"Oh. That's cool," she smiled.

"How about you?"

"I don't do anything. I live off alimony from my ex and have a good time!"

"Wow." Julian did not think she looked old enough to be married, let alone divorced.

"You ever been married?"

"No," Julian smiled and shook his head.

"Good for you. It's overrated. The best part of my marriage is the check I get every fifteenth of the month. I took him for everything I could get and then some."

"Sorry it didn't work out."

"Don't be, I'm not. Do you wanna dance?" she tossed a peanut into her open mouth.

"Sure," he said, even though the dance floor was tiny and the music was old, wafting from a jukebox in the corner. He forgot all about the ballgame as he wrapped his hands around her lean waist. She was nearly as tall as he was, with very long legs. For a moment he felt awkward, as most women did not reach his face while dancing. He pulled her tightly against him and they danced for a long time, slow and fast, then back to slow. During the second round of slow songs he let his hands slide down her back, reaching as low as he dared. She didn't seem to mind and began nuzzling his neck with her nose. The game was almost over when they went back to the bar. Janice brushed a damp piece of hair from her face and ordered a beer, smiling at him.

"I'll take another as well," Julian said. He pointed to his nearly empty glass, not even realizing it was his third drink.

CHAPTER 21

Face stood behind the pane glass window of the store, dragging on his third cigarette and watching the night slip into morning. He coughed a few times, and spat a greenish wad into a tissue. The streetlights flickered off, and the newspapers were warm and soft. He took his usual copies, tossed his soiled tissue into the trash and pulled up his stool when his first customer came in. He was a young man in his early twenties. His rumpled clothes and slight stagger reminded Face of himself ten years ago, when a night out was really a night out. The young man poured himself a large black coffee, spilling some on the counter, and his arm. Then he gingerly walked to the register, put his coffee down and began fumbling through his pockets for money. Face had a vision of his own formerly handsome face, eyes blazing with cocaine or dulled with heroin, women anxiously pressing against him, wanting him. He glanced at the rumpled ten-dollar bill the kid had placed on the counter. He was a nice-looking kid, despite the wildness of his dark hair and the newly sprouted stubble along his chin. Face thought he'd seen him around before, maybe in the park.

"Hey pal," Face peered under the kid's lowered head. The remnants of a summer tan made his eyes seem almost too bright. "You okay?"

The young man pawed the air in dismissal, and the smell of him made Face recoil, as well as remember, as he gave him back a five and four singles. Face's breath seemed to stall deep in chest for a moment, and he grabbed for his stool as a familiar, woozy feeling came over him.

The young man had not noticed Face's sudden discomfort. He steadied himself and returned the boy's change, then went to wipe up the mess on the coffee counter, trying to ignore the dizziness that had been plaguing him recently. Alongside the spill, the young man had left a set of keys on a silver key chain with a Honda emblem engraved on it. Face turned to find the kid on his cell phone by the door, speaking too loudly in a tearful, pleading manner to the person on the line.

"Cathy? It's me, Julian."

Face did not hear him say anything else, because it was then that he noticed the blue Honda Prelude parked in two spots outside the door. *Julian. Honda Prelude. Holy shit!* Could this be him? He watched the young man's slumping shoulders, his shirt hanging out of the back of his pants, babbling into the phone, and he held the keys more tightly in his hands. Could this rumpled, smelly, kid sobbing into the phone be the same perfect postured suit he'd seen in court? It had been a while and Face wanted to be sure. The kid hung up his phone and held onto the metal magazine frame with both his hands, almost like he could not stand up. Face considered calling the cops, reporting him for drunk driving, but he hated cops, and the kid had gotten away with it last time. Now, here he was, plastered at five in the morning, no one but the two of them. Veronica's murderer. Face stuffed the keys into his pocket, his chest burning, as the kid took his coffee off the top of the garbage can, and then began looking for his keys. He emptied his pockets, turning them inside and out, pausing for a sip of coffee between each one. Face watched and almost pitied him, knowing that in his years of dinking and drugging he had never looked as pathetic as this little punk. Finally, the young man lumbered back to the counter.

"Hey, you,…ya seen some key?"

Face stared at him, lit a cigarette and exhaled slowly, his face hot. "Keys? Keys to what?"

"My…car…keys…" Julian spoke slowly, looking confused and pointing out the window toward the car. *The car.*

"You think you should you be on the road, pal?" Face watched his dulled expression, suppressing a desire to spit in his face.

"Shut up," Julian murmured.

"Do I know you?" Face asked with mock innocence.

"Humph. I dun think so."

"You're a good-looking kid. I think I must have seen you on TV or something. Are you an actor?"

Julian found this funny and started laughing, a wet, gurgling, laugh with his head tilted back.

"Yeah, that's me. Fuckin' famous."

"So I was right! You *are* on TV, or are you a model? What have you been in?" Face grinned at him, exhaling his cigarette through his nostrils, the stream of smoke broken by his cough.

"You're not, like queer or something are you?" Julian stepped back a bit, and it was Face's turn to laugh. He tried not to take his eyes off Julian as his hand reached under the counter rummaging through extra cash register paper and matches, for a small baseball bat he kept there for emergencies.

"Nah, kid. Do I look like a faggot? I just know I seen your face before…were you, in the papers maybe?" Face found the bat gripped it, feeling the blood racing down his bony arm, pumping into his fist. He wished he were well so he could kick this punk's ass without the bat. Face began to walk around the front of the counter, sweat moistening his forehead, his heart beating so fast that it felt sore.

"Look, I gotta go…" Julian began looking in his pockets for his keys again, suddenly afraid of something he saw in this man's eyes. Face looked outside to see if anyone was around, then he walked toward the back of the store, and dangled Julian's keys like doggy treat. "This what you're looking for?"

"Yeah…" Julian walked toward him, and reached for his keys.

"How do you think it would feel to be left dying in the street?" Face asked him. Julian's eyes clouded over with confusion and Face watched his throat as he swallowed hard.

"Wh…what are you talking about?" Julian babbled. Face swung the small bat over his head, with all his strength, putting all his energy into it, for Jimmy. He wanted to make him feel pain and prove to Jimmy that he was not the same person who had taken Veronica's jewelry.

The bat hovered over Face's head, wobbling a bit as though his arms could not bear the weight of it. He began to push it down, toward Julian's head, but the force of the blow was diverted when he heard the door chimes, and turned to see a young woman rushing in. The bat landed squarely on Julian's right shoulder rather than on the top of his skull, where Face had intended to plant it. Julian fell to his knees, gripping his shoulder as the young woman raced over, screaming his name. Face's heart beat faster, and the sweat dripped from his brow, and he strained to catch his breath, the room spinning in front of him.

"What the fuck is happening?" She screamed, kneeling down next to Julian. Her head darted around the store, trying to find some clue as to what was going on.

"Cathy…" Julian sucked in his breath and coughed, spit flying from his mouth, "get me outta here."

Face dropped the bat and slumped to the floor, his breath caught in his chest. The room began to spin and a hot sensation began to tingle at his feet, working its way toward his eyes, which closed as he fell to the floor.

"Julian, what is happening?" Cathy screamed and dragged him upward. "Why did that guy do this? What's wrong with him?" They both looked at the unconscious man next to them. He was breathing, but he was quite pale. "Let's get outta here!" She half dragged Julian toward the door.

"Should we call the cops?" Julian stood looking at Face on the floor and rubbing his throbbing shoulder. "He was trying to assault me!"

"Why do you want to call the cops? So they can arrest *you…again*?" She indicated the car and shoved him away from her.

"But look at him, there's something wrong with him."

"He's crazy, that's what's wrong. He was trying to bash your skull in. Why did he do that, Julian?"

"Lemme just call for an ambulance, then we'll leave…"

"Okay, I'll put my car on the street. You call. Then I'll come back and *I'll* drive your car. Don't use your cell." She scooped Julian's keys from the floor, and ran out. He picked up the bat and went to the payphone and dialed 911.

CHAPTER 22

Later that same morning, Professor James Lawson had to listen to a list of recent complaints about him, three of which were formally filed with the Dean of Students.

"Jimmy, I know this has been a difficult time for you…but I cannot continue to make excuses for your behavior, there have been too many complaints to ignore. And now I hear about this girl? This girl is just the last straw."

"She's an adult." Jimmy leaned back in the small chair, which sat in front of the head of the Humanities Department, Lou Zaits. The suddenness and urgency of this summons had given Jimmy a clue as to what this was about, and he found himself angry with Melinda and her big mouth.

"I'm aware that she is an adult, but *you* are a member of this faculty and therefore *your* actions reflect upon all of us. This sort of thing does not sit well with members of the administration. We feel we must take a stand on this relationship, especially in light of all the other complaints about your behavior."

Jimmy snickered, "I don't need your approval for my personal life, Lou."

"There's no need for sarcasm. I called you here to discuss this because I consider you a friend. I could have just suspended you, a letter in the mail, and you know it. Some of these complaints are serious, Jim. You could lose your pension if you're not careful." Lou's tone was short. He removed his glasses and ran his hand over his face.

"Suspend me? Fire me? For carrying on a consensual relationship with another adult?"

"She's a student at this college, Jimmy!"

"But she's not *my* student."

"That doesn't matter. You know the administration frowns on it. This kind of thing makes us look...*seedy*. Plus, Jimmy...you must know this girl's reputation."

"Reputation?"

"She's well known as a drug addict Jimmy, come on, everyone knows it."

"She's not using anymore."

"Think about how this looks. She goes around campus talking about using heroin, she gets together with you, and you start acting...strange. What are people supposed to think?"

"This is such bullshit! I'll piss in a cup if you want me to!" Jimmy turned sideways in his chair and rolled his eyes. Lou walked to the front of his desk and leaned against it.

"Jimmy, listen to me," he grabbed a stack of papers and fanned them in front of his face. "This is a stack of complaints from students, *and* a few parents." He began leafing through them, "cancelled classes, late for class, grades not returned to students...incoherent comments in class...you told one young man his comments were full of shit...you drew a grotesque, violent drawing in the margin of one student essay, and a somewhat sexual drawing in another."

"I was doodling. They were just shapes." Jimmy waved his hand in disgust.

Lou thumbed through the papers in front of him and pulled out a photocopy of one Jimmy's doodles. It was a faceless woman, her head severed from her body, blood spurting forth from her neck. Jimmy looked at the drawing but did not speak.

"I think you need help. I know this has been a difficult time in your life. Look at all you've been through. It's only natural that you might..."

"You think I'm a drug addict, Lou? Or do you think I'm nuts?"

"Don't be ridiculous! You know what I'm talking about. Why don't you think about taking some time off? Go on sabbatical...work on your book. Don't you remember how excited you were about that book? It's all you talked about last spring."

"Honestly, Lou, I don't even remember what it was about."

"Well, you're going to have some time to work on it. As far as anyone else is concerned, you are on sabbatical to finish your book, but as of now you are officially suspended with pay until May—then we'll talk. I'm sorry, Jim. You know this is not my choice. Use this time, Jim. Get some help. No one can go through what you've had to deal with without some help."

Jimmy left Lou Zaits without shaking his outstretched hand and walked over to his office to gather some of his personal belongings: a couple of books, a dead plant, a photo of Veronica which sat in a frame on his desk. He knew Lou was right. Lou had done what he had to do. He knew that he had not been keeping up with his work. And then there was Melinda. Was it wrong that he wanted to sleep with her, all the time? It seemed that there was a small piece of the old Jimmy, inside of him, and that piece was watching himself—this empty mess cocoon—being blown around by whatever breeze was the strongest. The old Jimmy would have been prepared for class, would not even have gone near Melinda, and would have called the few people who kept leaving messages to assure them he was okay even if he really wasn't. That Jimmy was cursing at him, frowning at him, sometimes screaming at him. That Jimmy was the one who was guarding Veronica...keeping her away from the Jimmy who was...nothing.

Later that night was the first time in his life that Jimmy had struck a woman. He hadn't really *hit* Melinda, it was more like a hard shove, but he knew it hurt her and he didn't really care. The old Jimmy was shaking his head, his arms folded in front of him like an angry father. His dad was always admonishing him never to hit girls since he'd kicked Mary somebody or other in first grade because she'd taken his pencil. He remembered kids from the neighborhood, like Face, who hated their fathers because they beat up their mothers. Face used to have to sit at the dinner table and pretend not to notice the black eye and tell his mother the mashed potatoes were good. Once when they were around thirteen or fourteen, Jimmy had gone to Face's house and been frightened by his mother's swollen eye. It was bright purple and so large that it looked like it might pop. But Mrs. Jenkins acted like nothing was wrong and gave Jimmy a piece of cake. Jimmy's father always professed to never having hit a woman, although he certainly had done his share of screaming.

James and Melinda had made love, roughly. The sheets in her bed wound around them like a large rope as he pushed himself into her so hard that her head hit the wall. She laughed and grabbed his buttocks, blurting vulgar terms of encouragement. He pushed harder, wanting her to cry out in pain rather than pleasure. He didn't know why he was so angry at her, but he was. He blamed her for being suspended even though he knew that none of it was her fault. He had not even recognized the drawings on the papers, yet he knew he had done them. He grabbed her tightly, squeezing her as they rolled around the bed and onto the floor until they were both panting and covered in a film of sweat.

"That was amazing," she crooned, trying to unravel herself from the tangle of sheets. Jimmy sat naked on the floor, feeling stupid.

"I was suspended today," he said, not really to her, but like he just wanted to hear himself say it. The inside Jimmy was laughing at him, telling him how ridiculous he sounded.

"Suspended? What are you, like, in high school?" Melinda laughed at herself, loudly, then crawled over to him, still dragging the part of the sheet in which her foot was entwined. She stretched her naked body across the hard floor, leaned her chin on his knee and looked up to him. "Why?"

"Why do you think?" He stared at her brown eyes, realizing that she really did not know. She looked at him the way a child looks at her father, and it angered him. How could someone who once stuck a hypodermic needle full of heroin into the skin between her toes be so naive? Yet she was. He stared at her, with a harshness that he knew she had not seen before. Part of him wanted to wrap his arms around her and keep her away from the world. The other part wanted to put her through the wall.

"What?" Her voice cracked, and she touched her throat as if to make sure it was still working. "Is it...me? Because of me?" She shook the sheet off her foot and stood up, biting her thumbnail, "fuck."

"I asked you not to go around telling everyone, Melinda."

She spun around, spitting out a piece of her thumbnail "I didn't go *around* telling everyone," she mimicked. "People talk, it's human nature..."

"You gave them plenty to talk about didn't you?"

"No! What do you think, I took out an ad or something?"

"My career...it's ruined." He opened his hands as if he'd dropped it.

"How can they do that? It's not like I'm in high school or something. I'm not a child!"

"They can. They did."

"Jamie, I'm sorry..." she squatted next to him and touched his arm. He didn't know why, but he pushed her away. He shoved her hard, and she fell back on her ass, her back slapping the wall so hard that it took her breath away. "Don't call me that."

"Fine!" she fought back her tears and stood up slowly, with a wince, rubbing her buttocks. "James. Jimmy...what the fuck do you want me to call you? How about asshole?"

"I don't want you to call me anything." He stood up, stepping into his underwear and pulling his pants off the chair.

"Look, I'm sorry, please...I know you are messed up...Ginny told me, about your wife."

"She had no right to do that." He yanked one pant leg over his foot, then the other. "I didn't want you to know, I would have told you myself if I wanted you to know."

"*Why* didn't you want me to know?"

He pulled his shirt over his head. "I just didn't want to talk to anyone about it. I was sick of talking about it."

"Ginny was just looking out for me. She didn't want me to get hurt. I told her I had...strong feelings for you." It struck Jimmy that she was still naked, and that she felt no urge to conceal her nakedness while they were fighting. He couldn't dress fast enough.

"Please...Jamie." She stepped toward him and touched his hands. "How can I help you? Tell me how. Just tell me what to do and I'll do it."

James pulled his hands away and zipped his fly angrily. "What do you think? That you can make me forget about her? You think you can fuck me and I'll just forget all about her?"

Jimmy looked at her; her black eyeliner smeared at the corners, her young breasts standing at attention, her bed sheets sprawled all over the floor. Her voice was meek when she spoke.

"I know I can never *replace* her..."

Jimmy laughed bitterly. "Do you really think you could even come close to her? You don't even belong on the same *planet!* She was *everything*. And what are you?"

Melinda stood, bewildered, still naked, her eyeliner caked below her eyes. Her breasts heaved up and down, simmering with anger.

"Get the fuck out of here, you bastard," she said calmly.

114

CHAPTER 23

That evening, with his shoulder still bruised and tender, Julian McPhee went to an AA meeting. After the convenience store incident, Cathy had driven him back to her apartment, made him more coffee, and let him sleep for a few hours. When he woke around ten that morning he was startled by the brightness of the yellow print on her couch. Cathy was sitting in a chair of the same print, watching him, her own coffee mug nested between her palms. She didn't say anything when she saw him wake up, she just tucked her feet beneath her, as if afraid to let them touch the floor.

"Cathy," his voice was thick. "I don't know what to say to you."

She bowed her head, whispering into her coffee, "There isn't much you can say. You were drunk, Julian. How could you?"

"I thought I could handle it." He slowly propped himself up on the couch. "I thought I could just have a few...like everyone else."

"And you drove your car? My God, Julian, I can't believe you drove your car! How could you be so stupid?" She put her coffee cup on the table and rubbed her arms as if cold. Julian took the blanket that had been thrown over him and handed it to her, in the process dislodging a small baggie of melted ice that had been placed on his shoulder. He carefully set it on the table.

"I know it was dumb. I could have caused myself another whole nightmare."

"*Yourself?*" The word flew out of her mouth with such venom that Julian was startled into silence. "You're worried about yourself?

115

What about someone like Veronica Lawson? Weren't you worried about killing someone? Didn't that possibility even cross your mind?"

"Look, I know it was stupid and risky, but that whole mess is over. I didn't hurt anyone last night, and I didn't kill *her*" He stood up angrily.

"Yes, you did!" Cathy screamed at him as he paced around her sofa.

He spun to face her. "What are you talking about?"

"You did it, Julian. You *were* driving the car that night," her voice was so low that he had to move closer to hear her words.

"How do *you* know? You weren't there! Nobody knows!" He was speaking in a desperate, frightened whisper, circling her chair. He sat down again, burying his face in his hands. "*I don't even know!*" He sat for a long time, pressing his palms against his eyelids. Cathy moved over to the couch, sat next to him, and gently touched his knee with one finger.

"It *was* you, Julian. You have to know the truth now."

"No, I don't want to know," he said without moving his hands.

"Maybe *not* knowing is even worse. Maybe you'll never get past it until you know," she said softly. "I think you have to realize what can happen, how out of control you are, what you're capable of when you're drinking...I think that's the only way you can help yourself."

"I want it to stop, Cathy. I do. I really want it to stop."

"You called me that night."

"What?" He jerked his head up, and dug the heels of his hands further into his eyes, as if to erase a blurred image. He shook his head violently, "No!...No." The blood drained from his face, "Don't tell me," he said.

"You were on a payphone." She stood up. "You didn't get to finish, you got cut off. I called you back on your cell, but I guess you didn't have it." She walked away from him and turned her back, afraid his face would prevent her from continuing. He sat on the couch, still shaking his head as if its constant motion would prevent her words from reaching his brain.

"You said it was bad...that she was bleeding, you ran."

"No, Cathy, you're wrong. It wasn't me." He fell against the back of the couch, exhausted. He closed his eyes and grabbed a few clumps of hair in one hand, slapping himself on the forehead with the other hand. "Why can't I remember?" he cried.

"Maybe it's your subconscious, protecting you. Your mind won't let you remember." She walked around the front of the couch and kneeled in front of him.

"I would not leave a woman to die in the street. I would *never* do that!" Tears ran down his face and he was silent for a moment, his eyes pleading with Cathy. "Do really you think I could do that?"

Cathy moved away again, back to the window, and turned her back to him again. "I know you wouldn't have done that when you are yourself, but when you drink...you are not the same person." She stood by the window, watching the same people she saw every day, almost angry at them for being unaware of what was happening inside her apartment. She heard Julian get up from the couch and she stood listening to him vomit into the kitchen sink. After several minutes he came to stand next to her at the window and spoke in a calm voice.

"Maybe I could have saved her. I could have helped her, called someone."

"Who knows if that would have done any good, Julian?"

"I'll never know."

"Julian, I didn't tell you this to hurt you. I just thought it might make you realize that you need help."

"Why didn't you tell the police?" He asked her as they watched retired Mr. Gerry set up his folding chair.

"Because...I didn't know what to do. I was afraid. I didn't want you to go to prison."

Before he left early that afternoon, he and Cathy sat quietly at either end of the couch, each too involved with their thoughts to talk. Julian sat with his head tilted back, feeling drained and afraid, yet determined that this would be the moment that changed his life. He thought about how he had read the newspaper articles about the accident with detachment, as if he had been reading about someone else's life. But maybe deep down he had known all along.

Cathy was curled up at the other end of the couch, watching Julian and thinking about how she felt about him. Sometimes she thought she loved him, other times she found him repulsive. She knew one thing was certain: she did not want his battle to be part of her life. She did not ever want to hear his drunken voice on the phone late at night again. Alcohol changed his voice—its pitch, its clarity, its warmth— all distorted, and she wanted no part of it.

"I want to make something clear to you, Julian." He was surprised at the sudden noise after they had been sitting in silence so long. "I never, ever, want you to call me again when you are drunk."

"Cathy…"

"No!" she held up her hand the way she had seen Grace do many times. "I mean it. I will change my telephone number to an unlisted one if I have to. I don't want to be part of this. Call me any time you are sober, but I will hang up on you if you are drunk. I cannot be part of you life until you have conquered this. I hope you get well, I really do. I would like to be part of your life, but only if you get help. Got it?"

Julian nodded. "It's over Cathy. Really." He took her face in his hands and kissed her softly. "I'm going to get my act together, Cathy. I promise you now. I want us to be together, and I'm going to make it happen."

"I hope so," she sighed.

She watched him turn and wave before he drove off in his car, wondering if she would ever hear from him again.

Julian pulled into the driveway of his home with a nagging feeling gnawing at his stomach. Once again he had disappeared all night without a word. He had forgotten that Darren was at a conference in Boston and was imagining the scene that would follow his entrance. It was time for Scene D, but he had no idea what Scene D would be like.

Unfortunately, the wrath of Maggie was far worse than that of Darren McPhee. He'd never before heard her use vulgar language, but she called him a "fucking bloody bastard," with the word fuck sounding like *fawlk* with her accent.

"Where's dad?" He'd whimpered, hanging his jacket in the closet. Maggie followed him like an angry gnat, swirling around his head.

"You're *fawlkin* lucky he went to Boston yesterday." She spat.

"Maggie. It's over. I'm going to get myself together this time."

"You woulda give tha man a heart attack if he'da known you was out drinkin'" Julian walked into the kitchen poured himself some water, and swallowed some Tylenol.

He choked when the Tylenol stuck in his throat, and sunk into the chair, putting his head down on his folded arms. Maggie continued talking, not seeming to notice that she was talking to his scalp.

"I tole ya, a long time ago, when your troubles were just startin. My dad was a drinker, so I know it. Like a person with a bad back knows it's gonna rain, I know when the drunk is on a bender. It's a feeling…right there. She stabbed her finger against her breastbone, several times. I used ta get this feelin' several times a week when I was a girl, but I thought those times were over. I don't like havin it again."

"Maggie. I *was*…drinking. I'm sorry."

She shook her head several times as she paced about the kitchen.

"It's over now. This was the last time I swear"

"Oh," she laughed bitterly. "If only I hadda dime for every time I heard that in my life…"

"No, really. It's different this time. Something's happened. I know I can't drink anymore. I found out something today." Julian picked his head up, and something in his face made Maggie sit down.

"What?"

"That woman. It *was* me. I did it. I ran over her and just left here there." The words did not sound real to Julian as he listened to himself say them.

"Sweet Jesus," Maggie whispered. "You remember?"

"No, but someone else knows. She's known all along, she was just protecting me. She told me today."

"Was she with you when it happened?" Maggie was rubbing her hand nervously across the table.

"No. I called her after it happened. Apparently I was pretty specific."

"You don't remember calling her?"

Julian's face fell back onto his arms as he shook it several times. "How could I do that Maggie? How *could* I? What kind of person does that?"

"I don't know…" Maggie whispered, stroking his hair. Memories of her father asleep at the dinner table came back to her as she looked at Julian's dark head of hair. More than once she had come home from school to find her father passed out on the couch. She always tried to clean him up and get him to drink some coffee before her mother got home, but she wasn't always able to hide his afternoon adventures. She let Julian stay with his head down on the table for a while, then she gently but firmly tugged his hair upward so he was forced to look at her.

"It's got to be done with now, Julian, you have to see that now."

He nodded.

I'm writin' down a number for ya." She fished through the pen and paper drawer and wrote down the name: Phil, followed by a phone number. She sat back down in the chair, took Julian's hand and pressed the paper into his palm, pushing his fingers closed around it.

"With God as my witness, Julian, I have tried not to interfere and to let ya work this out on your own. God knows I love ya like ya were my own son. But I'm tellin' ya this now…and ya know I always mean what I say. If ya do this again…If ya don't call my friend Phil—I've known him a long time and he's a good man who's been where ya are now—and get yourself some help, I'll not look ya in the face again."

Julian stood and embraced her, crying into her wild red hair, but she pushed him back and wiped his face. "I mean it," she whispered. She patted him on the shoulder, causing him pain that he struggled to hide from her, and put some water in the teakettle.

"I'll make ya a cup a tea before dinner."

A while later, Julian went up to his room where he sat memorizing Phil's telephone number and rehearsing the conversation. He wondered how Maggie had ended up knowing some alcoholic guy named Phil. He wondered if she had really meant what she said. He had known her long enough to know that she was no pushover and usually stuck to her word. But could she really never speak to him again? He did not think she would abandon him, but he was not positive. Then there was Cathy. Had she meant her ultimatum? Part of him wanted to believe that she would not turn her back either, but again, he was just not sure. He had to call Phil. Maybe this guy could help him. He really wanted all of this to be over.

He was taken aback when a woman answered Phil's phone.

"Uh, yeah, is Phil there?"

"Who is calling, please?"

He was not sure what to say. He did not know much about AA except the stuff he had heard in rehab, but he hadn't really been listening then. He had looked at everyone there, judging them, never considering himself one of them. But he did know that AA was supposed to be private. How would he explain who he was? After a long pause he said only his first name, fearing a question about why he was calling, but she just said, "hang on." and he heard her yell for Phil to pick up the phone.

"Hello?" Phil's voice was both friendly and powerful.

"Uh, hi. My name is Julian. Maggie O'Neill gave me your number."

"Oh yea? How is Maggie?"

"Good. She said you would have information about joining Alcoholics Anonymous."

"Sure. Are you drinking now?"

"What?" The question surprised Julian. "No."

"Do you think you'll drink before seven tonight?"

"Seven? No, Definitely not."

"Okay. How about I pick you up around quarter of or so, and I'll take you to a meeting with me."

This sounded weird to Julian. Why would some guy he had never met want to come over and pick him up? "I can drive."

"It's no problem for me to come and get you, really."

"No, I'll meet you. Just tell me where it is."

Phil rattled off some simple directions to a church in Little City.

"You meet in a church?"

"Yeah, there's a big room downstairs."

"Oh. Okay."

"If you feel like you're going to drink before that, I want you to call me right away. And if you change mind the offer to drive you there is still open."

"Okay, thanks."

"See you later."

Julian hung up the phone thinking that Phil was kind of strange and again wondering how he knew Maggie. He fell onto his bed, feeling the movement of the water against his back. He closed his eyes for a moment when a vision of a telephone shot into his head. It was a blue payphone receiver, dangling from its silver wire. He saw himself crawling on the floor of a phone booth, trying to retrieve change that had flown out of his pockets in every direction. The receiver was swinging back and forth, bumping into whatever part of his body obstructed its path. A voice, a panicked voice was radiating out of the small holes: *"Julian, Give me the number, I'll call you back."*

He bolted upright on his bed, his heart pounding. *"Please deposit thirty-five cents."* The sound was real, piercing. He could feel the closeness of the booth suffocating him. Panic spread through him, as it had that night; his body not responding to thoughts that ran through his head...*Money. I have money. Put the money in. Where the fuck is my cell? Cathy? Cathy?*

Julian got to the church in Little City a little after six-thirty and was surprised that a number of people were already there. He was still frightened by the memory that had suddenly come to him and wanted to clear his mind. He walked slowly to the downstairs room, looking around the church to see if people saw him and knew where he was going. The large room was filled with rows of metal folding chairs and smelled like stale smoke. Two large stainless steel coffee urns sat on a long table in the corner next to a large platter that had been stacked with Oreo cookies.

"Julian?" He turned around, wondering how anyone knew who he was just by looking at him. "Phil." He extended his hand, which Julian shook. Phil was short with a ruddy complexion and curly brown hair. "Glad you made it," he said. "A lot of first timers lose their nerve and go to a bar instead." Julian was not sure if Phil had intended this to be funny, so he simply smiled politely.

"You want some coffee?" Julian nodded and they walked over to the urn where Phil filled two Styrofoam cups and handed one to him. "How are you doing?"

"I'm not quite sure at the moment."

"That's honest." Phil laughed and lightly slapped Julian on the back.

"How do you know Maggie?" Julian sipped his coffee and was surprised that it was very strong.

"I was a friend of her husband, Joe. I haven't seen Maggie in years, though. How is she?"

"She's well. Except that I guess she's worried about me."

"Then it's good that you're here." Phil used his chin to point at a row of chairs, "let's take a seat."

As the meeting started, a man stood up and introduced himself as Chris, an alcoholic. He said it like it was his last name: Chris Alcoholic. Julian jumped a bit when the entire room greeted him with a loud, "Hi Chris." He looked around, waiting for someone to laugh. It sounded like a kid's cartoon, *Hi Chris, Chris Alcoholic. Let's say it together!* He expected the room to break into song any moment. Chris picked a few others that he seemed to know and handed them sheets of paper, which they read, after receiving their big hello from the group. As they read Julian looked at the other people in the room. He had thought he would be the youngest one there, but he wasn't. There were several people there who were his age and even a few younger. There were a few very old people in their seventies or eighties, and everything in between. There was even a pregnant woman, which struck Julian as odd, though he didn't know why. When the readers were finished, Chris introduced a woman named Marci and told everyone she was celebrating her third anniversary. She walked up to the podium and introduced herself as Marci Alcoholic and was greeted as the others had been.

Marci described how she'd left her three small children unattended so she could go get drunk, and a neighbor called the police. Her kids were taken away from her by the state. "I lost my kids, but even that didn't stop me," she said flatly. Julian felt restless, feeling Phil watching him as he listened to Marci, whose kids were still in foster homes. Marci was petite with cute dimples, but Julian couldn't help but wonder what kind of woman would leave small children unattended. He also wondered what had happened to her husband.

"It took a trip to the hospital, where I almost died, for me to get sober. I had drank so much that my brain didn't work. I was too drunk to even breathe on my own. The doctors told me I would die if I kept drinking, so I came here, where I met my sponsor, Sharon. I wasn't ready, until then, to surrender to a higher power."

Julian looked around as people clapped for Marci and she hugged hers sponsor, Sharon Alcoholic. Everyone there looked nervous: chain smokers, nail biters, coffee junkies. *What the hell am I doing here?*

"So what'd you think?" Phil handed him another cup of coffee after the meeting was over.

"I don't know. It was different than I expected."

"In what way?"

"I don't know. I guess I was expecting you guys to tell me how to stop drinking."

Phil chuckled, "You thought there was a magic cure?"

"I don't know," Julian shrugged. "Maybe."

"It may not seem like it, Julian, but this is the key. Marci's story is different from yours, I'm sure. But sooner or later, and more than once, you *will* see yourself up there."

"You think so?" Julian did not think anyone had gone through what he had. "You ever have anybody who ran over a person when they were drunk?" Julian had surprised himself. He was not accustomed to spilling his guts to strangers, and he had certainly not planned to tell Phil *that*.

Phil furrowed his brow. "Not recently. But we did have a woman who killed her own daughter driving drunk."

"Oh my God!" Julian studied Phil's face to see if perhaps he was embellishing the story for impact, but decided he was not exaggerating.

"She got up there? She told that to everyone?"

"Yes, she did." Phil stared at him for a few moments. "You're not alone here, Julian. That's the point."

"What…what do I do next?"

"You don't drink, and come back tomorrow, and keep not drinking, and keep coming back."

"For how long?"

"As long as it takes. Some of us are going to the diner down the street. Why don't you come with us, meet some people."

"No, no." Julian said quickly.

"You sure?" Julian nodded and Phil shook his hand. "You call me if you get itchy. Any time."

Julian nodded again and shook Phil's hand again.

Julian got into his car, and watched Phil and some of the others walk down the street toward the diner. The street was quiet as he swung his car out of the parking lot, not realizing he had made a wrong turn until he was totally lost. After about twenty minutes he thought he must be in Orchard Park, as neatly groomed colonial homes began to replace the multi family homes of Little City. The streets here were much darker than in Little City where the streetlights were supplemented by the blazing lights of local businesses. He slowed down as he drove past glowing lights in the windows, wondering what things were going on inside the houses. Families were eating dinner, watching movies, playing board games as he and his problems passed them by. As time passed he realized that he was completely lost and perhaps he should try to back track. He pulled into a small paved road, which he thought, at first, was a dead end. But as he pulled the car forward in an attempt to turn around he noticed the stone pillars and iron gates. Across the top was a large sign: Orchard Park Memorial Gardens. The name rang through his head *Orchard Pak Memorial Gardens.* He stared at the sign, blinking as it seemed to sway. *Entombment at Orchard Pak Memorial Gardens.* He could see the words in front of him as clearly as he had seen them in the newspaper so many months ago. He shut his car off and got out.

CHAPTER 24

Jimmy left Melinda's apartment and drove to Marion Lake Park. It was after midnight, but he still did not want to go home. The air was cold, and the sleeping ducks grumbled in protest as he walked around the lake. The park was deserted, but this was not the oppressive quiet of his home. The ducks snored and occasionally flapped a wing. The owls and crickets were out in full force, and the water lapped at the shore with a soft, sucking sound. He sat for a while on a park bench, under the dim glow of a streetlight. He opened his briefcase, and took out the never graded papers, Tanya Hill's American Drama essay on *A Streetcar named Desire* still on top. There were twenty-four of them, and he graded them all. He lost himself in the words, wrote comments and grades, and piled them neatly on the bench beside him. His eyes grew achy and blurry from the dim light, and his head throbbed. He took out Veronica's picture from his briefcase and stared at it for what might have been hours. He closed his eyes and tried to picture each feature of her face, wanting to engrave them into his memory. He took the dead plant that he had stuffed into his briefcase and flung it into the lake, listening to the splash and echoes it created as he slid out of his shoes and socks and rolled up his pants. He picked up his belongings and walked toward the water, feeling the coolness of the mud sliding between his toes. He plopped down at the water's edge, dampness oozing against his buttocks. He took Tanya Hill's paper—a B+ and thumbed through the pages…*Blanche DuBois, while guilty of hurting others, is never deliberately cruel; in fact, she says, "deliberate cruelty is the one unforgivable thing…"* Jimmy peeled off the top page, then laid it on the water, watching it slowly float away, the words growing darker as the paper absorbed the water. The rest of the pages followed, then the other pages from the other students…all sent floating across the water—like stepping stones to get to the other side—until he had no more papers to set on the water. As he watched the papers floating away, he became more unaware of his surroundings. He stopped feeling the water against his ankles, the mud against his feet. He did not hear the slight wind, or the occasional snore of a duck. He had stopped hearing all noises, including the footsteps that approached him around three in the morning…

James was still at the lake as the sun came up. Some of the papers were still floating, like little sailboats, others were stuck on rocks or had accumulated in a pile along the storm drain that fed into lake. By this time the cold morning air was frosting in his breath and steaming off the sweaty film that covered his forehead and upper lip. He stared out across the water, watching it as if he was looking for something, or waiting for something to happen. His arms were wrapped around his knees, his feet hanging in the water. As he watched the sun float up out of the lake, he knew that all of his years with Veronica, all of his education, his profession, his intelligence, had not removed him from the rage that had lived inside of him most of his life. He'd managed to hide it from Veronica for a long time after his fight with Face. He'd kept it dormant, hidden from her. But now it had fully awakened. He had gone back to being what he had tried to suppress for so many years. The sky was fully light and the streetlamps had clicked off when he dug a hole in the mud next to where he sat, and buried Veronica's picture.

CHAPTER 25

After the convenience store incident, Face spent several hours in the emergency room. His boss, Gary, who was called by EMS when they responded to a call from a customer that the clerk had passed out, insisted that Face take some time off, and the emergency room doctor agreed.

"You should not be doing anything physical, even standing for long periods or lifting piles of newspapers," the doctor told him, glancing at Gary, who was standing in the corner. "It's okay," Face told him. "He knows."

"Well," the doctor continued. "You *have* to rest, period. In your weakened condition, any type of excessive stress or physical exertion can cause this type of reaction. You need to take it easy. You have an acute bronchial infection, which is working its way into your lungs. Cut back on the smoking, too. You'll need to see your regular physician tomorrow."

Face nodded, but knew he would not go, just as he had not gone to his last two appointments.

So after Gary got him home that day, he stayed in bed, played with his cats, watched every talk show on TV and read the five newspapers that Mrs. Murphy had gotten him from the newsstand. But that was enough. He had never been one to stay in bed because it made him feel worse. He felt better after a good night's sleep, and the extra drugs were kicking in, so he set out shortly after dawn to watch the lady joggers in Marion Lake Park. He got to the jogging track where it wound around the lake just after the sky had fully lightened. He saw one jogger, on the far end of the lake, doing her warm-up stretches, which he also loved to watch. He was tempted to walk up there just to watch her muscles flex beneath the clingy spandex; almost nothing was more beautiful than a woman bending forward to stretch her hamstrings, but he was too tired to walk over there. He walked over to one of the nearer benches, and noticed an unusual amount of trash floating in the water. He blamed local teenagers who sometimes partied around the lake after the movies had let out and the "teen clubs" had closed for the night. He'd once spent a week trying to catch a duck that had the plastic ring from a six-pack entwined around its foot, but he was never successful and lost track of the duck. He took his usual place on his bench, waiting for the jogger. He looked up the hill to see her sitting with her legs apart, reaching for her toes. He looked across the lake to see if the ducks were awake and foraging for food yet when he saw him. On the edge of the lake, a man was sitting, fully clothed, his pants rolled up to just below the knee with the bottom part of his legs in the water, his shoes sitting neatly alongside him with a sock balled in each heel. He was just sitting there, frosty breath smoking from his nostrils like a cartoon bull. Face looked around to see if anyone was with the man, but there was no one else in the immediate vicinity. Face approached the man slowly, thinking he must be an escaped mental patient. He gave his moustache a few bewildered strokes, and looked around again, unsure of what to do.

"Hey, fella?" Face remained at a safe distance, at the top of the small incline that led to the water, and spoke slowly. The man turned to look at him. "You need some help?"

"Oh my God!" Face catapulted down the small slope, nearly unable to stop himself from sliding into the water. "Jimmy?" He knelt down in the mud, next to his friend, looking around again, trying to figure out what was going on. "Jesus Christ." Face stripped off his jacket and draped it around Jimmy's shoulders, feeling his back muscles quivering.

"Face? It that really you?" Jimmy whispered, his voice hoarse.

"Yeah, it's me buddy. What's going on?"

"I didn't recognize you, you've aged."

"What are you doing out here, Jim?"

"Ah, Face…" Jimmy looked at him for a second, then returned to looking out across the lake. "I couldn't go home. I just couldn't. I got nothing left."

"Jimmy, I am *so sorry*." He draped his arm around his friend's shoulder, feeling the vibration of his chattering teeth. "I heard about what happened to Veronica, man, I know this has to be tough."

"My life is totally screwed up. I don't know what to do, Face. I lost myself, I'm out of control."

Face watched him for a few moments as the joggers began rounding the path and sending a few curious glances in their direction.

"Nah, you're okay. Come on." He tugged Jimmy's elbow upward but nearly fell himself. The cuffs of Jimmy's shirt were damp up to the forearm, like he'd stuck them in the lake. They walked to the bench and Face handed Jimmy his shoes. His feet were ice cold and very pale. "I live around the corner. Can you walk?"

"Yeah, I can walk." Jimmy seemed to be scanning the lake, looking for something.

"You're okay, Jimmy. You'll be okay. You just need to get warmed up."

Face was relieved that Jimmy was able to walk on his own, because he knew he would never get him back to his apartment if he had to support him. Face took his arm, and they walked slowly out of the park. Jimmy stopped every few feet or so to look back at the lake. Face held on to Jimmy's elbow, steering him back toward his apartment. Once there, Face told Jimmy to shower and gave him some of his "fat" clothes that now did not stay up. Jimmy came out and plopped himself on the couch. Face had been considering taking Jimmy to the hospital, but now he noticed his friend looked much better. Face handed him a blanket as the girls circled his legs curiously. Face picked Donna up and put her into Jimmy's lap where she soon curled into a comfortable ball and was joined by the other two.

"Who are these guys?" Jimmy asked, petting Donna's arching back.

"Best pussy in town. They're warmer than a blanket." He handed Jimmy a cup of coffee and sat down next to him. "They're they only pussies I get to see these days." Jimmy looked like he was forcing himself to smile. "Wanna talk?"

"There isn't much to tell."

"You mean sitting in mud and goose shit at the crack of dawn is typical behavior for you these days?"

"I don't have typical behavior these days. I'm not...myself."

"Clearly." Face lit a cigarette and studied the eyes he had not seen in years, yet still knew so well.

"I don't know what to do, Face. I don't even know where to begin to fix my life. After all these years, I'm right back where I started."

"Is where you started such a bad place?"

"For me it is."

"Why don't you get some sleep right now, we can talk later."

By the middle of the afternoon James was sleeping soundly for the first time in months, covered by two blankets and three cats, while Face Jenkins sat smoking, reading, and occasionally studying his friend's sleeping form, wondering what had caused his friend to end up in such a state. He knew losing Veronica had to be tough on him, but he was Jimmy "The Cat." Could his wife's death have destroyed him so fully? For a moment he felt a pang of the old jealousy when he realized he had never experienced that kind of love, and now he would never have the chance.

CHAPTER 26

Detective Steve Curtis was also awake early, but only because his sleep had been disturbed by his baby daughter, Katie. It was the first day he had been off duty in two weeks and this is not how he had hoped to wake up. His wife, Wendy had jumped out of bed quickly, as was her habit when Katie cried.

"I think she's getting spoiled, Wendy."

"She's just a baby," Wendy called from Katie's room across the hall. Steve sat up in bed, scratched himself and turned on the radio. He picked up the book he was reading and leaned against the headboard as Wendy came in carrying Katie, who was quiet but still had fresh tears on her face.

"I just think maybe if you didn't run in there so fast every time she makes a noise she might not cry so much."

"Steve!" Wendy placed Katie over her shoulder and rubbed her back. "The reason I *run* in there is so that she doesn't wake you up when you have to go to work."

"Oh." Steve closed his book and tossed it on the bed next to him. "Sorry. But look at her now, she's fine now that you're holding her."

"She's a baby. Babies need to be held. Besides, I think she's getting a tooth."

"Already?" Steve leaned up as Wendy sat on the bed next to him and tried to pry open Katie's mouth.

"I thought I felt a little bump yesterday," Wendy frowned, rubbing her finger across the top of Katie's gums. "You wanna see Daddy?" She placed Katie on Steve's bare chest where she wriggled around, grabbing hold of a fistful of chest hair. Steve screamed in pain as Wendy tried to pry her daughter's fist open.

After Katie had been fed, burped, changed, and cajoled back to sleep, Wendy crawled back into bed and cuddled under Steve's arm. They had both just dozed off when the phone on the nightstand rang. Wendy reached over and greeted the caller in a sleepy voice that Steve found quite sexy. She barely lifted her head up as she pulled the phone off her ear and held it out for Steve.

"It's Darren McPhee," she said.

It was later that morning that John Singleton placed a call to the offices where Julian McPhee had been employed, asking to speak to anyone who might have seen or talked to Julian in the last forty-eight hours. Susan directed the unusual call to Cathy Colfax, as everyone knew they were close. When Cathy sprinted out of her office a few minutes later, the place grew ominously silent. It took her only ten minutes to reach the McPhee home where John Singleton, Julian's father, and a young blonde detective were waiting.

"Darren McPhee." He stood and extended his hand as Cathy entered the living room. Cathy was taken aback by the introduction, as she had met him once or twice before. She shook his hand, noticing how the curve of the hairline on his forehead was identical to Julian's.

"Yes, we've met, Cathy Colfax. Has he called or anything?"

"No, not yet," Darren cleared his throat and sunk into the sofa.

"We didn't mean to alarm you, Ms. Colfax," interjected Singleton. "We're sure that Julian is somewhere…"

"Drinking, or passed out. You can say it. I know him well."

"We just want to find him before there's any trouble."

Cathy swallowed hard. "How can I help?"

"This is detective Curtis," Singleton indicated the tall man with the blonde crew cut. "He is a friend of the family. Nothing is official. We're just trying to figure out what's going on with Julian. You said you saw him yesterday?"

"Yes." Cathy looked around as Curtis stepped forward with an air of authority that contrasted with his age and boyish face.

Steve Curtis had only met Julian a few times over the years. The first time was as a new detective, when he was called by Darren to investigate an employee who he suspected of stealing from him. Julian had interrupted the meeting, drunk and belligerent toward his father. He'd called Curtis "Five-O," told his father he was going up to a friend's house in Vermont for a week, and belched on his way out. Curtis had been disgusted at Julian's behavior, even at the way Darren had tried to excuse it by talking about how much pressure the kid was under. Darren had also called on Steve a few times when Julian had gotten himself into trouble. Now he'd been called again, this time because Julian had not come home, and Darren feared he was driving around drunk somewhere. The Lawson incident had really scared Darren, Steve had heard it in his voice this morning.

"What time did you see him?" Curtis stepped toward Cathy. Darren sat looking out the window, his fist resting below his nose.

"Um...early in the day."

"He came over to your apartment?"

"Not exactly. I picked him up."

"When was this?" Curtis furrowed his brow.

"About five in the morning. He called me from a convenience store in Little City. He'd been in a fight and needed help, so I went there and got him."

"Was he drunk?" Darren's voice came from across the room, his face still turned to the window.

"Yes," Cathy said quietly, not sure whether to direct her answer to Darren McPhee or Steve Curtis. "But he said it was the last time. He swore he was going to change things. This time, he really sounded sincere."

"Who was he fighting with?" Curtis asked with interest, rubbing his hand across the top of his hair.

"It was a guy who worked there."

"Do you know what they fight was about?"

"Not really. It looked like he was trying to beat Julian's head in with a bat."

"A baseball bat?"

"Yeah, but small. Like the kind you get on bat day."

Darren started to laugh bitterly, "If he was drunk, he probably picked a fight with the guy, or the guy thought he was trying to rob the place or something."

Curtis proceeded without seeming to notice Darren's comments, asking Cathy where the store was located and writing her directions on a small pad.

"How long was he with you?"

"A few hours." She looked at the three men, feeling uncomfortable about what she thought must be going through their minds. "He, um, fell asleep on my couch, then when he woke up we talked for a while. Then he left."

"Did he mention any plans to go anywhere after he left you yesterday?"

"No."

"Did he say he would call you later or anything like that?"

Cathy felt a pang of guilt. "No. I wasn't expecting him to call."

"Do you know any of his other friends, anyone he might have gone off somewhere with?"

"No, no one."

"Darren?" the loud voice from upstairs was followed by a hurried set of feet pounding down the staircase. "I spoke with my friend, he said Julian was at the meetin', and he left around eight-thirty or so." The woman noticed Cathy as she stopped speaking. "Hello. I'm Maggie O'Neill."

Cathy introduced herself and smiled, but the desperation in the woman's voice frightened her. Something was wrong, she felt it.

"So we know his whereabouts until that time. That's very good news, Darren. He has not been gone that long. He'll turn up. This happens a lot with young guys, trust me. He's probably off somewhere with..." Curtis stopped short when he looked at Cathy. He patted Darren's shoulder, "He'll turn up."

"Thank you for coming over, Ms. Colfax," John Singleton was guiding her toward the door by her elbow, even though she did not want to leave. "We're sure we'll find him, there's no cause to worry. Please do us a favor and be discreet about this." Cathy nodded.

"Please call me if you think of anything," Curtis called into the foyer.

In the other room, Darren's voice was full of anger. "You should have told me, Maggie. Obviously everything was *not* just fine while I was in Boston! He was drinking again Sunday night, Maggie, you should have told me!"

"I didn't think ya needed to know, Darren. I thought he was gonna be okay this time. I sensed it. I really thought he was ready this time."

"He didn't ask *you* for that phone number did he?"

"No. I gave it to him, I *made* him take it." Maggie lowered her head. "I'm sorry, Darren."

"How could I believe such a stupid story. Why would he come and ask *you* about AA, he doesn't know your friends. How did I fall for such a stupid lie?"

"You're tellin' me I am a bad liar, Darren. I can't help it I haven't had a lot of practice."

Darren ignored her and turned back toward the window.

CHAPTER 27

By late afternoon Cathy was back in her office, having marched silently past the questioning eyes and into her office where she kept the door closed all day. She screened her calls, doodled on her legal pad, and kept looking out the window, watching all day, until the sky began to grow dark. "Where are you?" she said aloud to the window, waiting for someone to answer.

Earlier in the day, Jimmy Lawson had awoken from the first truly restful sleep he'd had in months, and was starving. He made a batch of scrambled eggs for himself and Face, feeling comfortable being back in Little City. It was where he grew up, and now it felt like it was where he belonged. The life he had worked so hard to create was now gone: no wife, no career, no book, no children. He had become what he had fought so hard to get away from. He was now the lonely, violent, promiscuous thug that his childhood had destined him to become. He felt like staying with Face for a while, hiding from his life again.

"Eat. You look like shit." He stared at his friend, the question in his face.

"I've had better days," Face shoveled a forkful into his mouth.

"Me too," Jimmy almost laughed. He took a small round ball of egg and dropped it onto the floor in front of Donna who gobbled it and licked her chops. Jane and Susie came mewing over.

"Now look what you did," Face admonished, "you got all of 'em started. They're cats, not dogs, you're not supposed to feed them from the table you idiot!"

"Ah, it's good for them…you're not eating."

Face had rummaged around on his plate a bit, making lines through the eggs with his fork.

"Face? I can't help but notice…what…what's wrong with you?"

"Take a guess," Face lit a cigarette and pushed his plate away, no longer willing to pretend to eat. "You know where I've been." Jimmy stared at Face for a moment, as if reading the words that his friend had just said in an invisible book in the air.

"Oh my god," Jimmy put down his fork as if the realization had made it suddenly too heavy to hold.

"So," Face sighed at sat back in his chair. "We know what my problem is, now what's wrong with *you*?"

"What do the doctors say?"

"They say I'm dying but I should take my medicine anyway. No matter how cranky it makes me or how limp it makes my dick."

"Wow. I don't know what to say."

"Ah," Face waved his hand through the trail of smoke. "I figure this is just payback. I should have been dead years ago, really."

"Can't they do *something* for you?"

"Don't you *read* anymore, *professor*? They don't know how to kill this shit yet. They've been close to the cure for how long now?"

"I don't know if you can call me professor anymore." Jimmy pushed his plate away.

"Why is that?" Face crossed his legs, the left one hanging completely over the right one.

"I was suspended."

"That like being fired?"

"It's a step in that direction." Jimmy looked at the bones protruding from Face's knees.

"What did you do?"

"Well, for one thing I fucked a student."

Face's eyebrows shot up and he leaned forward, "I'm listening."

"I did some other things too. Missed class, not prepared, drawing weird shit on student papers…"

"What the hell is wrong with you, Jimmy?"

"I don't know," he zoned out for a moment, having been suddenly overcome by a thought. "I just don't know who I am anymore. It's like I made this great life with Veronica, but without her I can't do it anymore. I have just become shit. I've fucked myself up, and I don't know how to fix it."

"Look, man…" Face touched Jimmy's elbow. "I know how much you miss Veronica. Hell, I was half in love with her and I only met her a few times…"

Jimmy laughed. "She had that effect on people. She was just so good…I don't know why this had to happen to her. She had everything to live for, she was a good person…sometimes…I just can't stand it that this happened to her, and I want to—" Jimmy's fist was tight. And the sides of his jaws twitched as he seemed to swallow a group of words. "I am just so damn angry all the time. I just can't stand it. I snapped, Face, I really snapped this time."

"Jimmy?" Jimmy looked up at his friend's thin, pale face. "Look at me. I used to be such a hot guy, you know how it was. Now look at this mug. I used get women, any woman I wanted. Now I got nobody, and I'm going to die alone. I've never done anything admirable in my life, in fact I've done more harm than good, and nobody's gonna miss me when I'm gone, except a couple a cats. But that's the difference between me and Veronica—she was never alone, and she didn't have to suffer. She was just gone…" Face snapped his fingers for emphasis. "*I* have to suffer, and watch myself whither away, and I *deserve* it, I'm not trying to say I don't. Veronica was good, so maybe that's why she just went the way that she did. God just took her. Me…he's got an axe to grind."

"He must have one with me too." Donna jumped into Jimmy's lap and he rubbed her ears. "God must be really pissed at me. Maybe he took Veronica because *I* deserve to suffer…" His eyes became vacant for a moment as Donna began to purr loudly. "I've got a lot to apologize for," he whispered. "Things I did. Things I didn't do."

"Like what?" Face sneered.

"Your nose, for one."

"Fuck you!" The words caught in Face's throat. "I deserved it. I shit all over you. You should have done more."

"Veronica was so mad at me. She hated violence. She was into all that social work crap…how sick *are* you?"

"As sick as I look."

"Okay, they can't cure it, but can't they do *something* for you, you know, to give you more time?"

"They have, but it's been a while. My time's running out."

"It's so hard to believe that they can't help you." They sat in silence as their uneaten eggs hardened on the plates, each lost in his own thoughts about the other.

"Face?"

"Yeah?"

"What can *I* do…for you? I want to help you."

Face laughed slightly, "If I think of something, I'll let you know. What about you?"

"What about me?"

"What can *I* do for *you*?"

"You already did it, this morning."

"I'm here, pal."

"Will you stay? If I need you? I mean, be there for me, as my friend, no matter what?"

"I'm behind you, Jimmy, but what the fuck are you talking about, anyway?"

"It's a long story, and I'm not ready to go there yet."

Face nodded and dragged thoughtfully on his cigarette.

When Cathy opened her office door shortly after five, she knew something had happened. Everyone was standing around, not working, not leaving. The phone rang and nobody moved to answer it. Cathy's heart began racing as the heavy silence in the room seemed to close in on her. Everyone was just standing there, looking at her.

"Cathy," Suzanne stepped forward tentatively, her glasses swinging slightly on the chain around her neck. "We've just had some news."

"What is it?" Cathy swallowed hard and placed her hand on her throat as if she were afraid Suzanne was going to strangle her.

"It's Julian, they found him. He's dead."

The words seemed to come out of Suzanne's mouth in slow motion, her mouth contorting with each word. Cathy blinked hard, trying to rewind time. She'd braced herself to hear about another accident, Julian in the hospital, in jail, a coma, even, but not this. She had not prepared herself for this.

"No," Cathy said calmly as she backed against the wall. "It's a mistake!"

"There's no mistake."

"Julian? They're sure it's Julian?"

"Yes, Cathy." Susan tried to take her hands but Cathy swung her wrists away. 'It's true. I just spoke to a Detective Curtis."

"No. No." She slid down the wall, shaking her head. "I just saw him. I was with him yesterday. He was getting himself together. What happened? What happened to him?"

Susan bent low to look into Cathy's face. "They don't know what happened. They found him in Marion Lake."

"In the lake?" Cathy looked up. "Why?"

CHAPTER 28

When Face saw the Wednesday morning paper and the headline, *Son of Comptech pres found dead*, followed by the sub headline, *police suspect foul play*, he dropped it onto the table and looked at his friend who was asleep on his couch, with Donna curled in a ball on his chest. "Holy shit," he whispered, watching Donna's body move with each of Jimmy's breaths. He skimmed the article quickly, his heart racing faster with each word: body found yesterday afternoon, caught in the storm drain in the lake, missing since the previous evening, car and wallet missing, facial lacerations and bruised neck, police are looking at a possible carjacking or robbery. *Jesus Christ* thought Face. *The kid was murdered, in the park where Jimmy was dazed and muddy.* He pulled at his moustache as if trying to stretch the sides of it to his chin. *What have you done, Jimmy?* He watched Jimmy breathing and wondered if guilt could be hiding beneath the regular, breaths, and the deep sleep. He recalled their conversation and Jimmy's words, *no matter what.* He felt a twinge in the decade old crack in his nose, and he saw the eyes behind the fist that had smashed it. Yes, Jimmy could be violent, but was he really capable of *killing* this kid? He understood Jimmy's rage, he'd wanted to pound the kid himself. But kicking someone's ass for revenge was different from murder, but then Face had not loved Veronica. Had Jimmy loved her that much? Maybe it had been an accident, he hadn't meant to do it, but a chance encounter had been more than he could handle and Jimmy's old cat rage had taken over. *My God, Jimmy. Did you do this? Are you capable of killing?* It would certainly explain his breakdown by the lake, and his reluctance to leave Face's apartment. Face examined the photo in the paper. The kid looked much different than he had the morning in the store. In the photo he was clean-shaven, his hair was neatly combed and he had the hint of a smile in the corners of his mouth. Face shook his head, volleying between disgust that this nice-looking kid killed his friend's wife, and sadness that maybe Jimmy had taken things too far. What would become of Jimmy?

Face threw the newspaper in the garbage, and decided that this was his chance to make amends for his past betrayal of Jimmy. He would just keep him here, where nobody ever noticed anything going on with the weird skinny man on the street. It might take a day or two, but Face would come up with a way to get Jimmy out of this. A plan. They needed a plan. He would *not* let Jimmy go to jail for this. No matter how tough he was, Jimmy would never make it in prison. Besides, the kid had it coming, didn't he? He had walked away free, no penalty—until now.

The cops did not even know that he and Jimmy knew each other, so they'd never look for him here. He knew he was taking a risk by helping someone who might have committed a murder, but what could they do to him? He and Jimmy could hide here for a few days, then maybe take off to Canada or someplace where nobody knew them. They could go whale watching, something he'd always wanted to do. As Face made these plans, he forgot, for a few short minutes, that he was dying, until he happened to glance at his kitchen counter and the small pharmacy that he no longer bothered to put away. He had to help Jimmy before he died, had to get him out of this. So far it looked pretty good. No one else knew that Jimmy had been in the park that night, and really, what evidence could connect him?

"Who?" Darren asked.

"Tanya Hill." Detective Steve Curtis, now officially working on the investigation in Julian McPhee's death, tugged at the pleats in his trousers before taking a seat next to Darren on the sofa. Maggie sat on the other side of Darren, as quiet as she had ever been in her life, feeling like everything happening around her was not real. She was making a mental list of every wrong thing she had ever said to Julian, and every sin she had ever committed. She was convinced that God had taken away her husband, and now the young man she had come to love like a son, for a reason. She must have done something in her life to deserve this pain, but she couldn't think of what it could be. Also running through her head were the phone calls that Darren had to make. He had asked her to help him as he went through his telephone book, deciding who should be called first. There were also other, more gruesome details to attend to, things she remembered well from her husband's death. She glanced at Darren's profile as he searched his brain for the name Steve had mentioned. He was trying to recall every friend of Julian's that he had ever met, and trying to hold himself together.

Darren was shaking his head, "doesn't ring a bell, Steve."

Curtis directed his eyebrows at Maggie who shook her head without looking at him.

"Who is she?" Darren asked.

"We're not sure. Several pieces of paper with her name on it were found in the lake, close to where Julian was found. It could be a coincidence, other papers were found elsewhere in the lake, but most were illegible."

"What type of paper was it?" Maggie asked, wondering if Phil had given Julian a paper with an emergency phone number.

"It looks like some sort of a report or essay for a class."

"That's weird," Darren said to no one in particular.

"Yeah, we thought so too, that's why we're checking it out." Curtis paused for a moment, assessing Darren's emotions. "Could Tanya Hill be a girlfriend?"

Darren shrugged. "I guess it's possible. He didn't really confide in me about that sort of thing. I don't know if he was involved with anyone." He stood up and walked over to the window. "I guess that was something I should have known, huh?"

Steve shook his head. "Don't do that to yourself, Darren." He was thinking about the fact that his own father did not even know his wife's name, or care that he had a granddaughter.

"But what about that girl who was here?" Maggie spoke up in a tired voice, "she seemed to be close to him. She was very concerned. I think she mighta been the girlfriend."

"Maybe Tanya Hill is a jealous rival?" Curtis offered the thought as it popped into his head.

"Wait a minute, Steve," Darren shifted his weight. "What are you getting at? I thought we were talking about a carjacking."

"That's our primary theory right now, but it's too soon for anything more than speculation. I just want to cover all bases."

"Do you think someone might have deliberately targeted him, that it wasn't just random?" Darren returned to the sofa and looked up at Curtis. Maggie impulsively patted his hand without looking at him.

"I'm going to be honest with you, Darren." Steve squatted in front of the couch, level with Darren's face. "It's possible that he was the intended victim, but I can't be sure. He was a big kid. I can't see someone trying to take his car without a weapon. And from the initial look, no weapon was used. But again, this is all speculation. I just want to be sure."

"Do you know…" Darren put his hand over his face for a moment.

"What, Darren, what is it?"

"Was he still alive when he…ended up in the lake?"

"We really won't know anything for sure until the autopsy is completed." Curtis stood to gather his jacket off of the chair in the corner, patting Darren on the back as he walked around the sofa. "We can't rule anything out until we get those results."

"When…" Darren cleared his throat, speaking in a hoarse whisper, "will they be done…with him?"

Curtis touched Darren's shoulder. "Probably tomorrow. I'll call you."

Curtis drove home gripping the steering wheel tighter than he normally did. A variety of murder scenarios played through his mind, none of them making absolute sense. But to him, none of this made sense at all. Darren McPhee was a good man who had lost his wife and now his son. Darren had lost what Steve's father had tossed away like garbage, and he felt that this was grossly unfair. His father was probably playing baseball with his young sons, waiting for his little wife to bring them some lemonade. And Darren, who cared for Julian so much, was now alone.

He leaned on the horn in annoyance when the car in front of him did not react to the changing light. "Move, idiot!" he yelled into the steering wheel, tightening his grip on it.

Maggie sat holding Darren's hand long after Curtis had left. Her grip was vice-like, yet comforting to him. He cried freely, watching the tears drop onto the back of Maggie's knuckles and slide down both sides of her hand. He watched them splatter against her pale skin, and felt the water pouring from his nostrils as well. They sat there for a long while, the room growing dark. It suddenly occurred to Darren that Maggie must want to move her hand away. She must want to dry it off, or scratch her nose or something, but she didn't move. She held his hand until he pulled his away to blow his nose. She spoke to him in a quiet, serious tone that was not familiar to him.

"I feel responsible Darren. It's my fault. I shoulda tole ya he was drinkin' the other night. You're his father and you had a right to know. God forgive me for keepin' it from ya."

"What do you think I could have done, Maggie? Clearly I had no control over him. This was bound to happen if he kept drinking. He was probably falling down drunk and somebody took it as a chance to get his car."

"He was tryin," Maggie cried and shook her head. "I seen him that day, he wanted ta change. I really thought he would *do* it this time. Ya know I know about this stuff. This time it didn't sound like malarkey."

"Ahh," Darren waved his hand in disgust. "He tried so many times, he said that so many times. He just couldn't get out of it. He wasn't strong enough to help himself. He had it too easy. I spoiled him too much, especially after Mary died. I made him weak."

"You're not God, Darren. You're not given a lump of clay ta shape. Some things are out of a father's control."

"That's for sure. But I don't know. I should have forced him to stay in rehab."

"And how could you have done that? He was a grown man."

"You know," Darren stood and walked to the window, as if waiting for an arrival. "I've pictured his death in my mind so many times when he was out drinking and I was sitting home waiting for the phone to ring. I played that call in my head so many times. When that woman was killed, I felt like I had written the script and was watching a movie of it. I pictured him in the morgue so many times, but it was so different, there was never that sense of finality. I guess I knew in the back of my mind that he would get home soon. But that's not going to happen now." He moved away from the window, as if he could not bear to look at the driveway any longer. "You know, for a long time I figured he would die in an accident or choke on his own vomit, but I never pictured him dead like this, in the lake. Someone killing him for that stupid car. I wish I had never given it to him. Mary would never have let me give him a new car."

"We don't know what happened yet, Darren."

"True," he turned to face her, leaning his back against the windowsill. "We don't even know if he'd been out drinking. Maybe he wasn't. You don't have to be drunk to be carjacked. Maybe we're assuming too much."

"I don't know Darren. I'm tryin' ta have faith that he didn't bring this on himself, but I just got my feelin', ya know?" She patted her chest. "I just got my feelin', God forgive me." She crossed herself.

CHAPTER 29

Curtis rang the doorbell of a small-off campus apartment near Collins University. The building was old with slightly peeling paint and too-sheer curtains on the windows. He was leaning over the iron railing on the front porch to try and peek through the curtains when the door opened. A young woman in a blue bathrobe glared at him in annoyance.

"Can I help you?" she put a hand on her hip and gripped the door handle, ready to slam it in his face if he tried to sell her something. Her brown hair was piled haphazardly on top of her head and her make-up free face had a puffy, reddish tint.

"Tanya Hill?"

"Yes?" her voice pitched with a sudden concern. He flashed his badge and watched her mouth drop open as he introduced himself and requested a few minutes to ask her some questions. She looked apprehensive, like she was afraid to talk to him, but afraid to say no. She tightened the sash on her robe and reluctantly stepped away from the door.

The apartment was small and cluttered with what looked like mostly second hand furniture. A pillow and blanket were rumpled on the worn orange and brown tweed sofa and the coffee table was strewn with balled up tissues and a bottle of Nyquil.

"You sick?"

"Yeah. I've had the flu for a week."

"Oh, sorry to disturb you," he said as his eyes scanned the rest of the room. There were books piled haphazardly in the bookcase in the corner, and a few stuffed animals were piled top of it, along with a few framed photographs.

"Can I ask what this is about?" she plopped onto the sofa and wiped her nose, balling the soiled tissue into her fist.

Curtis took a seat in a black imitation leather chair opposite the sofa. It made an offensive noise as he sat, but Tanya seemed not to hear it. "I'm investigating the death of Julian McPhee."

"Who?" she balled up her most recent tissue and added it to the pile.

"Julian McPhee."

"Who is he?"

"You don't know him?"

"No. Does he go to school here?"

Curtis shook his head and took a large Ziploc bag from his pocket. He handed it to Tanya who tried to open it until he admonished her to look at the contents without taking it out. She nodded and held the bag out in front of her face, squinting and wiping her nose again.

"This is my American Lit paper," her voice crackled with confusion. "Why do you have my paper? Where did you get it?"

"Marion Lake."

"What?" She tugged at the sash on her robe again and tucked her feet underneath her.

"Do you have any idea how your paper might have ended up in Marion Lake?"

"I don't have a clue!" Tanya sneezed and exhaled heavily as Curtis watched her face, which first showed genuine bewilderment, followed by a slow realization that slid across her face. "Oh my God. What a psycho! What a freakin' psycho!" she shook her head several times and repeated "freakin' psycho."

"Excuse me?"

"That psycho professor Lawson! He must've thrown my paper in the lake! He *must* have."

"Your professor? Why would he throw your paper in the lake?"

"Oh, I know exactly why! I filed a complaint about him so he threw my damn paper in the lake!"

"What was your complaint about?" Curtis took back the bag that Tanya handed him.

"He's nuts," she held her palms out. "He has just gone completely crazy. Ever since his wife died he's been…"

"Wait a minute!" Curtis held his hand up as a scenario began creeping into his brain. *"Professor Lawson?* Professor James Lawson? Is that who your teacher is?"

Tanya nodded vigorously. "Yeah, that's him. *Psycho.*"

"Oh my God!" Curtis rubbed the top of his crew cut. "His wife, was her name Veronica Lawson?"

"I don't know," Tanya screeched. "How the hell should I know what his wife's name was?"

Curtis left a bewildered Tanya Hill with her pile of tissues and got out of there. Of course! He felt like slapping himself in the head. Jimmy Lawson. Julian had walked out of court a free man after running over his wife while drunk. That was certainly quite a motive. It could be just a coincidence, but somehow he did not think so. He wondered what he might have done to Julian if he had killed Wendy. He tried not to think about it, but he knew what *he* would want to do. And *he* had gun on his hip.

Face left Jimmy sleeping in his apartment, no longer sleeping peacefully, but in a sweaty dream. He walked toward the park to see if he could hear anything. He felt like shit, and he'd coughed blood last night. His chest felt heavy, like his lungs were full of cement. He sat on the bench on the north side, looking at the ropes of police tapes in various spots. Some cops were still there, skimming the lake, poking through the grass. The atmosphere seemed intense, like they were looking for something specific. He thought about the plan that he had come up with during the sleepless hours of last night, and realized it had been forming in his mind for a while, and had grown fully when he saw the spray of blood on the tissue last night. The last thing he needed for his plan had landed in his lap the morning he found Jimmy in shock by the lake. He knew the whole Jimmy thing was fate showing him that the time had come to put the plan into action. He knew it was time, and the fact that this was also his chance to make amends to Jimmy was a bonus. Something good had to come from his sorry life, but it was now or never. Jimmy would be okay. He slipped his hand inside the pocket of his jacket, fingering the fifty dollars in cash that he'd just withdrawn from the ATM when a uniformed officer asked him what he was doing there.

"I'm not doing anything, just sitting here," he said without looking at the officer.

"Sitting? Why?"

"Is there something wrong, officer? Am I committing a crime?"

"No, I would just like to know why you are sitting here."

"Because I'm dying. It's all I *can* do." The young officer was taken aback and looked him up and down, apparently deciding from his appearance that he was not exaggerating his condition.

"Look I'm sorry. I'm just doing my job."

Face nodded his forgiveness.

"Do you come here often?"

"Are you trying to pick me up?"

"Sir, can you give me a break please. We had a possible homicide in the park."

"I know, it was in the papers. Such a shame." He saw some officers digging in the mud, next to the spot where he'd found Jimmy sitting.

"Yeah. Young kid."

"Do you know what happened yet? Face held his breath, wondering if Jimmy had left footprints, or if fingerprints could be found in mud.

"Do you come here everyday?"

"Just about. I like it here early in the morning."

"Did you notice anything unusual yesterday or the day before?"

"Not a thing." Face lit a cigarette and touched the money again. The digging officer motioned for another officer to come over, and he slipped a rubber glove onto his hand. The other officer had a big tweezers-like instrument, and he pulled a framed photograph from out of the mud. Face felt a tightening in his chest, as he leaned forward a bit, trying to see what the officers had found.

"Yo, Starskey, I think Hutch has found something over there," he told the officer. The officer turned around quickly and peered over his shoulder. He pulled a business card from his pocket.

"This is the detective in charge of the case." He handed the card to Face. The name STEVE CURTIS was printed in blue across the center. "If you think of anything you can give him a call, okay? Any time, just leave a message."

"Absolutely, sir. I want this bastard put away. I want to be able to feel safe in my park again." Face giggled to himself, enjoying his performance.

The officer thanked Face for his help and went to the edge of the lake.

Face dragged himself off the bench and walked to the bus stop, where ten minutes later he boarded a bus he had not been on in years.

There was no answer when detective Curtis and two uniformed officers rang the doorbell at the home of Professor James Lawson in Orchard Park. Curtis noticed three untouched newspapers and an overflowing mailbox.

"Looks like someone's on vacation," he said to his uniformed bookends. He strolled around the property, climbing through the shrubs to peek into the windows. Nothing seemed out of order. He directed the uniforms to ask around the neighborhood as he wandered back toward the garage. The flower gardens by the back patio were overrun with weeds, the flowers dry and dead. Curtis had felt an obligation to call Darren, as he had promised to keep him fully apprised of all aspects of the investigation. Darren's voice was full of concern, and he reminded Curtis that the charges against Julian had been dropped in the case of Veronica Lawson's death.

"I know," Curtis had said. "That's what concerns me."

Could this be revenge? Curtis pondered the thought as he wandered around the Lawson's backyard. A literature professor hardly seemed the type, but Curtis knew the anger that could erupt when someone felt that the person who'd hurt their loved one was getting off easy. He'd seen it before. He'd even been in a courtroom eight years earlier when a distraught father tried to shoot the man who'd just been acquitted of raping and strangling his fourteen-year-old daughter. The irony was that the father went to prison, and the rapist, whom police agreed was likely guilty despite the jury decision, was free. He poked his head around some bushes, not really expecting to find anything, wondering if he even *wanted* to find anything. As fond as he was of Darren, Curtis thought of Julian McPhee as a punk. He wondered again what he himself might do if he'd been in James Lawson's shoes. Lawson could possibly get life. Did he deserve that? He kind of already had a life sentence, didn't he?

One of the uniforms returned, interrupting Curtis's thoughts, saying that no one had seen Lawson for several days, and a neighbor had positively identified the photograph dug up by the lake as the late Veronica Lawson. Curtis phoned the station to say that Professor James Lawson was wanted for questioning and then he left to visit Darren.

CHAPTER 30

Jimmy was gone when Face returned from his bus trip. Jimmy's first thoughts of the morning had been that he should stop hiding. He was afraid to leave Face's apartment, but his mission now was to help his friend. He had some research to do, and calls to make to various clinics. He knew some people in the science department of the university who might be able to direct him to some experimental drug, some study that could be the cure. He was desperate to buy Face more time. If his own life as he knew it was over, so be it. He would deal with that if he had to, but right now Face was his concern. So he scribbled a short note: *I have to check out a few things, gone home. I'll be back later—JL*

Face was shocked to find the note; he was convinced that this apartment was where nobody would ever find Jimmy. He sat at the table for a moment, feeling slightly dizzy and wondering if he should give up the plan. Maybe Jimmy wasn't a suspect at all. But what the hell was he doing? He should be here, laying low. He sat breathing heavily for a few moments, but then got up; he had things to do. He took two pet carriers from the closet and gathered up the cats, who screeched in protest as he put them in the carriers. Donna had one to herself while Jane and Susie had to share. He went into his bedroom and took a small package from his jacket pocket and buried it deep inside in his sock drawer, then called a cab.

He told the cab to wait outside the veterinary clinic, then lugged the carriers inside and heaved them onto the countertop.

"Good Morning," a perky young girl behind the counter picked her head up, "can I help you?"

"Randy Jenkins. I called this morning, for boarding."

"Oh, yes, right." She rummaged around the counter and found a piece of paper on a clipboard and pen. "Fill this out please."

Face scribbled details about shots, eating habits and other vital information. Then he opened the cage containing Jane and Susie and patted their heads, "no fighting, you two." He scratched each one behind the ears until they purred, then he closed the cage. He pulled Donna out of her carrier for a moment and held her up to his face. "You behave yourself." He kissed the top of her head and put her back in the carrier. "Can they be kept together please?"

"Oh sure, Mr. Jenkins." Little Miss Perky waved at him as she picked up the cages, not seeming to notice how heavy they were. "Don't you worry, we'll take good care of them. They'll be perfectly fine."

"I know they will," he said quietly. She walked through a door and put the cages down. Face took a piece of paper from his back pocket and handed it to her when she returned.

"Listen, a friend of mine is going to pick them up for me a week from Saturday."

"Okay, that's fine," she smiled. "I'll just need his name..."

"It's all right here for you," he handed her the paper. "Would you do me a favor, sweetheart?"

"Sure," she leaned closer, as if he was about to tell her a secret.

"Would you call him? If he forgets? He might forget, he's busy."

"Not a problem, Mr. Jenkins. Don't you worry about a thing." She smiled at him again in that cute and perky way. He extended his hand to her, and when she shook it, he drew her hand to his mouth and kissed it. "Thank you, sweetheart."

"Okay," she blushed. "Bye."

On the way home, Face had the cab driver stop at a small liquor store where a dark haired Spanish-speaking girl with large breasts happily sold him a small bottle of Jack Daniel's. He gave the cab driver a generous tip and mockingly greeted the toothless pumpkin wreath that decorated the downstairs door. He bounded up the stairs, but was breathless halfway up. He sat at his kitchen table, exhausted, waiting to hear padded feet and feel soft fur against his ankles. He listened to the quiet of the house for a while, afraid of it. He imagined what it might be like for Jimmy, waiting to hear the shower turn off, or her heels on the floor, or her sneezing or cursing under her breath when she stubbed her toe, and hearing nothing. He noticed the light blinking on his answering machine, which did not happen often, and he ran through a mental list of bills he might have forgotten to pay before he pressed the button:

"Face, it's me, Jimmy. I'm okay. I'm at the police station. I can't go into details now, I'll explain later. I just didn't want you to worry. I'll be in touch later."

Face whistled and opened his bottle of JD. He was surprised at how quickly the police had found Jimmy. He took a swig from the bottle and cringed a bit as he felt it burn down the length of his throat. It had been years, but he had not forgotten. He sat back and closed his eyes for a moment, enjoying the mellow tingle that spread through his veins after each sip. He drank a toast to Nurse Samantha and another to his favorite lady jogger in the park, his cats, and Angela. Lovely Angela. After he had toasted all that was important to him, he took a pad from the kitchen drawer, and dug the newspaper out of its hiding place in the trash. He re-read the article about Julian's death, making a note of his injuries, then began to scrawl a letter. The plan was in action.

The coroner's office had completed the autopsy on Julian by late Thursday morning and released his body to his father who had it sent to the funeral home. He followed the van in his car, even though people at both the morgue and funeral home told him this was not necessary. He drove behind the van, imagining his son's body in the back, wrapped in a black bag. He wondered what thoughts went through the driver's mind as he drove bodies from one place to another. Did he sing along with the radio? Did he curse at drivers who cut him off? Did he ever get a ticket for making an illegal turn? These thoughts disturbed Darren, made him question his sanity. Why was he thinking about such nonsense? He stopped in front of the funeral home as the van pulled around the back. He thought about following, but he did not want to see the black body bag again. He sat out in front of the building for a while, looking at the lush grass and colorful flowers which seemed to flow out of the front of the building. Then he decided he could not do this alone, so he went home and asked Maggie to come with him.

Later that day, Maggie and Darren walked around the room full of coffins, searching for what they thought would suit Julian, who was to be buried next to his mother. Maggie was quiet, reliving this same moment from her husband's death. In fact, the moment was so similar that she could not breathe. But she did not want Darren to see how this disturbed her, and realized that he must be thinking similar thoughts about his wife's death. They chose a dark cherry wood lined with pale blue satin, thinking that it was what Julian would have wanted, but who ever really thought about what coffin they wanted? Who *wanted* a coffin? They sat together in a pair of elegant looking chairs in the funeral director's office. Neither of them ever saw the man's face, only the gleaming expansive of the dark mahogany desk that separated them. They chose flowers, not really caring about them, and scheduled wakes the next afternoon and evening, followed by a funeral on Saturday morning.

"It's real now isn't it?" Darren asked her on the way home. "He's really dead. It didn't seem real before, but it does now."

"It still doesn't see real to me," she whispered.

"I called everyone on the list, right?"

"Yes, I double checked it."

"Aunt Rose and her girls are flying in tomorrow."

"Will they stay at the house?"

"No, I'll put them in a hotel. I don't want anyone staying at the house."

"Okay, I'll get a car to pick them up at the airport."

"Good idea. I called that guy, the old roommate, right?"

"Yes, you did."

"We have to find something, for him to wear." Darren did not remember who had picked the dress that Mary had worn.

"I think the navy suit."

"He always looked good in that."

CHAPTER 31

After leaving Face's apartment, Jimmy had walked to the street adjacent to Marion Lake Park and found his car where he had parked it the other night. That night. He walked quickly to the car, glancing around at the police tape. A bunch of guys who looked like they could be cops did not seem to notice him as he walked by. He walked fast, keeping his head forward, afraid to see the lake. He wondered if leaving Face's apartment was such a good idea. He could have stayed there forever, sleeping on the couch, hanging out with Face. It reminded him of being young, in high school. But after seeing his friend's condition, he felt like his problems were less insurmountable than they had seemed just two days before. He didn't have to watch himself wither away. He was still alive, and he had things to live for. His life was a mess, but not yet completely beyond repair. He wrote Face a short note and decided to go home to shower and change and then go to the library and find some material on AIDS, and call his friends in the science department. Something good had to come of this whole mess, maybe he could find someone to help Face. Part of him had convinced himself that this was his sole motivation for going to his house, but he was curious as well. He wanted to see what was happening at his house.

He wished he could erase the last six months of his life, but he knew he had to just get himself together and move forward. It was over now. As he turned onto his street, he braced himself for what might be waiting. His house looked lonely with its overgrown shrubs, pile of newspapers and overflowing mailbox. He hesitated as he turned the key, almost afraid to go inside, but he knew he had to do it. His movements seemed echo a bit as he walked through the living room and into the kitchen where he rifled through the mail and listened to the twelve messages, taking a deep breath before each one. He was only listening with one ear as he sorted the mail into his and her piles, but he stopped when he heard the voice he feared:

"Mr. Lawson, my name is Steve Curtis. I am a detective with the Orchard Park Police Department. I have been trying to reach you in regard to a current investigation. I need you to call me immediately at the following number…"

Jimmy put down the mail and sat at his kitchen table, and went to the front porch and gathered the newspapers that were still sitting there. He looked through the papers over the last three days and found several articles about Julian McPhee. Dead. Found in lake. Foul play possible. Then he read the date. Marion Lake. Marion Lake the same night that he'd been there. The police wanted to talk to him. The house seemed incredibly empty as he looked at the shadow of the table leg on the floor. He breathed through his nose, trying to slow down his heartbeat as he took out his address book. He dialed the number for his lawyer, Brad Fischer.

"I'm sorry, Mr. Fischer is in a meeting. May I take a message?"

"This is Jimmy Lawson. I need to speak with Brad right away. It's an emergency."

"Can you hold for a moment, please?"

"Yes," Jimmy said through clenched teeth. Tedious music trickled from the receiver, as Jimmy stood and began pacing.

"Jimmy? It's Brad. What's going on?"

"I think I'm in trouble. Big trouble."

"What kind of trouble?"

"The police want to question me."

"About what?"

"Julian McPhee's murder."

"McPhee, isn't he the guy…"

"Yes. He's the one."

"Have you spoken to the cops?"

"No, they left me a message."

"Listen to me, Jimmy. I don't want you saying anything to them. Hang up and don't answer the phone and do not let them in your house. I'm coming over."

"Whoa! Brad, slow down." Jimmy's heart pounded. "Do you think that's necessary?"

"The guy who walked away from a manslaughter wrap for killing your wife is dead. What do you think they want to talk to you about, Jimmy?"

"Okay. You're right." Jimmy closed his eyes.

"Sit tight, don't answer the phone. I'll be right over."

Jimmy sat in the living room, peering out between the curtains at his driveway, waiting to be raided by a swat team. He saw Brad's gold BMW come bounding into the driveway, but he still jumped when the doorbell rang.

"Tell me everything," Brad was out of breath. In a way he seemed almost excited.

"I didn't *murder* that kid, Brad."

"Okay, sit down." They sat on Jimmy's couch. "Where were you on Monday night?"

"Well, Brad. That's the bad news. I was there. Marion Lake."

"Jesus," Brad whispered. "Please tell me you're making a sick joke."

"I wish I was."

Jimmy spent nearly an hour filling Brad in on the details of the past few days, and more importantly, the details of the night he had spent at Marion Lake. Brad was understandably concerned about the circumstances, but suggested they both go to the station to see where they were in the investigation.

"We have to cooperate with them, Jimmy, it's the best way."

While they waited in the hallway for detective Curtis to be free, Jimmy called Face who was not home. He left his friend a short message, afraid that he might be arrested and Face would hear about it elsewhere. Brad took three calls on his cell phone and then shut it off when it rang a fourth time. His idle hands seem to distract him so he took his pen from his pocket and clicked in nervously. The station was busy; people were bustling in and out of every door and hallway, except for the doorway next to them. It sat still, silent. Curtis was in there, talking to someone, presumably about this case, but they did not know who. They both stood when the door opened and a young woman stepped out, followed by Detective Curtis.

"Melinda!" James stepped in front of her, and she glared at him. "What are you doing here?"

"Well, *Professor Lawson*," she stressed the name, saturating it with sarcasm. "I was being interrogated about where you were on Monday night, what time you left," she put her finger against her chin in mock thought. "Oh, yeah and any violent tendencies I might have noticed about you." She stepped around him without looking at his face, rubbing her backside.

"Melinda? Wait." He took a few large steps and caught up with her, touching her elbow. "I'm sorry about everything. I really am."

She turned to look at him, her eyes examining every inch of his face as if she were looking for a particular pore. "Yeah, whatever," she mumbled. She turned to walk away and when Jimmy called her name again, she held up her hand and did not turn around.

"Shit," Jimmy whispered to himself.

Steve Curtis had watched the interaction between Melinda and James Lawson from his office doorway. Curtis sensed that Lawson's lawyer was nervous as Lawson spoke to the girl, but she had not really given them anything solid. He motioned with his head for Jimmy and Brad Fischer to come into the room, and they obeyed quietly. Curtis gave Jimmy a cup of strong black coffee that tasted like oil, and handed Brad Fischer the can of Diet Coke he had requested. They each sat in beige wooden chairs around a large table, which was full of coffee rings, pen marks and nicks.

"I suppose you know what we wanted to talk to you about?" Curtis pulled his chair forward as he sat down.

"Yes."

"The officer informed you of your rights?"

"Yes."

"You're not under arrest Mr. Lawson. You are strictly here for questioning on this matter. But we do need you to clear a few things up. I am required to inform you that we are video taping this statement."

"Okay," Jimmy glanced at Brad.

"How did you hear that Julian McPhee was dead?"

The question struck Jimmy as odd, as he retraced his steps. "I read it in the paper."

"Today's paper?"

"No, actually it was Wednesday's."

160

"So you knew he was dead on Wednesday?"

"No, actually I read that paper this morning."

"Why did you do that?"

Jimmy swallowed hard, recalling Curtis's message. "I hadn't seen the paper in a few days. I had just gotten home."

"Where had you been?"

"Staying with a friend."

"Melinda Deveraux?"

"No. I had not seen her since Monday night."

"As you know, Melinda was just here. Nice girl."

"What's your point?" Curtis was taken aback by the sudden sharpness of Jimmy's tone.

"We asked her if she's ever seen you behave violently."

Jimmy took a deep breath as if to speak, but Brad put his hand on Jimmy's shoulder.

"I'd like to see her statement," he told Curtis. Curtis handed him a legal pad on which notes were written. Brad read it swiftly, making whispering noises as his eyes moved down the page.

"She said no, Curtis. Move on."

"Okay." Curtis opened a drawer and placed several items on the table: the framed photograph of Veronica, and a pile of waterlogged papers, which had been fished out of the lake. Jimmy's mouth fell open and he looked at Brad.

"Do you recognize these items?"

"Yes."

"Do you know how they ended up in Marion Lake?"

"Yes."

"Care to explain?"

Jimmy had followed Brad's instruction and answered the questions without elaboration, but now it was becoming more difficult. He glanced at Brad who nodded.

"I threw them into the lake. Well, the picture I buried in the mud."

"Any particular reason you did this?" Curtis was writing notes on his pad, and did not look up this time.

"I had just been suspended from my job. I was kind of upset, so I threw my stuff away."

"How long did you stay in the park?" Now Curtis looked directly at him, studying his face.

"A long time. All night, actually."

"What were you doing there for all that time?"

"Thinking."

"About what?"

"Things..."

"Like your dead wife?"

Jimmy looked up. "Among other things," he said sharply.

"Maybe you were thinking about the guy who killed her."

"Maybe."

"Maybe you were thinking that he should pay for what he did."

"He did deserve to pay. But I didn't kill him."

Curtis regarded Jimmy for a moment, and his interrogation instincts almost softened as he watched Lawson's pathetic face looking at the muddy photograph on the table, but only for a moment.

"We found Julian McPhee's car." Curtis stood, now avoiding Lawson's eyes. "Do you know where it was?"

"No, I don't."

"Orchard Park Memorial Gardens." Jimmy's eyes followed Curtis as he walked around the room.

"What was he doing there?" Jimmy asked angrily.

"We think he might have been visiting your wife's grave."

Jimmy's breath was strained. "Why? Why would he do that?"

Curtis shrugged. "We thought you might know."

"How would he know where she was?" Jimmy's voice was louder now, and Curtis was looking for signs of a temper.

"It was in all the papers, James. It obviously stuck in his memory."

Jimmy sat forward, leaning his face into his hands.

"James, do you think maybe he was sorry? Maybe he *really* felt bad."

Jimmy sat back quickly, but held the words that were in his mouth when he felt Brad's hand grip his leg. He took a deep breath and composed himself.

Curtis sat down in the chair next to James and pulled it forward, leaning in close to his face.

"Did you see Julian, at the park that night?"

Brad grabbed Jimmy's leg again and cleared his throat. "I have advised my client not to answer that question," he said.

Curtis sat back, undaunted, challenging Fisher with a tiny smirk. "Maybe it was an accident. You didn't mean to do it, but you saw him in the park, started fighting. It got out of hand? I understand how that could happen, Jimmy."

Brad glared at Curtis. "Don't say a word, Jim."

Curtis sat alone in the interrogation room long after James Lawson and his attorney had left. He figured by the next day they might be ready to arrest Lawson, but something was holding him back, a sort of sympathy for Lawson. He had seen criminals in his career, and James Lawson was not the type of person he was used to sending to prison.

Things were no better at home that night, Katie screaming at least four times during the night. Wendy would jump up, wide-awake as soon as the wail began, which amazed Curtis. By the time Katie had gone back to sleep, Wendy would be like a zombie, feeling for the edge of the bed in an effort not to disturb him, not knowing he was wide awake next to her. He felt like making love to her, feeling her thin nightgown brush against him, but he was almost afraid to mention it to her.

By the time he'd finished his letter, Face was quite drunk, but not too drunk to admire the work he'd done. He felt sorry that he hadn't paid more attention in school, as he was clearly a gifted writer. Even the handwriting was a work of art. He held the pad up, admiring the delicate curves he had created. Even the spacing was perfect, every word, every letter separated by the same amount of space. After admiring his work, he went into his bedroom and dug into his sock drawer for the package he had purchased earlier. He sat on his bed, placing the letter on the pillow next to him, in plain sight. As he spread himself across the bed, next to the letter, memories of Claire, the prostitute, suddenly flooded his head. He saw the scar in the corner of her eyebrow, and the way she laughed with her mouth open, her tongue out. He saw the crusty sores on the infected tracks on her arm. He could hear the small noise she used to make as she shot up. It was a combination of a yelp and a deep sigh that Face had found wildly exciting. He began to slowly unwrap the purchase that was folded into a brown lunch bag like the ones he used to bring to school. The contents looked foreign to him, like things he had never seen before, yet he prepared it quite deftly. It was like riding a bike. He closed his eyes tightly, determined to enjoy the first one, and traced the inside of his arm, looking for the place where the scars were not so thick. He slapped at his skin a few times, feeling it bounce back beneath his fingers. His arm felt hot as the needle pinched through the old scars, and he found he minded the pinch more now. Then a mouthful of vomit erupted from his throat; he'd forgotten that part. He spit it onto the side of his bed, wiped his mouth on the shoulder of his shirt, and sat back against the pillow. The feeling was not *exactly* as he remembered, but then what ever was? He closed his eyes, seeing the back of his eyelids speckled with colors. A prickly feeling swam through the center of his skull and his blood was warm as it swam around his body, specks of the bug laughing as they chewed through his veins and escaped into his body, gnawing at him. He felt the crack in his nose widen into an earthquake fault that swallowed him up. Jimmy was there with him. Jimmy would love the plan. Fuck them all.

With a shaking hand, shot up again, then a third time.

"Fuck them all. We win." he said through the vomit that slid from the side of his mouth. He thought of Angela Pavone's toes, the most beautiful thing he had ever seen.

Darren spent the next afternoon and evening standing stoically alongside his dead son's coffin. The coffin was closed, as Julian had a black eye and bruises around his neck that were disturbing to look at. In fact, his face in the morgue had been haunting Darren since he had been required to identify it as his son's. When returned home from the evening wake he poured himself a scotch, then took a call from Steve Curtis. Steve cringed when Darren answered the phone because he realized that this was the day of Julian's wake, and he had missed it. But now at least he could tell Darren that it was over, the case was closed.

"I'm sorry to disturb you, Darren, I just have some important things to tell you. It's been a busy day."

"First of all, I got a call from a Nicolas Cole, he owns a tavern in Little City. He had Julian's wallet. Julian had left it there the night he disappeared. He didn't know what had happened to Julian or he would've called sooner, he just thought Julian would come back to get it."

"He was a regular, huh," Darren's voice was bitter.

"There's more, Darren. But if you want, it can wait. I know you've had a tough day. I probably should have waited to call."

"Tell me, Steve. It helps to know, the uncertainty hurts more." Darren walked around the house with the phone next to his ear, and ended up in Julian's room. He ran his hand over Julian's computer and across his desk.

"We got the car, too. It was parked outside a cemetery in Orchard Park."

"What cemetery?"

"It's called Orchard Park Gardens."

"Why would Julian go there?"

"Well, I don't really know, but Veronica Lawson is buried there. That's the only connection I find."

"Good God." Darren sat on Julian's bed and picked up a shirt, which was thrown across its edge and held it close to his face, smelling his son's skin within the fibers.

"Did you talk to him, *Lawson*?"

"Yes, we did. But he didn't do it."

"How do you know?"

"Someone else confessed, Darren. It's over."

Curtis had been called to an apartment in Little City in the wee hours of Friday morning to examine a note that had been left by a man who had overdosed on heroin. The landlady had found the body when she came to collect his rent check, as she did every other week. The body of a man named Randolph Jenkins was still in bed with a needle sticking from the forearm. A piece of paper rested on the pillow next to him.

"There's the note." The young uniformed officer indicated the paper, "I didn't touch it, I called you right away when I saw the reference to the McPhee case."

"Thanks, good work," Curtis smiled at the young cop who seemed annoyingly eager to please. His memory of himself as a uniform cop kept him from being impatient with him. Two men from the medical examiner's office were milling about. Curtis knew one of them quite well. Zack, a stout, bald man in his late forties had met Curtis while working on a variety of gruesome scenes as an assistant in the medical examiner's office.

"What's up Zack?" Curtis was already scanning the room with his eyes.

"Not much. How'd like this guy? He's got tracks that are older than you are."

"Very funny. Take a good picture of his face, okay?"

"Will do," Zack whistled an unrecognizable tune as he focused the camera above the dead man's neck. Curtis winced as the flash seemed to reflect off the man's open, still eyes.

Curtis walked out of the bedroom and began to look around at the contents of the small, cluttered apartment. There were newspapers everywhere; obviously Mr. Jenkins was well informed on current events. Most of the papers were bundled neatly on one of the chairs in the kitchen area, corners lined up perfectly, ready to be tied up for recycling. The coffee pot was half full and still on and a full ashtray sat on the table along with a lighter and a half empty pack. An empty bottle of Jack Daniel's was also on the table, next to the pad from which the note on the bed had been ripped. Curtis pulled out a small scrap of paper that was sticking out from behind the pad. It was a note from someone who had gone home, signed with the initials JL. Curtis also noticed a stained, folded newspaper next to the pad. He picked it up and recognized it as the first article about Julian's murder. On the countertop in the kitchen were a dozen or so prescription bottles. Curtis began looking at the bottles, not recognizing any of the names of the medications.

"What do you think, Zack?" he called into the bedroom.

"Oh, he offed himself, all right."

"Can you tell if he was ill? He's got quite a little pharmacy out here." Curtis picked up a few of the prescription bottles, rattling off the names to Zack.

"Sounds like AIDS. He looks like he was on his way out, anyway. Maybe he just couldn't take it."

"No possibility that it was accidental?"

"Nah," Zack waved to Curtis to join him near the body, where he pulled on Face's arm, stretching it out flat. "These scars, like I said, are years old. I don't think he's shot up in sometime before this."

"Did you bag the note?"

"Yeah." He picked up the note, now enclosed in plastic, and handed it to Curtis. "It's all yours."

"We're taking him out now. You need anything else?"

"No, go ahead," Curtis said, leaning against the doorframe and reading the note again.

"Zack? One more thing?"

"What's that?"

"What do you think this guy weighs?"

"Ah…Zack put his fingers around Face's wrist, lifted his shirt and looked at his ribs. "I can't be sure but I'd say about one-forty or so. I can let you know after we weigh him."

"It not important." Curtis surveyed the note again. Then he walked back out to the kitchen and played the answering machine. Jimmy Lawson's voice sounded too loud as it echoed off the walls. Zack and the other man, both in white shirts, passed by Curtis, pushing a stretcher with a black bag on it toward the door. Zack waved to Curtis before he headed out.

Curtis sat on the sofa, trying to get a feel for the dead person. He often did this in homicide investigations. He truly felt that the answers could often be found in the ordinary surroundings of the victim. It also made him think of the dead person as real. He could smell them, picture them in their own surroundings until they became more than just a body. He imagined Jenkins reading the paper, smoking, taking his pills with his coffee in the morning. He had difficulty, however, picturing this man doing what his letter had stated:

I smashed that kid in the face, choked him until he passed out, and rolled him into the filthy lake where he belongs.

Curtis read the page long note two more times, then walked back over to the kitchen table. He looked again at the folded newspaper, skimming the article about Julian's death. *The victim had facial bruises and lacerations as well as marks on his neck indicative of strangulation.* Curtis thought it odd that the note had listed the cause of the injuries in much the same way that the paper had listed them. He walked around the apartment for a while, wondering just how well this guy had known Jimmy Lawson.

CHAPTER 32

Darren curled up on Julian's bed, his designer suit and shiny shoes contrasting with his fetal position. All the details Steve had relayed to him kept playing in his mind. Julian had been the intended victim, someone was out for revenge. He had been sure it was Lawson, but now it turned out to be someone Lawson knew. A crazed heroin addict bent on revenge on his friend's behalf. Then the coward had killed himself. Darren would never get to face the man who had murdered his son. But at least it was over now. He was startled out of his thoughts by a small rapping on the doorframe.

"Darren?" Maggie's voice was hoarse. Darren sprung himself into an upright position, fisting his face free of tears. The waterbed moved beneath him.

"Maggie, I didn't hear you come in. I'm sorry."

"I...I didn't want to go home," she stepped into the room, knotting her hands like she did not know what to do with them. "I just wanted to come here." Her face was pale and tired, Darren was suddenly acutely aware of her pain.

"I know, Maggie," he shook his head several times. "This is too much to bear. It's just too much."

Maggie sat next to him, and pulled him against her breast, soothing him like a child. Darren closed his eyes tightly, feeling Maggie's despair press against him, mixing with his own. He reached around her and held Maggie against him, relating the things Curtis had told him.

"How could somebody do that to another human being, no matter what they done? Julian's was a mistake, not murder. There's a big difference."

Darren nodded his agreement, thinking about where they had found Julian's car, wondering what his son's last hour had been like.

"Why did he go there, Maggie? Why was he at the cemetery?"

"He was lookin' for peace, Darren."

"From her? From that woman?"

"Yea." Maggie put her feet up on the bed and hugged her knees. "He was askin' her forgiveness. He musta been."

"But he was convinced that he wasn't driving the car. I thought that whole thing was over. We still don't know what really happened. Julian's dead and who knows if he was the one."

"He was the one, Darren. He knew it, too. Someone tole him. He tole me the morning of the day he died. Someone he knew was protectin' him, but he was the one who did it. I think he always knew, deep down. He just couldn't deal with it."

Darren touched the back of Maggie's hair with his hand. "What have I done, Maggie? What did I do to deserve this? First Mary, now Julian? What else can happen in my life? Why did all this happen to me?"

Maggie touched Darren's cheek. "They're together now, Darren. Just keep thinkin' about that. Julian is seein' his mother." She wiped a tear from Darren's face. "Maybe she needed him, maybe she asked the Lord to bring him to her."

"She wouldn't have done that," Darren whispered.

"I don't know why, Darren. But he must be at peace now. I know he is. He is in a better place than you and I."

"Do you really believe in Heaven?"

"Of course I do," Maggie said loudly. "Don't you?"

"I don't know. I really don't know."

"Ya gotta believe, Darren." She grabbed both his hands and tugged at them. "You're puttin' a body in the ground tomorrow. But it's just a body. It's just where your son lived. You gotta believe that or ya won't be able to do it. He was a good boy, in his heart. He had some troubles, but he never intended to hurt ya, or that woman, or anyone. He's gotta be in Heaven, Darren. He never, ever woulda hurt anybody on purpose."

"But what about *her*?" Darren had moved himself to the corner of the bed, sitting cross-legged like a frightened child.

"Who?"

"Lawson. Veronica Lawson. What if she's there, with Julian?"

"If she's there, Darren, she forgives him."

"And the man who killed him? What about him?"

"I hope with all my soul that he's burnin' in hell."

Darren put his head down and wept. Maggie moved next to him and held him as he cried. "I just feel so empty. I'm nothing. All I have...it's like I sold my soul to get everything I could ever want and now I'm paying for it."

They sat together, clinging to each other and being rocked to sleep by the gentle movement of the waterbed. They dozed off after a few hours, sleeping propped together against the wall behind Julian's bed. They slept in soundless, dreamless oblivion, exhausted by the exertion of emotion.

Darren awoke before dawn. He wanted to move the arm that was stiff and bloodless under Maggie's face, but he did want to disturb her peaceful sleep. He had seen the pain on Maggie's pale face last night, and he felt she was relieved from it as she slept against his shoulder. His eyes felt sore and dry, his neck stiff. He moved his neck and Maggie stirred a bit. He watched her eyes begin to move beneath her eyelids, her lips spread slowly apart. He was suddenly struck by the smoothness of her face and could not resist the urge to touch a freckle on her cheek. He had brushed the flat part of his finger against it, softly, but to his surprise she woke up. She blinked at him several times, a question hovering in her brow. They were past the time when they should have moved apart, disentangled themselves from their sleep position, but neither of them wanted to move. Maggie patted the back of Darren's hand very softly, without saying anything. He touched her face again, with his uncovered hand, and she didn't say anything when he kissed her. Her mouth was dry, but warm and soft. It was a comfortable kiss: soft and slow with a sense of anticipation. Darren felt a longing that had been dormant for years, and his body tingled with feeling as she began to return his kiss, softly touching his tongue with her own. He stopped for a moment and looked at her eyes—stormy eyes brimming with pain and tenderness at the same time. He slid his hand to the side of her face, kissing her more hungrily and then kissed her eyelids, her chin, her hair. They slid down from against the wall, gripping each other as if afraid, the softness of the waterbed conforming to their bodies as they moved. Her name reverberated deep inside him, echoing along his ribs as he trembled above her. All of his pain pulsated through his flesh as they made love. His blood pumped, his mouth tasted her skin. He felt the softness of her hair, the heaviness of her breasts. He held her tightly, wanting her breath to be his own, her moans to be in his mouth as her knees rolled against his. He pressed himself harder against her, trying to feel each pore of her skin, visualizing the prints of each of her fingers as they slid along his back. He was able to lose himself within her. He wanted to float with her in this timeless, spaceless moment forever, not wanting the final shudder that signified the start of the inevitable, horrible day.

Maggie stood next to Darren as they lowered Julian's coffin into the ground, but she had been unable to look him in the face since that morning. After they had made love, she'd left abruptly and driven to her apartment. She ran a steaming shower and stood letting the stream of water redden her skin as she sat on the floor of the tub, crying. She thought of Joseph and the day she had buried him. He had been sick for so long that Maggie's life had revolved around cooking small, bland meals that he was unable to eat, bathing him with a sponge, doling out medication and cleaning the incisions after each surgery. She felt a sort of betrayal when Joseph died, like he died in spite of the time and energy she had put into caring for him. Rationally, she knew that this was nonsense, but that speck of anger had remained buried within her and had now begun to surface. She was angry at Julian for dying, and now she was angry at Darren for being vulnerable, but mainly she was angry at herself for losing control. She and Joseph had never had time to have children, so she thought that God had given her Julian, maybe to make up for taking Joseph away and denying her a chance to be a mother. But now he was gone, too. Killed by some low life junkie who was angry that Julian had gotten off hit-and-run charges. Her anger about Julian's death was now mixed up with her confusion about what had happened that morning. She wrapped her hands around her body, hugging herself as her thoughts moved to Darren. There had been no other man since Joseph, but all Maggie felt was ashamed. Making love with Darren had cleared her mind of all the sadness, but that was no excuse. His body had felt so good against her own, but this was no time to be ruled by desires of the flesh. She had almost forgotten what it was like to feel that close to another human being, to be stripped of every mask, every front, to be completely vulnerable. Her cheeks burned as she began to tingle with the memory of Darren's touch, so she stood and quickly turned off the shower. She sat on her bed in a robe for a long while, her wet, wavy hair dripping down her face and onto her shoulders unnoticed. She thought about what she and Darren would have to do in the next few hours, ashamed that she had forgotten the task this morning. Her life would be different from this moment forward, and she had to take control of it. She knew she had to do something. Her hand reached out for the phone next to the bed, and she dialed the number of her mother who lived in Dublin.

Later as she watched the coffin she and Darren had so carefully picked out being lowered into the ground, she was acutely aware of the proximity of Darren's hand to her own. If she swayed to the left, her knuckles would brush his, so she stood with rigid posture, afraid of any accidental contact. She felt like Aunt Rose and Julian's cousins were watching her, like they could smell what had happened between her and Darren. Their eyes seemed to be condemning her for seducing the grieving, wealthy father. Part of her wanted to take Darren's hand as she felt him begin to quiver a bit, but she was unable to move, to reach out to him. When the service was over, the funeral director invited friends and family back to the house for the customary repast, and a few people began talking to Darren. She went to the car and sat waiting, watching small groups of mourners slowly dispersing. She felt isolated from them. After all, what was she really? She was not Julian's mother, she was not even a relative. She was just a housekeeper. Now she was even worse: she was a housekeeper who had slept with her boss. As she watched them through the window of the car, she knew she had made the right decision.

Back at the house she was able to avoid Darren as she busied herself putting out the platters of food that had been delivered after she'd left that morning. She felt a slight twinge of guilt for not being there to deal with the caterer, but she had completely forgotten the arrangement when she left. Darren must have handled it fine, though, because everything had arrived on time and was correct. She watched Darren closely as he shook hands and let himself be hugged and kissed. He seemed devoid of emotion, even slightly embarrassed by the emotions of others. It struck her that the Darren she knew was quite different from the Darren that he presented to the world. To others he was the wealthy, sophisticated, successful businessman. He was the strong, serious widower who raised his young son on his own. He was a man full of grace and dignity. No one else had seen him cry over the loss of his son, or the anger that filled him at how it happened. He seemed so reserved with others. As she watched him shake hands with a young man who had known Julian in college, he looked up for a moment and caught her gaze. His eyes held hers for a second, but with an intensity that frightened her. What was he trying to convey to her with those eyes? Afraid to wonder about this, she sought out more to do, even though nothing needed to be done. She scooped up the ice bucket and went into the kitchen to fill it. As she stood by the freezer door she noticed a pair of legs in the sunroom, and wondered who might be sitting in there, all alone. She could only see the feet, which were clad in navy blue pumps and linen colored stockings. She took a few steps toward the door and leaned her head in slightly, not wanting to intrude. It was the girl, the one who had been at the house the other day. She was sitting, deep in thought, looking out at the backyard.

"Hello, you were here the other day, right?" She sat down tentatively in the chair next to the girl. "I'm Maggie."

"Yes, I remember," the girl smiled slightly, not willing to completely turn her eyes away from the yard.

"Cathy's your name, right?" The girl nodded. "What are ya doin'? Why are ya sittin' in here all alone?" Maggie patted the girl's knee.

"It's kind of silly," she chuckled to herself a bit, "but I'm trying to picture Julian playing in this yard, when he was a little boy." Cathy looked down at her hands, which were folded in her lap.

"It's not silly at all. I've done it a few times myself. I didn't know him until he was, I guess, twelve or so." Maggie sat back in her chair. "I always wondered what he looked like takin' his first step. I've tried to imagine him toddling around in those big shoes."

Cathy smiled, "we never got to talk about the kid stuff."

"What do ya mean?"

"You know, when you get to know somebody and you kind of give them your life story. Me and Julian never had a chance to do that, to tell about all the stuff that happened to us when we were kids: the broken bones, braces…mean teachers, grade school crushes, all that stuff."

Maggie nodded in a surprised way. "Yeah, you're right, life stories, I guess they're important. I never thought about it before, but ya gotta know that stuff, it's true."

"I wish I could have known Julian more…I mean I feel like I *knew* him but…I guess *completely* is the word I'm looking for. I think I knew him well, but I didn't know him *completely.*"

"I hope ya don't mind my askin' but you loved him, didn't ya?" Maggie leaned toward her a bit.

"I don't even know. I mean I never had the chance to really *be* with him, everyday, to see every part of him. You know, the good, the bad, the ugly, that sort of thing. I don't know if you can truly love someone without knowing all sides of them. I never knew Julian when he was cranky, or had a cold. I never even saw him get a pimple. I never got to buy him a birthday present or even a card. We never had the *little* moments. We just had bad things getting in the way all the time."

Maggie watched the girl's face intently as a realization came over her. "It was you, wasn't it?"

"What? What was me?" Cathy was startled by Maggie's sudden volume.

"You're the one who tole him he killed that woman, aren't ya?" she lowered her voice at the last part.

"Yeah, it was me." Cathy lowered her head and swallowed hard. "But now I feel like I shouldn't have told him. He died feeling horrible about himself, and I can't help but feel like I could have prevented that."

"Oh, my dear, you can't take the blame for that, I'm afraid. He felt horrible about himself anyway. It's better he knew the truth since he was going to die. At least he had a chance to ask for forgiveness."

"I should have done *something,*" Cathy breathed heavily. "Detective Curtis showed me a picture of the guy who killed him, and it's the same guy he was in a fight with. Remember I told you guys when he was missing, that I picked him up after a fight? The guy who killed him was that guy. I should have done something."

Maggie patted her knee again.

"I should have called the police, but I was afraid Julian would get arrested, he was driving around drunk. But if he'd been in jail, maybe he'd still be alive. Or the guy, he really should have been in jail for assault, but because of me he was free, free to kill Julian."

"Ya can't go around if-ing yourself to death," Maggie touched her shoulder. "I believe everything happens for a reason, reasons we can't understand. Julian had his short life, it had some purpose, we just don't know what it was yet. Maybe we'll never know, maybe it's not our place to know."

"Thank you, Maggie, for talking to me about him. My friends never understood."

"I'm sorry that ya didn't have a chance to really be in a relationship with him. I think you woulda done him some good."

"I tried, Maggie, I really tried."

"We all did, but he just wasn't ready."

"Thanks," Cathy squeezed Maggie's hand.

"Why don't you go mingle with some of the people out in the living room, maybe you'll feel better."

"Nah," Cathy sat back further in her chair. "I like it here."

Maggie smiled at her, and they both looked out into the yard.

By mid-afternoon the guests had retreated and Darren had left to drive Aunt Rose and her daughters to the airport. Maggie buzzed about the kitchen, feeling obligated to have the house in good order before she left. She wrapped the leftover food in portion-sized packets that Darren could easily heat in the microwave. She washed all the counter tops, made a list of telephone numbers that Darren would need: cleaning service, landscaper, pharmacy. She added some helpful hints: garbage Wednesday and Friday, drycleaner open late on Mondays, Field's supermarket would deliver groceries, the date the heath club membership had to be renewed. She was anxious to leave before Darren returned, but she could not resist visiting Julian's room before she left.

The door creaked slightly as she pushed it open, making her heart race. The bed still looked rumpled in the spot where she and Darren had made love. Her eyes avoided looking there as she tugged the comforter into place, smoothing it with her open palm. She straightened some things on his desk: disks, pencils, a few pieces of mail, some old magazines and a pocket dictionary. His desk seemed sadly empty—no coffee rings or love letters or framed photographs of friends. She opened each drawer only to find the contents even more sadly unremarkable. A few pages of old newspapers—classifieds—sat folded in the top drawer, blue pen circling some job ads, a few doodles in the corners. The address book was neatly organized, all names and numbers written with the same pen, something Maggie had never been able to accomplish. At the bottom of the drawer she found a yellowed newspaper clipping of his mother's obituary, which she read twice. In the side drawer there were a few trinkets from college and high school like yearbooks, old report cards and certificates of participation. She pulled out one certificate for participation on the seventh grade soccer team. It was folded around a photograph of a thirteen-year-old Julian happily bouncing a soccer ball off his knee. Maggie put the photo in her pocket, closed all of his drawers, and sat touching the keys on his computer keyboard. She wondered what letter he had touched last, what were the last words he had typed? She hung a shirt that had been on the back of his chair in the closet, sliding the hangers down the pole, imagining a time when he had worn each of the shirts that hung there: the red sweater last Christmas, the blue t-shirt when he played in a company softball game, the striped button down when they'd gone out to dinner on her birthday. She turned on his television, just to see what channel he had last watched, and took a compact disc out of his stereo and returned it to its case. She sat on the bed for a few moments before she returned to the kitchen, where she heard Darren come in.

She stood waiting, listening to the movement of his feet from the front door, the sound of him hanging up his coat and putting his keys in their usual place in the marble dish in the foyer. The shadow of his legs approaching reached her eyes first as she watched the floor, waiting to see his feet.

"Hi," he said with uncertainty, leaning his shoulder against the kitchen doorway.

"Did ya get Aunt Rose and the girls off alright?"

"Yes." He sat down at the table.

"The service was just lovely this mornin', don't ya think?"

"Yeah, I guess so," he said quietly.

"Who was that nice young man, with the dark hair and the earring?"

"He was Julian's roommate in college." Darren watched Maggie buzz around the kitchen, wiping, fixing, taking things out and putting things back. He knew that in reality she was doing nothing.

"Maggie, I think we need to talk."

"You're right." She stopped moving around the room and sat across from him, folding her hands in a business-like way. She felt drops of sweat sliding down between her breasts and goose bumps lined her skin. Darren had noticed the list on the table and was reading it.

"What's this?" His face was pinched, his voice raised.

"I'm goin' away, Darren."

"What? Where?"

"Well, Darren. I don't wanta leave a mess behind, so I made ya some lists and stuff that ya might need."

"What are you talking about, what mess?"

"I'm leavin', Darren."

"What? What do you mean, where are you going?"

"Home, to Ireland. I spoke to my mum this mornin'."

"Oh God, Maggie, is she ill?" He impulsively reached toward her hand, but she began fixing the cloth placemat to avoid his touch.

"No," she looked up to face him. "I'm not leavin' to go take care of anybody. My mum's perfectly well. You might think that's all I do is go around takin' care of people, but this is about me. I just need...to go."

"Okay, okay." Darren nodded and then rested his intertwined fingers against his lips. "How long will you be gone?"

"I..." she stood and turned toward the sink, looking into the yard. "I'm not comin' back."

"Ever? You're not ever coming back?"

She stood by the sink and shook her head. Darren closed his eyes for a moment as if trying not to comprehend her words. He recalled the feel of her skin as he pressed his forehead against his tightly intertwined hands.

"Why, Maggie?" His voice was so faint that at first she was not sure he had spoken, but when she turned around it was clear that he was waiting for her to answer.

"I'm not gettin' any younger, Darren. It's about time I started findin' my own life, and stopped tryin' to be someplace where I got no business bein'."

"What are you talking about? *This* is your life."

"What, Darren? What is my life? Being a substitute wife? A stand-in mother? Julian's gone now, you're a grown man, you don't need me."

"No," he whispered without looking up. "Please, no." His voice was thick and strained. Maggie gripped the edges of the sink. She pressed her lips together tightly as if trying to hold in any words that might escape.

"Look, I know what this is about. I know why you're angry. I'm sorry. I didn't mean to take advantage of you, I should not have let myself get out of control like that." He walked over to the sink and placed his hands on her shoulders. She turned and looked up at him, touching his cheek.

"You're wrong, mister. I took advantage of you. You were hurt, and grievin' and *I* shouldn't a let it happen. You just lost your son; naturally you were all emotional and mixed up. I shouldn'ta even come back here. I had no business bein' here. Who do I think I am?"

"Don't kid yourself, Maggie. I knew exactly what I was doing, and you are not a *substitute* anything!"

She turned away again, walking into the doorway of the sunroom.

"Julian was like a son to you." Darren continued, following her. "You're hurting too. You loved him, but I never let you fall apart. I always look to you to be strong. I never considered your pain. I'm always too wrapped up in my own pain to worry about anyone else. I see it now. I've been unfair to you. I've expected you to be everything, except a true partner."

"So what was that this mornin'? Some kinda employee bonus?" she spun to face him angrily.

"No, no, no." Darren grabbed her hands and held them tightly. "It was me acknowledging what I've been ignoring for a long time. You have meant so much to me, Maggie, you have been my one true friend in the world. No one knows me like you do."

"Oh really? Did ya ever have a broken bone when ya were a kid?"

"What are you talking about?"

"I don't know that about ya, do I?" Maggie flicked the tears away from her eyes. "We should be ashamed of ourselves, that was no way to behave right before we're putting that boy in the ground..."

"I'm not ashamed, Maggie, and you shouldn't be either. What do you think Julian would say if he knew?"

"Oh lord…" Maggie wrenched her hands free, shaking her head.

"He'd be happy. You know he would. He would say something like, 'way to go, Dad. What took you so long?' We were feeling so many things, but all of it was real." Maggie turned away again.

"Please don't go, Maggie," he placed his palm on her back "I need you."

"I don't know, Darren. I don't think you are thinkin' clearly right now. I don't know if I am either."

"I am devastated that Julian is gone, Maggie, but I am not confused about my feelings for you. I'm certain about that. I need you in my life."

"Ah, Darren," she waved her hand without turning around. "You can find somebody to run your life for ya."

"You know that's not what I mean." He ran his hand over the top of her head, and through her hair. "I don't want you to *run* my life, I want you *in* my life. You are a huge part of my life, not just what you do, but who you are." He pulled her around by her shoulders. "I can't stand the thought of you not being here. Not talking to you, seeing you, knowing you're listening for me to walk in the door. Maggie, please. I can't even fathom the idea of being here without you. And just so you know, I broke my collarbone when I fell off a horse in the fourth grade."

He covered her mouth with his own, too frightened to hear her refusal, wanting, again, to stop time. Her mouth softened against his as she tried to imagine what changes this would bring in her life. How would her world be different with Julian gone, with herself in Darren's bed? Thoughts of this unknown world frightened her, but she was unable to resist the images of Darren's touch, of waking up next to him. She pulled away from his kiss.

"I've got to call mum," she said, shivering a bit.

CHAPTER 33

Steve Cutis had been awake all night, watching his wife Wendy sleep soundly alongside him. She was so exhausted that even when he had gotten up to feed the baby at four in the morning, she had not stirred. He sat in the living room, feeding his daughter in the rocking chair by the window, only the glow of the streetlights lighting the room. She sucked eagerly at the bottle with a funny slurping noise, her big blue eyes wide open, looking at his face. He wondered what she was thinking about him, what she saw with those bright eyes that were so much like his own. He stroked his free hand across the thin tuft of white hair that sometimes stood straight up on her head. She stopped sucking the bottle for a moment, loosening her lips into a wide smile beneath the dangling nipple. Curtis smiled back at her, locking his eyes with hers. After she had finished her bottle and spit up on the shoulder of his pajamas she fell back into a deep sleep and he put her into her crib. He showered, dressed, and left early, before Wendy woke up.

As he drove he wondered if his father had ever had a moment with him like he had just had with his daughter, a moment where you think you could never love anything that much again in your life. Of course, he must not have, or he never would have been able to leave him and his mother. He wondered if his father had bonded with his new sons, who were teenagers now, and if he was more successful at fatherhood the second time around. His thoughts moved to Darren McPhee, and what it might be like to have a father like him, a father who really cared, a father who gave his son everything he had. Steve's dad had sent money until he was eighteen, but not enough to keep Steve and his mother in their home. They had been forced to move to an apartment complex where Steve's bike was stolen the first week he was there. After he grew up and became a cop, he often entertained the strange fantasy that his father's young wife had thrown him out and he'd become destitute trying to get back East. For many years he imagined that every drunk or homeless suspect he arrested would look up into his face and recognize him as their son. He wondered what he would do if he found his father in such a state. He thought it possible that he would do nothing at all.

When he had reached the morgue, it was still too early for anyone to be working, so he parked in the lot and walked to a nearby diner to get a cup of coffee and then walked back. The building was open so he went inside and sat on one of the hard plastic chairs in the hallway.

He sipped his cup of too hot coffee and waited for Zack to get in. His lip stung a bit, so he blew across the top of the cup, which was almost too hot to hold. His body felt tired, from lack of sleep, but electrified by the small details that had pried his eyelids open every time they started to close. Something was not right here. The plastic blue chair felt hard against his back as he thought about Julian McPhee. Curtis had long ago classified Julian as a spoiled, lazy bum who had been given everything, then shit on it. While he had always been willing to come to Darren's aid, he was angry that Julian had gotten off the manslaughter charge. He thought some time in jail was just what that little punk needed. Curtis had no doubt that Julian had been driving the car, but he also knew that they never would have been able to get past reasonable doubt in a trial. He also felt sorry for James Lawson, imagining how he would feel if something like that ever happened to Wendy or Katie. He had once punched a guy who grabbed Wendy's ass at a club before they were married, and he wondered what he would be capable of doing to a punk like Julian if he hurt the woman he loved.

Steve's thoughts were disrupted by Zack's familiar whistling as he strolled down the hallway.

"Hey!" He said when he saw Curtis. "What's going on, detective?"

"Couple of questions."

"No problem. C'mon in." Zack fumbled with a large ring of keys, balancing a coffee and a little bag from the bakery as he opened the door.

"It's about that guy—the overdose, Jenkins." Curtis cringed at the formaldehyde smell that stung him despite the number of times he'd been in that room.

"Well, he's gone. The doc checked him out, and released the body day before yesterday."

"That was quick."

"Yeah. Pretty straightforward stuff."

"They found a relative?" Curtis wondered suddenly.

"No, all dead."

"Who took the body?"

"Lemme look," Zack yanked open a file cabinet and pulled out a manila folder with a blue label on it. "A James Lawson."

"Holy shit," Curtis said without intending to.

"What?" Zack had removed a lab coat from the closet and was buttoning it over his navy blue chinos and plaid shirt.

"Nothing. Never mind. What did the doc say about Jenkins's physical condition?"

"Advanced AIDS related pneumonia. Perforated ulcer," he read from the file. "The guy was in rough shape, Steve. Didn't have long. I saw his lungs, man, they were like fly paper—all kinds of shit stuck to 'em. I figure he was at least three packs a day, along with the drugs."

"Thanks for ruining my breakfast."

Zack held up his coffee cup in a mock toast.

"Do you remember the *kid*, the floater from last week?"

"Yeah, McPhee. Young kid. In fact, I was going to call you this morning. We just got the final report from the autopsy late yesterday."

"Good," Curtis said. "Maybe it'll clear up a few things. What was his general condition like, before death?

Zack returned to the files, pulling another folder out. "Body of twenty-three-year-old male," he read to himself, his finger following the words. "Scar on left knee...oh here's what you want. Toxicology report," Zack whistled. "Negative on narcotics, but 2.5 on the booze"

"Christ!"

"Yeah, I'd say our friend was more than a few sheets to the wind, but he had water in his lungs which means he was alive when he went into the lake. The bruises around his neck were consistent with strangulation, but it looks like whoever started it, didn't finish the job. He could have been unconscious, though, so the perp might have thought he was dead and then shoved him in the lake."

"Interesting," Curtis frowned and made some notes. "Even if it didn't kill him, the force around his throat had to be pretty strong to make those bruises, is that what you're saying?"

"Basically." Zack had pulled up a stool and taken his jelly doughnut out of the bag.

"What was his height and weight?"

"6 feet 2, one eighty seven."

"Pretty big kid." Curtis opened his briefcase and removed the plastic encased note found next to Face's body. "Let me ask you something, Zack." He held up the note. "Do you think its possible that Mr. Jenkins, the overdose, who was four inches shorter and forty some pounds lighter, and walking around with AIDS related pneumonia, could, and I quote, *'smash that kid in the face, choke him, and shove him into the filthy lake where he belongs?'"*

Zack laughed, licking powdered sugar off his fingers. "Not without help."

"We can totally rule out accidental death, right? He couldn't have fallen at the bank of the lake, right? It's mostly mud. He wouldn't have gotten bruises from the mud."

Zack wiped his hand with a napkin and took some photographs from the file. He showed Curtis a photo, a close-up of Julian's neck. "What's that look like to you?"

Curtis sighed. His neck had finger shaped purple marks on each side. "Looks like someone was choking him. But even though McPhee was that drunk, I don't think it could have been Jenkins."

"You're the detective."

"Can I see the other pictures?"

"You sure you want to?"

"Come on, Zack. It's not like I've never seen a dead body before."

"You ever see a picture of a two day floater? They ain't pretty."

"I hear you, I can handle it."

But looking at the photos of Julian's face had been a mistake. His one eye was swollen and bruised, but both eyes were wide open, as was his mouth. There was mud on his teeth and on the sides of his lips. The skin on his face looked like paper. Curtis felt nauseous, yet glued to the photo. "Why is his mouth open?"

"My guess is he was gasping for air or screaming when he died."

"Jesus," Curtis whispered. He handed the photo back to Zack who looked at it like it was a postcard.

"I thought this was all a done deal or I know the doc woulda kept Jenkins another day or two."

"It is, officially, but I'm not convinced. Thanks for your help."

"See ya." Zack took a bite of his doughnut, some jelly leaking out the side.

"I don't know how the hell you can eat that shit in here." Curtis shook his head as he walked out.

Curtis sat in the parking lot for some time, watching his breath that was slightly frosty now that the weather had grown colder. He thought about Darren McPhee, who didn't deserve the pain, and James Lawson who didn't deserve the pain he was in either, and the kid in the middle who caused it all and left a mess behind. *He died gasping for air.* The image kept flashing into his mind and he wished he had never looked at the picture. Part of him wanted to forget the entire matter, to let Jenkins go down in history as a murderer, to let Darren get on with his life. But the other part of him, the detective, knew that something didn't add up. Did Lawson help Jenkins and then let Jenkins take the blame? Was the suicide part of the plan from the beginning? It seemed somehow easier to think that Julian fell into the water unconscious and just never came up. It was somehow nicer to picture him peacefully floating under the surface than spitting out mud and swallowing lake water. What would finding out do to Darren? *He died gasping for air...*or screaming.

CHAPTER 34

The body of Randolph Jenkins was cremated following a small service, which was attended by Jimmy Lawson, Mrs. Murphy, and a young blonde nurse named Samantha something. Jimmy thought of Veronica's funeral, how crowded it had been. She had relatives, friends, colleagues, acquaintances. Face had none of these. He imagined that Julian McPhee's funeral had also been crowded with friends of his father and friends from school. How did this happen? How had such a good looking, funny, intelligent, caring man ended up alone? He wondered if Face had planned the suicide before the morning he found Jimmy at the lake, or if he'd decided to do it after Jimmy had said he was at the police station. Or maybe suicide had been in the cards all along, and the note was just added for Jimmy's sake. He could not be sure. What made Face want to help him after all the years that had passed? He had thrown away his name, his reputation as a good man to save Jimmy. Why? Jimmy thought about a time when they were about to graduate from high school and they stayed up all night drinking beer on Face's front porch while his parents were in Atlantic City for the weekend.

"I can't wait to get out of this place," Jimmy had said.

"Really?" Face was surprised. "Why?"

"Come on! You actually like this hole?"

"It's not so bad Jimmy, it's our home."

"It's not my home for long. I am leaving and I won't look back. I am not going to end up living across the street from my parents."

"You could do worse, you know." Face had a small stone in his hand and was rubbing it against the cement steps of the porch.

"Come on, Face. You really want to sit here the rest of your life watching your dad use your mom as a punching bag."

"Shut the fuck up. What do you know about it?"

"I know I wouldn't be able to stand it."

"No? But you can stand your dad screwing every piece of ass he can find?"

Jimmy drank his beer quietly. "I didn't know people knew about that."

"Everybody knows, Jimmy. Everybody knows everything around here." The rock had worn down into a tiny nub.

"See what I mean? I don't want to stay here and become like all of these people. I'm going to make a better life for myself. I want a yard with kids and dogs, and a nice green lawn, a garden, a two-car garage."

"I don't know. It's going to be weird, not being here, where everyone knows everyone else. People here look out for each other, you know."

"How do you know it won't be the same at school?"

"I won't know anyone. There's no history."

"Yeah, no Angela, is more like it." Jimmy had slapped him on the arm, the young, strong, arm that he once had.

"Don't remind me," Face had sighed. "I almost don't want to go anywhere 'cause of her."

"She's going, Face. She won't be here either." He sucked the last bit of beer from the can and then crushed it beneath the heel of his sneaker.

"I wish things didn't have to change. I want to be young forever. I don't want to work everyday for the rest of my life and go on vacation once a year."

"What do you want to do?"

"I don't fuckin' know!" Face had laughed, but with a tone of trepidation. "How friggin pathetic am I? I know what I *don't* want, but I don't have a clue about what I *do* want. I just hate the fact that everything we do seems to be preparing for something else."

"What do you mean?"

"High school, for one," Face tossed the tiny bit of rock that was left between his fingers onto the sidewalk below. "You spend four years getting ready for college or whatever and then you go to college to get ready for a job, then you work to get ready to retire. Where the fuck does it end?"

"Jesus, Face. You sound like my grandmother."

"I just don't know what my life is supposed to be."

"Why don't you be, I don't know, like a musician or something?"

"What the fuck am *I* gonna play?" Face laughed.

"Play the guitar. You'll get laid a lot."

"Fuck you, I'm devoted to Angela. What do you want to do, Jimmy, I mean, for the rest of your life?

"Hmm," Jimmy sighed. "I just want to get up everyday and not be pissed off. I want to be happy, to have a job that I don't hate. I don't want to be miserable like my Dad. I want to be the guy who wears nice clothes and carries a briefcase and has a summer house at the shore."

"I don't want to just be happy," Face had said. "I want to do something important, something people will remember."

"Don't worry about that, who could forget you?" Jimmy had meant it to be a joke at the time, but now the words rang true.

Jimmy still remembered that old Face. Those bright eyes and smooth skin that made the girls seem afraid to look right at him. That straight nose that Jimmy's own fist had shattered, and the engaging smile that let him get away with almost anything. Jimmy wondered how their lives would have been different if Face had not changed so much during college.

Face had stayed around taking classes at the local community college. But Jimmy was away at school, so was Angela. Jimmy had noticed the changes in his friend when he came home that first summer. Face had dabbled with some stuff at high school parties, but now he seemed to be constantly hunting for what he could get next. His original plan had been to go to a four year-school after getting his associate's degree, but his need for cash led him to working full time before the end of his second year. What if Face had not been sucked into drugs? Would they have remained friends? What if he had confronted Face about his drug use, before they began drifting apart? Would both their lives have tuned out differently? Would Veronica be dead?

Jimmy's thoughts were interrupted by Mrs. Murphy who came to shake his hand. She thanked him for a lovely service and said how much she would miss him, he was a nice man and never caused any trouble, and she was sorry for all his problems. The young nurse shook Jimmy's hand but did not say anything.

When Jimmy got home, he was smacked with the memory of walking into his empty house after he had buried Veronica. He closed his eyes for a moment, thinking about that silence that seemed to suffocate him as he closed the door. His footsteps had seemed to echo on the wood floor. He felt that now...the quiet...like breath being held. But then he was jolted into the present by a mewing sound. Three cats stood in the hallway in front of him, demanding their dinner. If they were human, they would have been standing with their hands on their hips, each tapping a foot.

"Okay, girls, give me a second here," he told them as he hung his keys on their hook. The cats ran ahead of him into the kitchen, tails upright and twirling at the ends as they paced around the three bowls in the corner. Jimmy had considered not taking them when the veterinary clinic had called, but he knew he owed it to Face. The cats also gave him a reason to go home. They were living, breathing beings who needed something from him. He had missed knowing that when he was walking through the door of his house, someone was on the other side of it, listening to his footsteps. Now he felt that again.

He looked at Veronica's mail, still in a pile on the counter, and he wondered what Darren McPhee would do with his son's mail. A sudden vision flashed before his eyes—Julian McPhee, his mouth open, lake water pouring in, his hands stretched out, gold watch gleaming in the moonlight. He shook off the image and sat at the table sorting the mail, until he thought about how pathetic it was that this was how he spending time. He took the pile of mail and hurled it onto the floor, startling the cats away from their bowls. He stared at the pattern that the colored envelopes made against the tile. He took the trashcan out from under the sink and noticed his answering machine blinking. He pressed the button then sat cross-legged on the floor, sifting through Veronica's mail, putting it into the trash. There were two messages on his machine, one from his mother asking him to come and spend the holidays in Ohio, and the other was from Detective Steve Curtis. He looked up at the machine and then stood and played the message again, wondering what Curtis wanted.

An envelope in Cathy Colfax's mail startled her. The McPhee address sat majestically printed in the upper left hand corner in gold letters. She realized it must be a thank you for the flowers she had sent to Julian's funeral. She opened it slowly, seeing the familiar signature that was printed on the bottom of her paychecks. There was also a small photograph of Julian playing soccer. Her face puckered with confusion until she turned the photo over: *Now you have Julian as a child — Maggie.* Cathy turned the photo back over and studied the face with its familiar, mischievous smile, which was covered by braces. He looked a bit thin and gangly and she thought she could see a pimple on his chin, which made her laugh. *Thank you, Maggie,* she thought to herself. His smile in the photo looked happy, like a cheerful, sweaty kid playing soccer. It gave her some comfort to know that he had been happy and carefree sometime in his life, and that maybe he was that way now. She studied the photo for a few more moments, then put it inside her high school yearbook, where it would remain. The doorbell rang as she was closing the book and replacing it on the shelf.

"Come in," she called, knowing it was Grace and Janine. They pushed the door open, each with a grocery bag in her arms.

"What's this?" Cathy asked as she ran over to grab the door.

"We're having a slumber party?"

"A what?" Cathy laughed.

"A slumber party. You're stuck with us until morning. We've got movies, munchies and three bottles of wine." Grace marched into the kitchen and set the bag on the counter. "How do you turn this thing on?" she fiddled with the oven controls. "We've got cookie dough."

"Cookies and wine?" Cathy's eyebrows went up as she sat on the couch and watched her two friends scurry about the kitchen.

"It's a great combination. Covers several food groups, and if you drink enough wine you don't care how many calories are in the cookies." Janine opened the cabinet above her head and took out three wine glasses, then began fiddling with the corkscrew. "I hate these damn things," she groaned. Cathy sat watching them invade her cabinets, gathering bowls and utensils.

"I know what you guys are up to," Cathy smiled.

"No, you don't." Janine handed Grace a glass of wine as she sliced cookie dough and placed pieces on a tray, then she went into the living room and handed Cathy a glass. "We're not trying to cheer you up, if that's what you think."

"Then what *is* all this?" Cathy's tone grew serious.

Grace and Janine looked at each other for a moment, and Grace came to sit with them on the couch. "We owe you an apology."

"Oh yeah? For what?" Cathy looked from one to the other.

"I, I mean *we*, feel like we haven't been very good friends to you," Janine said softly.

Cathy took a sip of wine. "I'm listening."

"We weren't real supportive of your feelings about him—about Julian. We should have talked to you about him more, helped you out. But we weren't very good listeners when it came to him." Grace took a gulp of her wine then placed the glass on the coffee table. "I just feel like we should have been more open to your feelings about him. We weren't willing to see beyond his problems."

"We were just looking out for you Cathy," Janine interjected. "We love you and we didn't want you to get hurt."

"I know that," Cathy sighed. "I just wish you would have gotten to know him better. I know you guys would have really liked him if you had seen in him the things that I saw."

"What matters is you, Cathy. We want to make sure you're okay." Grace touched her hand. "We know this has been hard for you, and we know you'll be sad for a while, but we just want to make sure you're going to come out of this okay."

"Why this sudden change of heart, about Julian?" Cathy looked at each of their faces.

"I don't think either of has changed our minds," Janine looked at Grace for approval. "If he was...alive, we would probably still be telling you to stay away, unless he was ready to change."

"We didn't realize how involved you were, Cathy. We didn't know how much you really cared about him. I'm sure you had reasons to feel like you did."

"I did have reasons to care about him, and I really felt like he was going to change, but I guess I was wrong. He *was* drinking the night he was killed. He had left his wallet in a bar. It was the *day after* he swore to me he wouldn't, the day after." Cathy bit her lip and sipped her wine. "He swore he wanted us to be together, but he could not even keep his promise for a day."

"Addiction is wicked, Cathy. Some people just don't have the strength to fight such a powerful force."

"I know that now. And I know that you were just looking out for me. You guys had good reason for not liking Julian, I just didn't want to see it."

"Are you going to be okay, honestly?" Janine asked. Cathy sipped her wine again, pondering the question.

"Yeah. I think I will be. I need some time. I keep thinking about what the future would have been like for Julian and I. Of course I once thought he would just stop drinking and we would live happily ever after, but that's not what I see now."

"What do you see?"

Cathy pulled her feet up beneath her on the couch. "I see doubt. I see myself never knowing if I would ever see him again every time he left. Never knowing what he would do when he was drunk. I realize now that there was no way I could have saved him." She seemed lost in thought for a moment. "I *will* be okay," Cathy nodded. "But I won't be so blind again. And I will certainly listen to you two from now on!" She hugged Janine, then Grace, and took a deep breath. "So what's on the agenda for this party?"

"We get drunk, eat lots of crap, talk all night and watch sappy tear-jerking movies."

"And don't forget the other one," Janine smiled wickedly.

"Oh, yeah, we have a very special movie just for you. It's called *Studs* and it comes in a plain brown box."

"You're kidding?" Cathy laughed.

"I do not kid about full frontal nudity, my friend."

"You guys are too much," Cathy laughed.

"What do you think about the three of us in Aruba over Christmas?" Janine asked, "I brought some brochures." She winked at Grace.

"Hey, uh, Betty Crocker," Cathy said to Grace, "I think your cookies are burning."

"Shit!" Grace bounded into the kitchen in what seemed like one step.

"Thanks, guys." Cathy squeezed Janine's hand.

CHAPTER 35

Jimmy Lawson was still having trouble sleeping. He went through the same routine each night, washed and changed, brushed his teeth, flossed, and went upstairs with the cats, who seemed to want to follow him everywhere. Then he would lie in his bed—at least he had progressed from the couch—and read for a while until drowsiness blurred the words. The cats would curl against him, and they would all breathe in unison, until Jimmy started tossing and sweating. The nightmares came on a regular basis. His only refuge was working on his book, and his only sound sleep was the small naps that would overtake him in the living room chair. Also on a regular basis, messages came from Detective Curtis, asking to speak with him, but never insisting he come in for questioning. He thought about calling Brad Fischer, he even dialed Brad's number but hung up without leaving a message.

The nightmares would vary in content and in intensity. Sometimes he would see Face injecting himself, choking, but then Face would change his mind and hold his arm out to Jimmy, calling him to stop it, to save him, pleading for his life, crying out. In these dreams Jimmy would watch his friend, unable to move a muscle, unable to save him. Another nightmare was Julian McPhee, choking, coughing, mud and water filling his mouth, cutting off his air, sinking under the water. Jimmy would wake up sweating, unable to breathe, feeling like he, too, was drowning, tasting mud. The old dreams were still there, too: Veronica's face against the windshield, smashed skin,

192

broken teeth, the screaming babies. He had even considered calling Melinda once or twice, but knew she would not welcome him as she had before.

Jimmy spent his days in a groggy, disheveled fog. He sat at his computer for hours at a time, trying to replace the contents of his brain with the words of his book. There were periods where he did not shower for days, and he ate only sporadically. His mother called from time to time, and he managed to assure her that he was fine, just working hard on the book, and he was thinking about coming for the holidays, he would let her know.

The cats were a source of comfort to him, and he realized that he might just stay in bed and die if they were not surrounding him, demanding food or nuzzling him for more personal attention. There were days when he spoke to no one except the cats. It seemed like the outside world did not exist, his only world was inside his house, and it was starting to suffocate him.

Steve Curtis also found the next weeks quite stressful. He was preoccupied with a case that was officially closed. Questions were constantly popping into his mind: Did Lawson help Jenkins kill Julian? Had Lawson arranged Jenkins's suicide somehow? Had Lawson hired Jenkins to do his dirty work? Had they gotten Julian drunk that night?

Then there was Darren to think about. Steve did not want this man to suffer any further, but on the other hand he felt Darren deserved to know the truth about his son's death, whatever that truth was. He decided that he should speak to James Lawson, unofficially, as the case was closed. Maybe, just maybe, Lawson would give him some clue about what really happened.

Curtis's preoccupation with the case had caused a bit of tension at home, as well. Wendy was tired and cranky from lack of sleep, and on more than one occasion she had addressed a question to her husband only to find him deep in thought, not having heard a word.

"I'm home all day, Steve, with no adult to talk to, and you can't even listen to me."

"I've just got a lot on my mind, honey, work stuff." He put a forkful of salad in his mouth and tried to be nice. "Great salad," he smiled with mock enthusiasm.

"Oh shut up." She shook her head and speared a small piece of her own salad, trying not to smile at him, but still annoyed. Curtis tried to be as attentive as possible during dinner. He gave Katie her bath and bedtime bottle while Wendy cleaned the kitchen. Their plan was to meet on the couch in a half hour, watch a movie and snuggle. He sat in the chair in the bedroom holding Katie as she sucked at her bottle and kicked her feet in a bicycle motion. He loved how Katie smelled after her bath, and he closed his eyes and tried to focus on her scent, her small slurping sounds, and the movement of her feet. But other thoughts kept taking his mind away from his daughter. He glanced at his cell phone which sat charging on the night table. He stretched toward it with the arm that was holding Katie, but he could not reach it without getting up. Katie let out a few squeals of protest when he stood, and the bottle came out of her mouth. He grabbed the phone and held Katie's bottle in place by pressing it between his chin and neck as he checked his messages. When he heard Jimmy Lawson's voice he knew the movie date would not happen.

"Come in." Jimmy opened the door and let Steve Curtis into his living room. Curtis was shocked at how awful he looked. He had lost weight, needed a good shave and a haircut and his eyes were puffy and dark from lack of sleep.

"Thank you for seeing me. I know you didn't have to." Curtis stepped into the room, looking around as he always did. The place was clean, but lifeless. No plants, no pictures, no books or even a cup on the table.

"True." Jimmy waved at the sofa and Curtis sat down, and a cat leapt onto the arm.

"What did you need to see me about?" Jimmy sat down in a chair across from the detective, his heart racing.

"Your friend, Jenkins."

"Face?"

"Is that what you called him? Why Face?"

"It's a long story," Jimmy shifted in his chair. "He used to be really good-looking when he was young."

"Oh." Curtis pictured the dull, bony face he had seen dead in the apartment, not believing that he had once been handsome. "I'm just curious, Mr. Lawson…"

"Call me Jimmy, please."

"Okay, Jimmy. I called you a few times, over the past few weeks. I kind of got the idea that you were avoiding me. Why did you suddenly decide to talk to me?"

"I just was wondering what you wanted," Jimmy said softly. "I couldn't stop thinking about why you might have called."

"I see. You know I am not here in an official capacity?"

"Yes. So what about him? What about Face?" Jimmy seemed impatient.

"He didn't kill McPhee." Curtis spoke slowly and watched Jimmy's face with each word.

"What are you talking about? You're the one who said he confessed."

"True," Curtis spoke deliberately, eyes focused on Lawson's expressions. He noticed a slight twitch in his jaw. "But he was lying."

"What are you talking about? Why would he do that?" Jimmy stood and began walking around the room.

"His confession was not consistent with the physical evidence."

"Oh, really? In what way?"

Curtis crossed his ankle over his knee and sat back in the chair. "Basically Jenkins was too small and too frail to have killed a big, young, healthy kid like McPhee. He must have had help."

Jimmy snickered. "That's it? That's your physical evidence? The kid was drunk!"

"How do you know that?"

"I don't *know*. I'm just assuming, after all, he was drunk when he ran over my wife. It's not too tough to imagine, is it?"

"You miss you wife, huh?"

"Don't start shit with me, Curtis!" He yelled. "I'll throw you right out of here on your ass. No head games. You're here because I let you come in, don't forget that."

"I'm sorry." Curtis put both of his feet on the floor, and swallowed hard. "I really wasn't trying to screw with your head. You just seem, sad."

"Sad?" Jimmy glared at him. "Sad? That word does not begin to describe the past six months of my life. Not even close. There are no *words* to describe what I've lost."

"I see that, I'm sorry." Curtis stared at Jimmy's face, seeing the fear in his eyes, which were shadowed by his long hair and lack of sleep.

"She was everything to me. She and I had a whole life together, and all of it died with her," Jimmy said softly. "Are you married, Curtis?"

"Yes." He was startled, and not totally comfortable, to be the one answering a question. "I am. I have a wife and a baby daughter."

"Imagine if they were just gone, one day. You came home and it was all over."

"I know you must be devastated." He looked away, unable to stay focused on Jimmy's face.

"Imagine your daughter, Curtis, never getting to be born."

This statement confused Curtis. "Was your wife pregnant?"

"No, she wasn't. But it was something we were planning to do. And I feel like it was supposed to happen. There are souls of children out there, and they will never be born because of *him*."

Curtis was frightened as he watched the man sitting across from him. The air around him seemed dark; he seemed so taut with emotion that Steve wondered if he should fear for his own safety.

"He didn't care about her," Jimmy continued. "He didn't care about me, or the children we were supposed to have. He just ran her over and left her to die."

"Look, Lawson, Jimmy. I understand your pain, but his case *was* dismissed. It's *possible* that the car was stolen and someone else ran her over. Maybe all this anger toward McPhee is misplaced."

"C'mon. He did it, Curtis, you know it as well as I do."

"I'll admit I have my doubts, but it's *possible* that he didn't do it." Curtis threw his arms upward.

"He *did* it! I know he did it!" Jimmy snarled as he stood up and stepped closer to Curtis. Curtis sat back when he saw the look in Jimmy's eyes.

"How can you be sure?'

"Because he fucking told me!" Jimmy flopped back into the chair, his chest heaving with each breath. Curtis ran his palm over his mouth, not sure if he wanted to hear any more. He thought of Julian, drunk, laughing, the woman's body flying onto his hood. He cleared his throat, unable to stop himself from continuing.

"When did he tell you that?" he nearly whispered.

"The night he died." Jimmy spat out the words, almost before Curtis had finished the question. "He told me that he killed my wife on the night that he died. I talked to him, at the lake."

"How did you both end up at the lake, together?"

"I was there like I told you before, putting my papers in the lake, having my breakdown or whatever you want to call it. I didn't even hear anything. He came up alongside me, and threw up in the water. He was stinking drunk; bombed out of his mind. I can't even believe he could walk. I didn't know who he was at first, it was very dark where I was sitting. I thought he was just some guy so I tried to help him. I got him over to the bench. Then we were under the streetlight, and I saw his face and I knew."

"You were positive, I mean you remembered his face, from court?"

"I could never forget his face. It was the last thing my wife ever saw."

Curtis leaned forward as he listened to Jimmy's story. He felt like he knew what Jimmy would say and he was afraid to listen to it, but could not resist hearing it. "What happened when you recognized him?"

"It was slow. His head was down when we first got to the bench. He was very groggy, but I pushed him back on the bench, so his head kind of fell back, under the light.

"'Holy shit,' I said. 'You're him, Julian McPhee?' He squinted at me and asked me how I knew him. He had *no idea* who I was. No *fucking idea*. Like the whole thing had never happened. Then I told him who I was, and he started crying, like a little pussy. He totally freaked out." Jimmy was sweating now, his hatred exhausting him like exercise.

"What do you mean, *freaked out*?"

"He stood up and walked away from the bench, then walked back toward me, he was mumbling some crap, I couldn't even understand what he was saying. Then he fell on his ass in the mud. I was scared. I thought he was totally nuts, then he told me he did it."

"What did he say, exactly?" Cutis was close to sweating himself, his heart beating faster with each detail.

"He said, 'It was me, in case you were wondering. I *should* be in prison. I killed your wife.'" Jimmy was crying now, spitting the words through tears. "He said he had not even seen her, not until she fell onto his hood. He said her face came right up to the windshield and he saw her eyes, she looked right at him, and then she slid off of the hood and landed on the road, hard. He says he sat there for a second, waiting, not knowing what to do, then decided to get out of there and he ran over her body as he tried to get away. He said he felt the bump…" Jimmy took a deep breath and stopped before he said the rest very slowly. "He felt the front and back tires *go over her body*."

"I thought he didn't remember anything."

"That's what I said to him, I was so angry. I thought he was totally full of shit, but he said he remembered, that he'd gone to her grave to look at it. He was standing there, talking to *my* wife, and the memory came back."

"Jesus!" Curtis had never before lost his instincts as a detective. He had always known what question to ask, what to say next, until now. He just sat there, his face resting on his hands, waiting.

"He was so drunk, Curtis. You would not have believed it. He was drooling and slobbering all over himself. I think he even pissed his pants at one point. And he walked into a tree. He just turned around and walked into it, that's how he got the cuts on his face."

"When did you punch him?" Curtis sighed and raked his fingers across the back of his neck, where his muscles were stiffening.

"When he said he talked to Veronica. I lost it. I screamed at him, asking him where he got his nerve and stuff like that and then I threw a punch. I hit him right in the eye. He felt down, right flat down on his back."

Curtis stood and walked over to the window, not sure he should continue, no longer feeling objective. "Jimmy, maybe you should call your lawyer before you say anything else."

Jimmy laughed. "What kind of a cop are you? I thought cops hated lawyers."

"I'm just trying to protect you." He spun around to look at Jimmy, who was staring vacantly forward.

"Do I look like I care anymore what happens to me? I really don't give a fuck."

"No, you don't look like you do."

"Don't worry about me, Curtis. I want to come clean with this. It's time."

"Go ahead, then." Curtis sat back on the sofa. "What happened when Julian was down on the ground?"

"I went over to him, I was going to pound him again. I was just going to give him a good beating, you know teach him a lesson."

Jimmy looked excited as he said these words, like beating someone up was something he found rewarding. "But he said it again. How she looked, her face was right in front of him. He looked her right in the eye, and all he could think about was getting away, so he ran over her again. He said he thought she would have lived if he had not run over her again."

"My God." Curtis started to approach Jimmy, but stepped back when Jimmy continued. "I choked him. I couldn't help it. I wrapped my hands around his throat and I just kept squeezing." Jimmy's eyes were distant, and with his hands he pantomimed the action. Then he put his hands down and walked back over toward the window. "But I couldn't finish. I couldn't kill him. I don't know why, I just let go. I knew what he had done, and I could not kill him."

"How did he end up in the lake?"

"He got up, he wasn't really hurt. He kind of stumbled around, like he was disoriented, and he kind of stumbled toward the lake. He got sick again. He crouched down at the edge, puking his guts out. He started losing his balance, almost like in slow motion. I saw him losing his balance, so I put my hand out. He reached for it, but he missed, and fell in."

"What did you do?"

Jimmy's face was gray as he spoke in a hoarse whisper. "I thought he was going to climb back out. He wasn't that far in at first, but he was so drunk that he didn't know which way to go to get out, he went out deeper. I walked as close to the edge of the water as I could get, I lost sight of him for a moment, and I thought he'd swum away, maybe gotten out further down, but then he started thrashing about, panicking. I stood on the side and tried to reach in, but by that time he was too far out. His hands were up and water was pouring into his mouth and he was choking and spitting. I was ready to jump in, I almost jumped in to get him out, when what he'd said came back into my head. He had looked into my wife's eyes, and let her die, he ran her over again."

"So you let *him* die?"

"Yes."

"What did you do then?"

"I stood there for a while, listening. I kept thinking I heard him moving or something, then I walked back to where I had been sitting and I buried Veronica's picture."

"Why did you do that?"

"It was like, she was gone, really. That was it. I think she was there, in spirit when I had my hands around the kid's throat. I stopped because of her, a promise I once made to her. But then I just let him drown. She would not have liked that, believe it or not. She was completely gone then, I destroyed her; everything she believed in."

The two men sat lost in their own thoughts for a while. Curtis replayed the scene in his head, Julian's mouth filling with water, the sound of thrashing in the lake that grew slower and slower and then stopped. He thought about Darren, imagining his face when he told him someone had watched his son drown.

"Did you tell all of this to Jenkins?" Curtis asked without looking directly at Jimmy.

"No, no. I never would have involved him in this mess."

"So why did he confess?'

"He did it to protect me. He felt he owed me something."

"But how did he know you were involved at all?"

"He found me at the lake the next morning, he saw that I was a mess. When he saw the paper, he figured it out. He knows me too well to think I could be in the same place with *him* without something happening."

"Quite a friend you had there."

"Yeah," Jimmy looked up at Curtis. "So what happens to me now?"

"I don't know. I'm not sure a jury would believe your story. They might not believe that you stopped choking him, they might think you choked him into unconsciousness and then pushed him into the water. That would be murder."

"Do *you* believe my story?" Jimmy looked Curtis in the eye, waiting for his answer, as if it were important to him.

"Why do you care what I think?"

Jimmy did not respond, so Curtis got up to leave. Jimmy stayed in his chair as Curtis walked to the door.

"Should I call my lawyer?" Jimmy called out.

"If I were you," Curtis said, his hand on the door. "I would get some help, some serious help."

Curtis drove home slowly, his fingers trembling as they gripped the steering wheel. The sky was overcast, like it might rain or possibly snow. Jimmy Lawson's words echoed in his head, and each bump in the road evoked the image of a tire running over Veronica Lawson as she lay in the street. He pictured Julian's face, frozen in terror as he went under the water. He felt like his own lungs were filling up. What would it be like to watch that happen to someone? How could he tell Darren? Was this worse than hearing that a junkie had killed your son for revenge? He thought about filing a report. Jimmy Lawson was guilty of attempted murder, or manslaughter at least. That was if Curtis believed his story, which he was not sure he did. He wondered if *he* would have been able to stand by and watch Julian flailing in the water and not help. Or was his story bullshit, a way to be guilty of a lesser charge? If he could convince everyone of this version of the story, Lawson could get away with murder.

When he got to his house he tossed his coat on the chair, poured himself a shot of scotch and tossed it down his throat. He stood feeling it travel down his body, tasting lake water. He looked around the small condo that Wendy kept spotlessly neat. The blue carpet in the living room had recently been vacuumed. He grabbed his coat off the chair and hung it up in the closet, knowing she'd be pissed if he left it there.

"Steve?" Wendy came out from their bedroom wearing a light blue bathrobe. She had a towel draped around her head, like she'd just finished taking a shower. She looked at the open bottle and the shot glass, then at Steve.

"What's going on?" Steve stared at her for a moment, and touched a strand of hair that hung down from under the towel. He cupped his palms around her face and kissed her softly, then pulled her into a tight embrace.

"What's wrong with you?" her voice was muffled against his shirt.

"I just love you," he said.

CHAPTER 36

Jimmy stayed in his chair and listened to the car pull out of the driveway, exhausted from his meeting with Curtis. He felt relief as Donna came over and jumped into his lap. He ran his hand over her back and she purred loudly. He closed his eyes for a moment and raked his fingers through Donna's soft fur. He heard the sound again, from deep within his mind—the thrashing in the water, the coughing and gasping. Then he saw them—the eyes. Those eyes had looked into his own, pleading, frightened, wide eyes that were lit by the angle of the streetlight. He heard the voice again, too. The small, cracking voice that now never left Jimmy's head.

"Please…help me."

The words echoed in his mind as he drove to Marion Lake Park. It was colder now than it had been that night. Maybe if *that* night had been colder he would not have stayed at the lake. He would have gone home, or maybe back to Melinda's. But maybe it had been fate that he was there when Julian came stumbling over. What else could it be? What were the chances of the two of them being there at the same moment? What were the chances of nothing bad happening when they met by chance?

He sat on the hard bench where he had sat with *him* on that night. He could feel the coldness of the wood through his jeans. The sky was dark but clear, and the park was empty. The water looked very still; no ducks gliding across it, no one thrashing about. He wondered how deep it was in the spot where Julian went under. He could pinpoint the spot from where he sat on the bench. The spot where he spoke his last words—*Please...help me.* The words began as a small cry, a plea from a child. Then they grew into a desperate scream. Jimmy had watched Julian's hands as they tried to grab anything, but could only find water. The last thing he saw, the last glimpse of Julian McPhee was his watch as it reflected off the water, his hand reaching for nothing.

Jimmy's memory of that night was vivid, and he thought about how lucky Julian had been not to remember seeing Veronica die. How lucky for him that he only relived her eyes against his windshield for the last few hours of his life. Jimmy felt like his own mind would replay the image of Julian dying over and over. He would never forget the feel of his hands around his throat. He had felt the veins pumping, his neck muscles bulging. He should not have looked at his eyes. He saw the fear, and he let go. Veronica had made him a coward.

After he had let go of Julian's throat, the kid was gasping so much it made him puke. That was another sound that kept playing in Jimmy's mind. The gasping, the words, *I'm sorry* between each breath. The sound of him retching, bent over the edge.

Jimmy could see him now, as if he was there again, squatting, off balance. Jimmy looked at the exact spot where Julian had been. He had stepped closer to Julian. Jimmy could feel the sensation of putting his foot out, pushing against his back with the tip of his shoe; just a small push. Had he done that? He was unsure if the sensation was a memory or a fantasy; like the hand that reached up and brushed his fingertips, and how his fingers had pulled away from that touch.

Veronica's voice rang through his head as he walked around the lake,...*What are you, some kind of thug?* Maybe he was. Maybe the real Jimmy was not the one who married Veronica, not the learned professor or successful author. Maybe the real Jimmy was a vengeful person, a person who could be guilty of the one unforgivable thing— deliberate cruelty. Maybe the real Jimmy was guilty of murder.

CHAPTER 37

Steve Curtis went to the McPhee home three times during the next two weeks, but each time he went no one was home. He had decided to tell Darren what he knew about the night his son died and let him decide if he wanted to go after Lawson for assault and /or attempted murder. He also left several phone messages at the McPhee home, none of which were returned. It wasn't until the week before Christmas that he heard from Darren again. He and Wendy and Katie were invited to the McPhee home to a party to celebrate the marriage of Darren and Maggie. They had gotten married while in Ireland visiting Maggie's family.

Wendy was excited about the party. She had not had much chance to dress up and socialize since Katie had been born, and Curtis was proud to show off his family as well. Wendy had tried on three dresses, two of which were still a bit too tight across her slackened stomach. Curtis sat on the bed and watched her check herself in the full-length mirror, turn around, stamp her foot and curse. Then she would head back to the closet for the next option. When the third dress fit perfectly, he was relieved.

The McPhee home was lavishly decorated with wreaths and gold bows and a large tree in the living room. Darren and Maggie looked happy as they gushed over Katie, who smiled as if on cue. People milled about the party enjoying themselves, but the overall atmosphere was subdued; Julian had not been forgotten. Curtis listened as several of the guests mentioned him. Their memories of him seemed to have softened quite a bit in the short time since his death. Nobody mentioned his drinking problem or the accident, or even how he died. Now he was just a son, a young man full of unfulfilled promise, a young man who had touched others. He watched Maggie and Darren sitting together sipping champagne that was being served by waiters in tuxedos who carried a variety of finger foods as well. He watched Darren's arm draped protectively around her shoulder and her smile as she looked up at him every so often. He wrestled with the knowledge he possessed, lingering after most of the guests had left, but stalling the conversation he dreaded.

He managed to get Darren alone in his study after all the other guests had left. Katie had fallen asleep in her carrier and Wendy was trying to put her coat on without waking her. Maggie stood by and watched intently, admiring the baby she called "the lil' sleepin' angel."

"I'm sorry I didn't get back to you, Steve. I know you called a few times while we were away."

"No, it's fine." Steve sipped what was left of his champagne. "I'm really happy for you, Darren."

"Well, one thing my life has taught me is not to waste a day." Darren had unbuttoned the collar on his suit and was loosening his tie. "I think Julian would have given us his blessing."

"Absolutely," Curtis agreed.

"So what's going on?" Darren sat on the leather couch and sat back with his legs crossed. "Why were you trying to hunt me down?"

Steve sat down next to him. He had planned this speech for weeks, but now he did not know what to say to him. *Lawson was involved in your son's death, he assaulted him and then watched him drown in the lake. We can press charges against Lawson for assault and attempted murder. He could go to prison.*

For a moment Curtis thought of the day when he had been in this house asking Darren about his murdered child's love interests, making him realize what he didn't know about his own child. Would it be cruel to dig this up again? Would the softened pain grow sharp again? He recalled the break in Darren's voice that day. He continued his speech in his head, afraid to say the words to Darren.

We can go after Lawson, but it will be difficult. They will try to make Julian look like a monster.

It struck Curtis that a case against James Lawson would be similar to the manslaughter case against Julian McPhee. No witnesses, not enough evidence.

"Hey, you two!" They were interrupted by Wendy and Maggie who had come into the study carrying the sleeping Katie, coat on, in her seat.

"Ready to go, Steve? She's all bundled."

"Yeah, I'm ready," he sighed, extending his hand to Darren. "Congratulations. I'm really happy for you." Darren took Steve's hand, then pulled him into a tight hug.

"Darren, did ya see this lil' sleepin' angel?"

Darren released Steve from his grasp and bent to look at Katie's face. "She's beautiful," he said to Wendy.

"I'm afraid Maggie has let the cat out of the bag on your little secret, Darren," Wendy smiled. Steve looked at Darren.

"What secret is that?" he asked his wife.

"Maggie has a young cousin, in Ireland, who is having a baby in six months. She's only sixteen and wants to give the baby up for adoption, so Maggie and Darren are thinking of adopting it."

"That's terrific," Steve smiled.

"So, Steve, did you have something to discuss?" Darren moved next to Maggie as he spoke. Steve looked at them and swallowed a breath.

"No, nothing. I just wanted to make sure you were okay."

Steve drove home with his wife and daughter, feeling happy with his decision to let sleeping dogs lie. Darren was making a new life for himself; maybe James Lawson was doing the same.

CHAPTER 38

James Lawson spent the first Christmas without his wife in Ohio, with his mother. They spent a sad, subdued holiday exchanging small gifts and having Christmas dinner in a lovely restaurant. When he returned home after the New Year, he went to see Lou Zaits, who agreed to give him a partial teaching schedule for the spring term at Collins University. He had finished his book, and his agent was sending it out to various publishers of academic materials. He had even received a New Year E-mail greeting from Melinda, who had moved to Phoenix to live with her new boyfriend, a thirty-five-year-old photographer. He had sent back his warm wishes, happy that she seemed well. He was also in therapy, twice a week, and was learning how to control his rage. Face's girls had also adjusted to their new life, waking Jimmy each morning. They had been fed by dawn for years, so if Jimmy slept later than eight they began nipping at his toes, then running ahead of him to their food bowls. Jimmy trod behind in his boxer shorts calling, "I'm coming ladies. I'm right behind you," as they waited for him.

By the second Christmas after Julian had died Maggie and Darren were the parents of a baby girl they had named Priscilla. Darren had partially retired from Comptech, giving more duties to Jeffrey Madison and Cathy Colfax, and was happily changing diapers and dishing out strained peaches. He often caught Maggie just admiring Priscilla, watching her sleeping or sucking her fingers or twirling her hair. He also spent time speaking at a variety of self-help meetings about his son's alcoholism.

Steve and Wendy Curtis had cause to celebrate as well. Wendy was pregnant with their second child, a boy who would be born that February. Darren and Maggie had already agreed to be godparents. It was that second holiday season, a week before Christmas in a crowded shopping mall, when Steve Curtis saw James Lawson again. He and Katie were looking for a bracelet for Wendy when Steve spotted James buying a wreath in a stand in the middle of the mall. He looked closely, unsure at first if he had recognized him correctly. He looked far better than he had at their previous meeting. His hair was neat and he looked well rested. He hung the wreath over his arm, dangling it on his elbow, and paid for it. When he turned away from the cashier, he spotted Steve Curtis watching him, his young daughter holding onto one of his fingers. James smiled and strode up to where Curtis was standing.

"Curtis," James extended his hand, which Curtis shook.

"How are you?" Curtis asked, looking him over.

"I am doing well, much better than when I saw you last. Who is this pretty young lady?" Jimmy bent at the knee to meet Katie's eyes.

"I'm Katie," she said with several fingers in her mouth. Steve smiled, but felt uneasy seeing Lawson talking so closely with his child.

"Look, Curtis, I wanted to thank you."

"For what?" Katie had turned away to watch the kids on Santa's lap, although she herself was afraid of him.

"I got some help, after I talked to you. I've been in therapy for a good while now, and it's helped me a lot. I've made peace with myself, for a lot of things."

"That's good, Jimmy, I'm happy for you." Curtis did not know why, but trepidation crept up the back of his neck.

"I also know that, well, you could have made things tough for me, and you didn't. I appreciate that, really. You could have really put my ass in a sling."

Curtis tightened his hold on his daughter's small hand. Jimmy's hand was extended again and he was smiling.

"I didn't do it for you, Lawson. As far as I'm concerned, you're no better than he was. Both of you let someone else die. I thought about opening the case again, I almost did. But I kept my mouth shut to spare Darren McPhee some pain, that's the only reason."

208

Jimmy's smile widened. "Come on, Curtis. You can't fool me." He took a step closer and spoke into Curtis's ear, not wanting the child to hear. "He got what he deserved. You know you would have done the same thing."

He patted Curtis on the back and gave him a broad smile before he walked away and was lost in the crowd. Curtis stood motionless, ignoring the impatient tug on his hand. What had Lawson seen in him that could have convinced him that they were alike? He had convinced himself he kept quiet to protect Darren, but was that the truth? Or did he suppress the truth because he felt that Lawson's actions were justified? The thought of watching a young man drown was repulsive to him, yet he wondered what he would be capable of if that person had taken Wendy from him?

You would have done the same thing.

Curtis shook his head and led his daughter toward the exit. He honestly didn't know.